A RAMBLING MAN

A RAMBLING MAN

ROBERT VAUGHAN

THORNDIKE PRESS
A part of Gale, a Cengage Company

GALE
A Cengage Company

LIBRARY OF CONGRESS CIP DATA ON FILE.
CATALOGUING IN PUBLICATION FOR THIS BOOK
IS AVAILABLE FROM THE LIBRARY OF CONGRESS.

ISBN-13: 979-8-88579-532-6 (softcover alk. paper)

Published in 2023 by arrangement with Wolfpack Publishing LLC.

A RAMBLING MAN

1

June 6th, 1864, Northern Virginia

Missouri was a state with divided loyalties, and while some of Sergeant Lucas Cain's friends from Missouri had chosen to fight for the South, Lucas chose to fight for the Union, because he didn't want to see America divided into two countries.

Lucas was with the Fifth Missouri, and they were in the seventh day of the Battle at Cold Harbor. Lucas ducked when a cannon shell launched by a Confederate Napoleon gun some three-thousand yards distant, came rushing in with a sound not unlike that of a disconnected freight-car rolling rapidly down the track. The twelve-pound missile burst loudly in an explosion of flame and flying pieces of shrapnel.

Sergeant Cain ducked the shell burst, then rose up to fire into a tree line on the opposite side of what had once been a field of cotton, lying fallow now, as it had for the last three years. On the other side of the field, drifting clouds of gun smoke gave proof that the Confederate soldiers were returning fire.

"You men, make sure you are adjusting your fire for distance," Lucas called.

"Hell, we're doin' that, Lucas," Dan Lindell replied. "This isn't our first dance."

Lucas was a sergeant and Dan a corporal, but the two men were friends and had served together since the war's beginning.

Another artillery shell came in and exploded, this one a little closer than the previous one, but still far enough away so as not to pose any immediate danger.

Lucas reloaded his musket, turned back toward the far treeline, and fired.

After shooting, he brought the rifle down and began pouring in powder in preparation for another shot.

"Sergeant Cain," Lieutenant Chambers said, hurrying up to him just as Lucas had finished reloading. "Go tell Cap'n Greenley there's only a few Rebs over there. We'll swing around, and get behind 'em."

"Yes, sir," Lucas answered. Finished with the reload, he fitted the ramrod back into its holder, then got to his feet. Lifting his musket to high port, Lucas started on his mission running through the forest, leaping over fallen logs, ducking under low branches, and splashing through meandering streams.

As he ran, the sound of his footsteps and his ragged breathing played a counterpoint to the sharp bark of musketry and the heavy boom of distant artillery fire. Then, when he reached an open space on the other side of the wood line, he paused for a moment. Seeing that it appeared clear, he dashed quickly across, then leaped over a knee-high stone wall, landing in the midst of several Union soldiers who were sitting around waiting to be called upon. The soldiers, surprised by Lucas's sudden and unexpected appearance, raised their weapons, but they relaxed when they recognized him as one of their own.

"Sarge, where'd you come from?" one of the soldiers asked.

"I'm with Lieutenant Chambers," Lucas answered. "Where's Captain Greenley?"

"Over there," the soldier replied, nodding his head toward a tree stump about twenty yards back of the stone fence.

"Thanks."

Lucas hurried to him and saluted.

"Sergeant Cain, I thought you were with Chambers," Greenley said.

"Yes, sir, I am. Lieutenant Chambers

wanted me to tell you that he doesn't think there are that many Rebs. He thinks we could swing around and get behind them and catch them between us if you would want to do that."

Lucas's report was followed by a rather heavy rattle of musketry coming from the other side of the clearing, in the same direction from where Lucas had just come.

"That sounds like there's more 'n just a few of 'em," Captain Greenley said. "See any more of 'em on your way over?"

"No, sir. The thicket is clear," Lucas said.

"How about cavalry? See any cavalry?"

"No cavalry, sir."

Another sharp round of shooting caused Lucas and Captain Greenley to look again across the clearing. "That sounds close," Greenley said. He stroked his beard and looked toward the distant tree line.

"All right, Sergeant, maybe Chambers is right. Go back and tell him to start movin' this way."

"Yes, sir," Lucas replied. He started back across the open field.

He followed the same path he had used before, jumping over logs and splashing through streams. Suddenly there was a loud popping sound in his ear, and a Minie ball knocked off his cap and spun him around.

10

Lucas hit the ground hard, aware that his face was bleeding from shavings thrown into his cheek when the ball smashed into the tree beside him. He dropped his rifle and it scooted out across the ground, winding up several feet in front of him.

Somewhat stunned, Lucas got back to his hands and knees, then started crawling toward his musket, when suddenly a pair of gray-clad legs appeared in front of him. Then another, and another still. Lucas looked up to see several Confederate infantrymen staring down their rifle barrels at him.

"Where do think you're a' goin', Yank?" one of the Rebels asked.

Lucas looked around for his rifle and finding it, reached for it.

"Better leave it there, Sergeant," someone said. The speaker was a mounted Confederate officer who was holding his pistol on Lucas.

Lucas felt his heart pounding and he took several deep breaths, fighting against the fear that was building up inside. Where did all these people come from? He began looking around, and saw that he was surrounded by Confederate soldiers.

The mounted officer made a motion with his pistol, indicating that Lucas should leave his rifle where it lay. Lucas stood.

"What do I do now?" he asked.

"Good that you had sense enough to ask that," the officer said with an asymmetrical smile that lifted one corner of his mouth up, while the other turned down. "On account of you won't be doin' nothin' unless we tell you to." He looked toward the Confederate infantrymen, picking out a Corporal. "Take him over and put him with the others."

"Yes, sir," the Corporal replied.

The officer galloped off as the Rebel soldiers marched Lucas away.

When Lucas reached the place where he had left Lieutenant Chambers not a half-hour earlier, he saw that all the others were prisoners as well. Lieutenant Chambers had a wound in his shoulder, and it was being bandaged by one of the soldiers from Lucas's company. Those from the company, as well as several from other companies, were sitting on the ground, weaponless, guarded by half-a-dozen Confederate infantrymen.

Looking around the battlefield, Lucas saw several Union dead, many more than had been there when he left on his courier mission. One of the Confederates who had been escorting him jabbed the business-end of his rifle into Lucas's back.

"Sit down!" the Rebel soldier barked.

Lucas sat on the ground next to Dan Lindell and the wounded Lieutenant Chambers.

"Are you hurt?" Lucas asked Dan.

"No. What about you?"

"Nothing," Lucas answered as he looked toward Chambers. "How are you, Lieutenant?"

"I'll be all right," Chambers said in a wheezing, gasping voice.

Just over the lieutenant's shoulder, and unseen by him, one of the other soldiers in the company shook his head slowly, letting Lucas know that the wound was much worse than Chambers was letting on.

"Turns out there were a lot more than I thought," Chambers said. "Sorry 'bout that, boys. I let you down."

Lucas glanced over toward some of the dead, then he let out a sorrowful sigh as he recognized one in particular. "Damn, they got Peter," he said.

Peter Carson could neither read nor write, so Lucas had written some letters for him, and had read the letters he had received. Peter was married, and had a small child.

"Sydney's gone, too," Dan said.

Lucas looked around at the others in his

company. Those who weren't dead were sorrowing for those who were. Dan smiled wanly at Lucas. "This hasn't been one of our better days."

"No, I wouldn't say so," Lucas agreed.

"Y'all lie flat on the ground," a Confederate corporal ordered. "Don't nobody stand — don't nobody do nothin', lessen we tells you to."

"What about them fellas, Corporal?" one of the guards called, indicating a couple of blue-clad soldiers a few feet away who were now digging graves. "Want them to quit and lay down, too?"

" 'Ceptin' them," the corporal said. "They can keep diggin'. And when they're done, bring 'em back here with the rest. You, you, and you," the corporal said pointing, "you'll stand guard around these prisoners. Shoot if even one makes a move. And if it looks like he's gettin' away from you, well then just shoot one o' these fellers here." The corporal pointed toward the men sitting on the ground. He gave an evil laugh as he walked away.

Lucas could still hear the sound of fighting, but any hopes he might have had of the Union army overrunning this position to rescue them quickly faded as the sound of musketry and cannonading grew more and more distant.

Lucas studied the men who had been taken prisoner with him. Their faces reflected disbelief, disgust, and fear, mirroring, he was certain, the expression on his own face.

Lieutenant Chambers was taken away, leaving Lucas as the senior man. Several times during the long afternoon, one of his soldiers would glance over toward Lucas, as if asking him what they should do. For three years these men had been good soldiers, obeying their orders without question in the innocent faith that no matter the circumstances, their leaders would get them through. They did everything that was expected of them, yet here they were, prisoners of the Rebels.

"It's up to you, Sergeant," they seemed to be saying. *"It is your job to tell us what to do to get out of here."*

The hours dragged on and the sun slowly sank behind the wooded hills to the west. Darkness crept in from the draws and notches, came down from the hills, and moved out of the woods. The stars popped out, one by one at first, then in clusters, then in great clouds until, finally, the night sky was filled with them.

"Blackwell," the Rebel corporal said. "Get

15

a fire goin'."

"Hell, whyn't you have one o' them Yankee sons of bitches do it?" Blackwell complained, nodding toward the prisoners.

"I don't want any of 'em movin' around out there in the dark."

"Yeah, well, it just don't seem right for me to have to be a' doin' it when we got prisoners that could do it for us," Blackwell said with the air of one who was being put upon. He put his musket down and started out into the dark to gather wood.

Lucas saw one of his men looking at the Rebel's rifle, and he knew exactly what the sullen young man was thinking. Lucas stared hard, until the soldier looked over at him, then slowly, Lucas shook his head no.

"You want to try 'n pick up that gun, Yank? Whyn't you jus' go right ahead," the corporal said matter-of-factly. "Onliest thang, by the time you touch it, I'll done have your brains splattered all over the place."

The Union soldier looked away.

Lucas had fought well and bravely throughout the war, coming through battles, great and small, without consequence until he was captured.

Now, he and more than three hundred

other Union soldiers who had been taken prisoner were waiting by a railroad station in Northern Virginia, some twenty miles from the scene of the battle. Here, they would board a train that would take them to a prison camp where they would be interned for the duration of the war.

When Lucas heard the whistle of an approaching train, he looked down the track to see a stream of smoke.

"Here it comes," Dan said quietly, "and what becomes of us now, God only knows."

Lucas watched the train arrive, then brake with a squeal of steel on steel and a cloud of vented steam.

"All right, you Yankee bastards, get on your feet," one of the guards shouted. "See how good we're bein' to you? You ain't a' goin' to have to walk. You boys are about to take yourselves a nice little train ride."

There were no passenger cars. Instead, there were two slatted cattle cars.

"There's too many of us to get into just those two cars," one of the prisoners complained. His protest earned a lash from the whip one of the guards was carrying.

"Anybody else got 'ny thing to say?" the guard with the whip asked.

Nobody responded.

"Get in them cars, now," a Confederate

sergeant ordered.

"Let's go, let's go!" the other guards took up the shout, hurrying the prisoners aboard by popping whips over their heads. And though none of the boarding prisoners was actually struck by the whips, their popping presence was enough to keep the men moving.

Lucas followed the others up the inclined plank and into the cattle car. There were so many men packed into the car that there was no place to lie down and barely enough room to sit.

Lucas and Dan were both slammed up against the side of the car, but all things considered, Lucas believed that if he had to be crowded into a car like this, it was better to be next to the slats where he would at least get some air.

Through the slats, Lucas watched as a man standing alongside the track waved his arm toward the front of the train. That was answered with two long whistles. Then with bone-rattling jerks, the train began moving.

During the exhausting three-day trip, the men were given very little water and even less food. Any need for a toilet was taken care of in the car, and despite any air that might be coming through the slats, the car was overpowered by the stench of human urine and feces.

Eventually, the men learned that even though there was no room to lie down, they could get some rest by leaning against one another. Lucas discovered how to disassociate himself from reality so that he could observe, rather than physically experience, the sights, sounds, smells, tastes, and tactile sensations of the crowded car.

Then, mid-morning on the third day, the train made a stop that was different from the earlier fuel and water stops. This stop stretched much longer, and the men began to have the hope that their long trip had ended.

"Hey, look," someone said, "look at all them guards out there. They's sure a bunch of 'em."

"Boys, we must be here."

"Yeah, but where is here?"

"I reckon we're about to find out," someone said.

The door to the car was thrown open and Confederate guards, standing on the ground just outside the car, started yelling.

"Let's go, Yankees! Everyone out of the car!"

Once all the men had off-loaded the train, Lucas, who was the ranking man of his unit, held up his arm.

"All you men of the Fifth Missouri form up here," he called out in his best military voice.

Dan Lindell, and a few other prisoners from the same unit, started to respond to Lucas's call. They were halted in their efforts to form up by guards who holding whips, lashed out at them.

"There ain't a' goin' to be no one a' givin' nobody no orders here but us!" one of the guards shouted. "Now seein' as how you boys are a' wantin' to form up, you just form up right here."

With pushing and lashings from whips that some of the guards were carrying, they managed to get the prisoners into the kind of formation they wanted. Once they were formed, a Confederate sergeant took charge and started the group moving.

"We aim to shoot any of y'all that ain't 'a keepin' up," one of the guards said matter-of-factly. "So, iffin I was you, I wouldn't be a' hangin' back none, neither."

The road they were on was going east by north-east from the Andersonville Railroad Station. They passed over one stream, then marched alongside another. Some of the exhausted men, who were by now maddened with thirst, left formation to try and drink from the stream. Their efforts were met with rifle-butt strokes and whip lashes, forcing them back into the march.

At the end of their march, they came upon a palisade of timbers, standing upright in the ground. All around the wall and located approximately one-hundred-fifty feet apart, were elevated sentry boxes manned by armed guards. A few of the guards were watching the new prisoners as they marched up the road, but most were turned in the opposite direction, looking down into the prison.

The prisoners were halted in front of two massive wooden gates. They looked at the closed gates and the towers with increasing trepidation.

"Hey, Reb," someone shouted, "just where we at, anyhow?"

"Why, don't you know? Y'all's in Georgia now, 'n this here is Andersonville Prison," the guard answered with a smile. "Why, this here's a' goin' to be home sweet home for you boys, all the way up 'till the time we whup all the Yankees, 'n this here war's over."

Once the huge stockade gate was swung open, the prisoners moved through. Then, when those entry gates were closed and barred behind them, they saw another gate leading into the prison compound. The second gate was not yet open.

"Now, a'fore we open up this here inside gate so's that you fellers can go through, I spec's I better tell you somethin'. What y'all are goin' to see oncet you get in there is a little fence that ain't no more'n knee high. That's what we call the dead line, 'n the reason we call it the dead line is on account if anyone tries to cross it, you'll be shot dead."

The second gate was open, and the newly arrived prisoners of war crossed into the stockade.

Lucas nearly gagged from the smell as he surveyed the scene before him. The prisoners were almost skin and bones, wearing clothes that were little more than rags. A stream ran through the camp, and though he saw someone drinking from it, he saw, also, that it was, literally, a cesspool of slime and filth.

"Well, what do you think, boys?" the guard asked with a wide, mocking smile. "This here's goin' ta be your new home. I hope you gets to liken it as much as me 'n all the other guards do." He finished his comment with a loud, cackling laugh.

2

"Fresh fish!" one of the prisoners called and several others laughed, if the cackling could be called a laugh.

"Fresh fish?" Lucas asked. "I wonder what he means by that."

"You've got me," Dan said.

"It means new prisoners," one of the prisoners who had already been there said.

"Who are you?" Lucas asked.

"The name is Ken. Ken Chapelle. Who was you with?"

"Fifth Missouri. Who were you with?"

"Third Ohio. Come on, I'll show you around."

Chapelle led the little group through the crowded camp until they reached a slow-moving stream. A cloud of flies and other insects hung just over the water.

"This here, we call the swamp," Chapelle explained. "As you can see, it just about cuts the prison into two halves. This here side is the north half. Cross the bridge over there," he pointed to a little footbridge near the wall, that crossed the stream, "and you'll get into the south side. There's two streets run across — Main Street right behind us, and South Street way down to the other end of the compound. Tell me, what do you think about our water supply?"

"My God!" Lucas said, turning his head away in disgust.

"Should'a warned you, I guess. It's a little fragrant if you catch it just right."

The stench was overwhelming, and the incessant buzzing of the flies was even louder than the constant chatter of the hundreds upon hundreds of men who were gathered around the stream. Some were bathing in it, others were doing their laundry, while a few were openly using it as a latrine. Despite all that, Lucas saw some people drinking from it.

Before they ever reached the edge of the water, the flies attacked them in droves. Lucas and the other new men began waving their arms madly to drive them away, whereas Chapelle and the older prisoners made only a few, half-hearted waves at them.

"What the damn Rebels did," Chapelle said, as if not even aware of the difficult time Lucas and the others were having with the swarming insects, "was build this whole place downstream from their own tents and horses and dogs and everything. So they do whatever they do to the water 'fore it even comes here. And, believe me, you ain't seein' a tenth of what we do to it."

"But, there are men actually *drinking* that water," Dan Lindell said.

"Yep," Chapelle answered. "But them that do's already gone crazy. A man with any sense'd die rather'n drink from it."

"Is that the only water there is?" Dan asked.

Chapelle scratched at his beard, pulling out a couple of lice. He examined them for a moment then, almost casually, tossed them aside. "Some boys and I are planning on digging a well up there," he said. "Want to see it?"

Dan was still looking at the swamp. "You mean to tell me they do . . . *everything* in there?"

Chapelle nodded.

"Then that's why this whole place has such a stink to it," Dan said.

"Ah, you'll get used to it. You'll get to where you don't even notice it so much after a couple months. C'mon, I got some pards I want you to meet.

"Now, this here road is the main street I was tellin' you about," Chapelle continued, pointing to a dirt road that ran east and west right through the middle of the camp, parallel to, but just north of the swamp. "My spot is just about a hundred yards or so north of here."

Continuing the tour, Chapelle led the little group away from the swamp, more toward the north end of the big, open field.

Lucas looked around the camp as they followed Chapelle. It was teeming with men, some moving about animatedly, others sitting lethargically, and still others lying down in the last stages of a lingering death. They passed a sign advertising a laundry and tailor shop. *This place is like a community,* Lucas thought. A community from hell, perhaps, but a community, nevertheless. "What are these things?" Lucas asked, sweeping his hand out.

"What things?"

"These . . . these shelters," Lucas said. "I see them on both sides of the swamp. They're everywhere, but they're not tents."

Chapelle chuckled. "We call 'em shebangs."

"Shebangs?"

"Don't know who come up with the name, but it seems to fit. When we first got

26

here we didn't have no shelter, none of any kind. The Rebs hadn't built no barracks, 'cause what wood they was able to come up with, they used in the stockade walls and such. What tents they had, they give to the rebel guards. Us, they just turned loose here in the open field and said this was goin' to be our home."

"What did you do?"

Chapelle sighed. "So, what could we do? We began putting tents together out of whatever we had . . . blankets, shirts, extra pants, haversacks. Some of 'em went up pretty quick, and some of 'em has got downright comfortable . . . what with diggin' a hole and buildin' up walls and coverin' it with a roof of sod, and all."

"Hey, look over there," one of the new prisoners from the Fifth Missouri said, pointing toward the Deadline. "What's goin' on?"

Lucas looked toward the Deadline and saw a prisoner calling, good-naturedly, up to one of the guards in the tower.

"Look at that guard," Lucas said. "Why, he can't be more than . . ."

"Twelve, thirteen, more'n likely," Chapelle said.

"I've seen youngsters as drummer-boys," Lucas said, "but that's a little young to be

27

guarding a bunch of prisoners, isn't it?"

"It's all the Rebs got left," Chapelle explained. "The real young ones and the real old ones, that's who guards the prisoners. Their fightin'-age men is off in the war."

"Sonny, you got something to eat?"

"Yeah," the young guard answered. "I got something to eat."

"What you got?"

"Got me two ears of corn."

"Give you a dollar for 'em." He held up the bill. "A Yankee greenback for both ears."

"What you think, Billy Bob?" the young guard called over to another guard station. "Should I give the Yankee this here corn?"

"Done told you, Wiggins. You plannin' on given any food away, you give it to me," Stevens answered.

"Watch this," Wiggins went on, grinning. "Hey, you, Yankee. Why'n't you come over here?"

The prisoner shook his head. "Not me, I ain't comin' over there."

"Ian, best you stay where you're at," one of the other prisoners called to the man who was standing at the Deadline.

"Don't worry none about me," Ian called back. "I know what I'm doin'."

Lucas felt Chapelle tense up. "What is it?" Lucas asked. "What's going on?"

"I don't like the looks of this," Chapelle said. "Look over into that other turkey roost, there."

"Turkey roost?"

"That's what we call the guard towers," Chapelle said. "You see what I see?"

Lucas looked toward one of the other "turkey roosts" and saw a Rebel lieutenant calmly watching the exchange between the prisoner and the guard.

"That there is Lieutenant Patterson, one of the most evil sons of bitches you'll ever run across," Chapelle said. "If he's got 'ny thing to do with it, even just a'watchin' it, it can't come to no good."

"You comin' over here to get your corn, or ain't you?" the young guard called, drawing Lucas's attention back to the drama at hand.

"I told you, I'm not comin' across the line," Ian replied.

"Why not?"

" 'Cause it's the Deadline. You'll shoot me if I do."

"Who says I will?" the guard called down. "Now, you want something or not?"

"Yeah, I want them two ears of corn," Ian answered.

"All right then, step across," the guard called. He held up one of the ears of corn, and took a tiny nibble. "Won't last long."

Ian turned to several of his friends, grinning broadly. "What do you think?" he asked. "Should I do it?"

"He's a Reb, ain't he, Ian? Don't trust him," one of the prisoners called back to him.

"Don't go, fella," Chapelle said, under his breath. "If you do, he'll shoot you sure as a gun is iron."

Lucas could feel the tenseness of the moment, but he couldn't understand why.

"Fellas, that's just a little boy up there," Ian said. "Why, I've spanked pups older'n he is. He ain't goin' to do nothin' to me."

"I think he's right," McSpadden said. "I can't see a boy that young doin' anything. Don't know what he's doin' up there in the first place."

"Told you, he's up there 'cause the Rebs done run out of men."

"Well, yes, but the boy is clearly just a playin'," McSpadden said. "Look at him. He's just havin' a good time, that's all."

Chapelle shook his head. "These kiddies scare me worse'n the soldiers do. Folks say they get a thirty-day furlough ever'time they shoot one of us."

"I can't believe that he'd really shoot," Lucas said. "He and the prisoner are teasing each other, aren't they?"

"Yeah, and that just proves how new this here Ian fella must be," Chapelle said. "I'm tellin' you boys right now, and I want you to listen to me. The Deadline is somethin' you don't ever want to mess with."

"But the lieutenant, he's watching it all," McSpadden said, pointing to Lieutenant Patterson, who hadn't taken his eyes off the developing drama. "Surely he'll stop it before it gets out of hand?"

"Huh," Chapelle grunted, "he's probably the one that'll sign the furlough."

"Come on, Ian, get away from there!" one of his friends shouted.

"Ah," Ian said, "he ain't gonna shoot me. Look at 'im. He's just a pup. He wants the dollar. Probably never had one before."

"Don't do it, Ian."

"I sure do want that corn," Ian said. He turned toward his friends. "Can't you just taste it?"

The young guard who was holding the ear of corn took another nibble. "Better hurry, then."

Ian hesitated for a moment, then he stuck his toe right up to the Deadline.

"Ian, no, do you want to die?" a friend pleaded.

"Damn, there's Mad Matthew!" Chapelle

said, pointing out a young man who was hopping around, crazily. The young man was dancing, and clapping his hands, and making faces at the guards.

"Mad Matthew? That what you call him? I saw him right after we got here."

"His mind is gone," Chapelle said. He sighed. "Truth is, it's a wonder ever'body's mind ain't gone, with what all we've had to go through here."

"The corn's goin' fast!" the guard warned. "You want it, you better come now." He took another bite, bigger this time, and made a show of enjoying it.

Ian looked around at his friends one more time. He smiled broadly, then he shrugged. "What the hell?" he said. "I'm goin' to do it, fellas. You watch me if I don't." He called up to the guard. "All right, here I come."

Confederate Private Stevens had been watching the interplay going on between the young guard and the prisoner, and he looked at the expression on the face of the prisoner. It was laughing, mocking even. Stevens could feel the hate for the prisoner filling his gut. He raised his rifle and sighted down the long barrel, putting the bead sight right over the center of the prisoner's chest. The prisoner was keeping a wary eye on the young guard, and didn't know that Stevens had just aimed his rifle at him. Trying to keep the young guard calm, the prisoner kept a smile fixed on his face.

"Was you grinnin' like that just a'fore you kilt my brother, Yank?" Private Stevens asked under his breath. He thumbed back the hammer.

"Ian, no!" someone yelled, just as Ian stepped over the Deadline rail and started toward the turkey roost.

Private Stevens didn't see a helpless prisoner making a benign move across the Deadline. What he saw was a murderous Yankee coming toward his brother. He pulled the trigger.

The hammer snapped down, the cap popped, then the musket boomed and kicked back against his arm.

The report of the rifle startled Lucas and the others and they looked on in shock as Ian staggered backwards, his hands clutching his throat, blood spilling through his fingers. Ian's eyes were open wide, more in disbelief than anything else. He fell back, falling just short of the Deadline rail. He flopped once, then he was still.

"You runty little son of a bitch!" one of the prisoners shouted, and several of the others began yelling and gesturing toward the young guard with the ear of corn.

"Weren't him what done the shootin'! 'T'was the other'n!" someone shouted, pointing toward Private Stevens.

Stevens brought his rifle back down while smoke was still streaming from the barrel. With hands shaking so much now that he could barely control them, he started reloading.

A couple of prisoners, including Mad Matthew, reached across the Deadline to grab Ian and drag him back.

"Don't nobody cross the line! Don't nobody else cross it!" Chapelle shouted in warning as he began pointing to the other towers. All the guards were holding their muskets at the ready.

"Hey, Patterson, you bastard! Give the little son of a bitch his thirty-day furlough . . . the dirty little coward."

"You Yanks all know the rules," Patterson called down to them. "You all know the rules."

Lucas saw the prisoners who had been most vocal turn and walk away, shaking their head in anger and disbelief.

"Thirty-day furlough," one of the old timers said. "What a Reb won't do!"

"My God," Dan said. He still hadn't been able to take his eyes off Ian's body. "These aren't people — they are worse than animals. Do they just shoot you for the fun of it?"

Thus began the first day of Lucas's time in Andersonville Prison.

3

It was night. Leaning over the railing of the towers were the guards, shadows upon shadows, keeping a vigilant watch on the prisoners below. Here and there, like winking fireflies, tiny candles flickered in the void, but they did little to push away the darkness.

This was the time for sleeping, but even when sleep did come, it provided little rest, for Lucas and the other prisoners were sleeping the slumber of the exhausted. Now, as during the day, they fought hunger, thirst, pain, mosquitoes, stench, and the numbing closeness of each other. Only the merciless beat of the sun was missing.

There was, however, one part of the camp that stood out from the rest. Like a brightly lit island in a sea of gloom, a group of men were gathered in the glare of a dozen or more torches. This was the area where a group of men congregated that Lucas soon learned were called the Raiders. The Raiders were also prisoners, but they weren't like any of the others. The Raiders were well-fed and better-clothed than the others, having earned these privileges by cooperating with the guards, turning against their own.

Tonight, they were singing bawdy chanteys, drinking whiskey, and having a party. Their raucous behavior was presided over by a large man in a gaudy, green coat.

Ben Brodie, the man in the green coat, watched as one of his "Lieutenants" slipped up to prepare a "hot-foot" for one of the more recent recruits to the Raiders. The recruit was unaware of what was happening until the burning punk reached his foot. When it did, he jumped up and let out a howl of pain.

"Ouch! Who did that?" he yelled. "What'd you go and do that for?"

The protest was met with an outburst of laughter.

"Lewis, way you was hoppin' around there, folks would think you was doin' a dance!" Eddleman teased, and again, the others laughed.

"Gimme some more of that whiskey," Brodie demanded, and in the gleam of the torchlight, the bottle changed hands. Brodie turned the bottle up and took several Adams-apple-bobbing swallows.

"Brodie, you think we'll ever get outta here?" Lewis asked, looking gingerly at his foot.

"Now, just why 'n hell would you want to get outta here?" Brodie replied. He took another drink of his whiskey. "You know, gents, we got it good here, better'n before we was captured, even. I mean, we was gettin' shot at ever' day, 'n we seen lots of our own gettin' kilt. Hell, I say let those fools stay out there on the battlefield and get their selves kilt. Long as you fellas stick by me, you'll have all the food, water," he held up the whiskey bottle, "and whiskey that you can drink. Now, you tell me. What more could a body want?"

"Maybe a pretty woman," Hedrick suggested.

"Hell, Hedrick, you never had no pretty woman before you was catched, what makes you think you ought to have one now?" Eddleman said.

"Pretty woman? Hell, somebody's ugly as you prob'ly never had no woman a'tall," Brodie added, passing the whiskey bottle around.

The Raiders laughed uproariously at their leader's joke.

"Lenny, m'lad," Brodie said.

"Yes, sir, Mr. Brodie?"

"I've a taste for some cheese scrambled in with my breakfast eggs. Take a stroll over to see our man Ferguson, and see if he can come up with any."

"What we got to trade?" Lenny asked.

"Take a couple dollars in Yankee greenbacks. That'll satisfy 'im."

"Yes, sir, Mr. Brodie," Lenny replied.

Brodie reached down into his pocket and pulled out a roll of money they had taken off the new prisoners. Ostensibly, he was the "treasurer" of the Raiders, so this wasn't his money — it was "their" money. But only he had the right to decide when, and for what, the money was to be spent. And if he spent it on himself, such as the cheese, eggs, pork, flour, peas, and other food products that he bought for his private mess, he also spent a lot for the rest of the Raiders. He bought all of their liquor, and their food . . . and if it wasn't quite as good as his own, it was, nevertheless, many times better than anything the rest of the prisoners were given.

"Hedrick," Brodie called.

"Yes?"

"The new fish arrived today. Know where they went?"

"You talkin' 'bout them Missouri boys?"

"Yeah."

Hedrick smiled. "They went over there with that Illinois bunch."

Brodie took another swallow of whiskey, then he passed the bottle over to Hedrick.

"Why don't you get a few of the boys together?" he suggested.

Hedrick drank deeply, then handed the bottle back and nodded. "I'll choose them as may be lookin' for a little excitement."

Some distance away from the Raiders' area, Lucas and a man named Wayne Ackerman were walking through the darkness. Although Wayne was swinging along on his crutches he was managing to keep up.

The two men were picking their way carefully through the shebangs stepping over, and around, sleeping and quietly-talking men.

"Need some whiskey! Got a shirt here to trade. Need some whiskey for a sergeant!" Wayne called.

"You know, Wayne, Ralph said it doesn't have to be whiskey," Lucas said quietly. "Says he'd rather have medicine."

"You haven't been here long enough to know, but I wouldn't trust any medicine as we might get from the Rebs," Wayne replied.

"Hi, fellas, what's up?" a young, not quite

40

sixteen-year-old boy asked as he joined them.

"We're tryin' to get some whiskey to use as medicine for our sergeant," Wayne answered. "Lucas, I'd like to introduce you to Newt Butrum. He was a New York drummer boy that got catched at Culpepper."

"You're kind of young for a place like this, aren't you?" Lucas asked.

"Young?" Wayne replied. He laughed, bitterly. "Hell, this boy ain't young. He's been right here in this prison ever since they built the damn place. So when you get to thinkin' about it, I reckon that makes him about the oldest man here. Now he's sort of the camp's good luck piece."

"I do bring folks good luck," Newt said. "Maybe I can bring your sergeant some." He began calling out with the others. "Got a good shirt here . . . need some good whiskey for a good sergeant . . . good shirt, good man, need some good whiskey."

"Whiskey," Wayne called.

"Need some whiskey," Lucas added, holding up the shirt to advertise what they had to trade.

"You wantin' some whiskey, you're goin' to have to see the Raiders," one of the prisoners said.

"I'd rather do without, than get anything

from them traitorous bastards," Wayne said.

After searching through the entire camp, they located half a bottle of whiskey from one of the prisoners who wasn't associated with the Raiders.

Now, in good spirits, or at least as good of spirits as they could be in such a place, they returned to the shebang where Sergeant Caviness lay, suffering with a leg wound that had become gangrenous.

"Here you are, Sarge," Wayne said. "Drink this, it'll help with the pain."

"Thank you," Sergeant Caviness said in a voice that was racked with pain.

"Here now!" Brodie said, coming upon them with at least ten men behind him. Unlike the other men of the Andersonville Prison, Brodie and the men with him were well fed. They were also armed with clubs and a few even had hatchets.

"There ain't no need o' wastin' whiskey on somebody that'll more 'n likely be dead tomorrow. Hand it over."

"Like hell, we will," Lucas said. "I'll break the damn bottle before I let any of you have it."

"Boys, we need to teach this here feller a lesson," Brodie said. "He needs to learn who his betters are."

Four men approached Lucas then, and

two on either side, grabbed his arms. As they held him, Brodie began to beat on him, showering punches until Lucas passed out.

For Lucas's remaining time in Andersonville, he learned more about the group of men that the other prisoners called the Raiders. The Raiders sold the guards information on the other prisoners. For their cooperation, they received an almost unlimited supply of food, clothing, whiskey, and anything else they might need to make their stay in prison more tolerable.

Four of the men who had been together with the Fifth Missouri made plans to escape. The four were Lucas Cain, Dan Lindell, Ely Bagby, and Jeremy Karnes. They had discovered that when the guards changed in the middle of the night, there was about a five-minute time period when they were not quite as observant.

They made their plans to escape at two o'clock in the morning, when all the tower guards would be changing. They chose the location of their escape very carefully, knowing that if they went out between guard towers four and five, there wasn't as much overlapping coverage. Also, there was less open space from the wall to the trees where they would have cover. Their plan was to tunnel under the wall.

When the time came for their escape, the four men gathered in the dark, then Bagby and Karnes started toward the wall. The flash of gunfire lit up the night, and Lucas saw Bagby and Karnes go down. He heard someone laughing.

"See there, I told you what them boys had planned." Four guards and Ben Brodie appeared out of the dark.

"Thank ya, boys, you just put me in real good with the guards," Brodie said.

A few days later, Brodie appeared outside a fenced enclosure where Lucas and Dan were being retained. The already starving rations the prisoners received had been cut in half for Lucas and Dan, and the two men were barely surviving.

Brodie was eating a biscuit. "Uhm, uhm, these bacon biscuits are real good. This here's my third one." He held the biscuit close to them so they could smell the bacon. "I need to thank you boys for tryin' to escape like you done. Them guards have been plenty good to me. If you're thinkin' 'bout tryin' 'ny thing else, let me know. No tellin' what I'll get next time."

Every day of Lucas's internment was a fight for survival until the day the war was over, and he was finally freed.

Forty-five thousand prisoners had been held at Andersonville under the tyrannical command of Major Henry Wirz. Due to the inhumane treatment, thirteen thousand Union soldiers died while in captivity.

As the prisoners were released, Lucas, Dan, and half a dozen others went looking for Brodie and the Raiders. They had a score to settle, and now that the Rebel guards had all been rendered impotent, there was nothing to keep them from getting revenge.

As it developed, however, they were denied their opportunity for retribution. Brodie and the others, knowing what they might face from their fellow prisoners, had finagled a way to leave before the other prisoners, so the quest for vengeance was denied.

Vicksburg, Mississippi – April 24, 1865
With the war's end, Lucas Cain, Dan Lindell, and every other Union soldier who had been held by the Confederates, were free to return home. Home for Lucas was Cape Girardeau, Missouri, a small town on the Mississippi River. And it was because of its location that Lucas would be traveling up river from Vicksburg on the side-wheeler riverboat, the *Sultana.*

45

Captain of the *Sultana,* Captain J. Cass Mason learned from Lieutenant Colonel Reuben Hatch that the U.S. government would pay steamboat captains five dollars for every enlisted man and ten dollars for every officer they transported home. Hatch guaranteed to provide former prisoners as passengers, if Mason would pay him a kick-back.

Mason agreed.

One of the *Sultana*'s boilers had recently sprung a leak. A mechanic recommended a seam replacement, but that would take several days, during which time Mason feared that another steamboat would come and take his promised load. Mason, there-fore convinced the mechanic to simply patch the leak.

"How many men did you say would be on the boat?" Lucas asked.

"Somewhat over two thousand," the Union naval officer who was processing the prisoners, answered.

"Will the *Sultana* hold that many?" Lucas asked.

The naval officer chuckled. "Well, you won't be getting staterooms, that's for sure. But then you didn't exactly have a stateroom in that Reb prison you just left, either, did you?"

"You've got that right."

"So, my advice to you, Sergeant, is to just find yourself a place somewhere on that boat, and hang on 'till you get to St. Louis."

"I'll be getting off before St. Louis," Lucas said.

"Well, there you go, then. Your trip will be over in just a few days."

Lucas walked down to the dock to look at the *Sultana.* This boat would take him to the home he hadn't seen in almost five years of war. It was a big boat with its name painted on the fender skirt that covered the side paddle wheel. He didn't care if he would be a deck passenger for the whole trip, he was going home, and that was his primary, glorious, thought.

"All right, you men, start boarding," someone shouted, and Lucas joined the long line of emaciated men shuffling toward the boat. He found a place on the hurricane deck, and even managed to sit down and lean back against the wall of the after-cabin. Passengers composed almost entirely of former prisoners of war continued to come aboard for nearly an hour longer. Lucas saw that one of the boarding passengers was Ben Brodie, the leader of the despicable Raiders. As they continued loading, he saw that Brodie was at the opposite end of the boat from him, and as crowded as it was, there was no way he could get to him. Although he had initially sworn to get revenge, the fact that he was now free and going home pushed any thoughts of revenge away.

When the last man had boarded, the ship's horn sounded and the first rush of steam burst from the pipes with a sound that reminded Lucas of cannon fire. The boat pulled out into the middle of the Mississippi River, pointed its nose north, then with the twin side paddle wheels beating against the water, started upstream. When the *Sultana* left Vicksburg, it was crammed with 2,427 passengers, sixty horses and mules, and over a hundred hogs.

As the boat started its journey, the men cheered.

"We're goin' home, Lucas, we're goin' home," Dan said excitedly. "I've got a five-year-old daughter that I haven't seen since she learned to talk."

"It'll be a happy reunion for you," Lucas said. "For all of us, I suppose."

As the *Sultana* beat its way upriver, conditions on the boat were nearly as bad as they had been in the prison camps. To begin with, the *Sultana* wasn't normally a passenger carrying boat; it was a cargo boat, so there were no quarters as such for the men.

And though the US government would pay five dollars for each enlisted man and ten dollars for each officer, there was no difference between the officers and men in the accommodations. Because of the number of passengers on the boat, they were lucky if they could find a place in the cargo hold or on one of the decks that gave them room enough to lie down. In addition to finding space, food was another problem. There was no specific dining area, so the men were given mostly hardtack and a small piece of ham to eat wherever they were.

Nobody complained, because although none of the few officers aboard had been prisoners of war, nearly all the enlisted men had been, and they had all come through even worse conditions in both the Cahaba and Andersonville prison camps. The fact that they were going home kept everyone's spirits up, and they shared their joy with each other, talking about parents, wives, and children who they were certain would be waiting for them.

The Mississippi River was more difficult to navigate than it normally was. Heavy rains had caused the river to rise, and created a stronger current than usual. In addition, there were tree limbs and other debris that Captain Mason had to avoid, so that sometimes the port wheel would go forward as the starboard wheel was put in reverse, causing abrupt turns which would throw the passengers off balance.

Then, at two o'clock in the morning of the 27th of April, the boat was struggling against the surging current of the Mississippi River eight miles north of Memphis, Tennessee, when suddenly one of the boilers exploded. The boat was ripped in half by the explosion, which also ignited flames and released scalding steam.

Lucas and Dan were sleeping on the after-hurricane deck and awakened to the gruesome scene of bodies, along with metal fragments from the boilers, splintered wood, and other debris raining down on the boat and into the water.

One of the two boat chimneys came crashing down on the hurricane deck, killing many.

"Dan!" Lucas shouted. "Come on, we have to get off this boat!"

"I can't, Lucas, I'm trapped under whatever the hell this thing is that fell on us."

Lucas worked his way through the flames until he reached Lindell where he saw that Dan's leg was trapped under part of the fallen chimney. He tried to move the chimney, but it was too heavy.

"Go on, Lucas, leave me," Dan said, his eyes brimming with tears. "This here boat's 'bout to sink. You need to go on."

"Not without you," Lucas said.

The flames grew higher and hotter, and try as he may, the chimney refused to move.

"Here, let me help!" someone said, and looking toward the speaker, Lucas saw one of the men he recognized as a deckhand on the boat.

The two men worked frantically trying to free Dan, then the boat crewman saw an axe.

"Try this," the deckhand said, handing the axe to Lucas.

Lucas began chopping away at the chimney while the deckhand cleared away the debris. As the two worked, they could hear others screaming in terror and pain.

Finally, Lucas chopped away enough of the chimney debris that he was able to free Lindell.

"Come on, Dan, we've got to get off this boat!" Lucas shouted.

"I can't swim," Dan said.

"That's all right, I can," Lucas replied. Lucas looked at the deckhand who had helped them. "You coming with us?"

"You go ahead, I'll be along shortly," the deckhand said.

"Good luck," Lucas said, then he and Dan jumped from the burning boat.

When Lucas hit the water, the cold took his breath away. The *Sultana* was near mid-channel and it was over a mile to either bank of the river. Beside him, Lindell was splashing about in absolute terror. Lucas saw a wide piece of wood floating by, and he grabbed hold of it with one hand while reaching out with the other to pull Lindell over.

"Dan, quit splashing and grab hold of this," Lucas shouted.

Lindell grabbed hold of the buoyant debris, then realizing he wasn't going to drown, quit fighting.

As the two men held on, they could hear the screams of panic and pain from those who were still on the burning boat, the flames of which cast an eerie glow into the night and onto the mass of live and dead humanity either thrashing or bobbing about the sinking boat. Chaos ensued as those in the water either tried to help one another or competed for handholds on every available piece of floating debris.

"Hold on, and if you can, kick your legs," Lucas explained, and with him and Lindell both kicking, they were able to generate some propulsion.

■ ■ ■ ■

One of the other passengers on the boat was Ben Brodie. Because Brodie had been one of the Raiders, he had managed to hide from the other prisoners. But when the boilers exploded, and the boat started to sink, he jumped into the water and started a desperate splashing, trying to keep afloat. He saw one of the other passengers clinging to a board to provide some buoyancy. He recognized the passenger as Lenny Eddleman.

Brodie managed to make his way to the board, then he grabbed one end of it. The board started down.

"This isn't big enough to support both of us," Lenny said. "You need to find another board."

"This one will do," Brodie said.

"No, it won't. I told you . . ." Lenny stopped in mid-sentence. "Brodie, it's you!"

"Good to see another Raider made it off that wreck," Brodie said, "but I think I'll just keep this board for myself."

"What the hell do you mean you'll . . . *unh*!"

Eddleman's grunt of pain was because Brodie, who had a knife with him, stabbed

Eddleman in the back. The sudden shock of pain caused Eddleman to lose his grip on the board.

"Thanks for the board," Brodie said, as he began kicking his feet to pull away from Eddleman, who was struggling in his death throes.

On the opposite side of the boat, Lucas and Dan finally reached the Arkansas side of the river. Even though it was in the middle of the night, the sound of the boiler exploding and the resultant flames had brought dozens of people down to the river's edge. Seeing Lucas and Dan, two of the onlookers waded out into the cold water to help them ashore.

The two men were both wearing the remnants of Confederate uniforms, and though but a few weeks earlier they had been bitter enemies, now they were doing all they could to help a couple of Yankee soldiers.

"I got a fahr in m' heatin' stove, iffen you two would like to come warm up a mite," one of the men said.

"Thank you, that's very kind of you, Mr., uh . . ." Lucas said, pausing to allow the man to give his name.

"It's Jackson," the man replied. "Theodore Jackson, but you fellers can call me Ted."

Lucas, supporting Dan as best as he could, followed the man about two hundred yards to his house.

"Marthy Ann, get these here fellers some coffee to help 'em warm up. They was on that boat that blowed up out there in the river."

"Oh, heavens," Martha Ann said. "Look at you two. You must be near on freezin' to death."

"Yes, ma'am," Lucas said. "We're cold, all right."

"I'll make some coffee."

"What was you two a' doin' on that boat?" Ted asked.

"We were trying to get home," Lucas said.

"You don't say," Ted said. "There'll be another boat comin' through a'fore too long, 'n I reckon you could go on it, lessen this here thing has you a' scairt o' ridin' on river boats now."

"No, I'm fine with getting on another boat, as long as it takes me back home," Lucas said.

"Me, too," Lindell added.

Martha Ann brought the coffee in, as well as a plate of doughnuts.

"Oh, thank you, ma'am," Lucas said, taking the cup of coffee with one hand, and grabbing a doughnut with the other. Lucas and Dan wolfed the doughnut down ravenously, then reached for another, and then another. Ted and Martha Ann looked on in wonder.

"You boys must be awful hungry, you must not o' et a lot, lately," Ted said.

"Almost everyone on the boat was a prisoner of war, and, well, they didn't feed us all that well in the prison camp," Lucas said.

"You poor boys," Martha Ann said. "I know it's early, but would you like some breakfast? I can cook up a pan of biscuits and fry up some bacon and eggs. Oh, and Ted and me — we like our grits if you'd like me to cook up a pot."

"Ma'am, if you had just offered us a thousand dollars in gold, it wouldn't be more welcome," Lucas said.

Lucas and Dan were lying on the porch of the Jackson home. "We shouldn't have eaten so much," Lucas said as he was experiencing severe stomach cramps.

"I know, but it was so good," Dan said. "It's worth the pain we're going through now. We could still be laying on the bank of the river, or worse yet, still floating on that piece of wood."

"Think of all those poor men who came through everything we endured, just to die on the way home," Lucas said. "It doesn't seem right."

Both men were quiet, each dwelling on his own thoughts.

"Lucas?" Dan said a little later. "What was the name of that deckhand that helped us?"

"I don't know," Lucas said. "With all that was going on, I didn't get his name."

"I hope he got off the boat all right."

"He struck me as being a pretty resourceful man," Lucas said. "I'd be willing to bet that he did."

"Yeah, I think I agree with you. But there's one bastard that I'm hopin' went down with the boat," Dan said.

"I'm thinking you mean Brodie and I'd say the odds are pretty good that he did go down with the boat."

"An awful lot of men did."

4

One week later, the stern wheeler riverboat *Caleb Malloy* put into Cape Girardeau.

"I wish you had time to come meet my folks, Dan," Lucas said.

"I'd like to," Dan said, "but we're only going to be here for half an hour, and I sure don't want to take any chance of missin' the boat when it leaves. I'm wantin' to get to St. Louis as fast as I can."

"I can't say as I blame you, with a wife and a daughter waiting for you." Lucas extended his hand. "It's been nice knowing you."

"You, too," Dan said. He smiled. "Especially since you saved my life."

Lucas chuckled. "Well, the only reason I saved your life, was because there was no beautiful young lady to save."

"What are you tellin' me? That I'm not purty?" Dan asked.

Both men laughed, then looked at one

another for a long moment. Each had been an important part of the other's life throughout the war, the prison camp, and now each wondered if he would ever see the other again.

"Take care of yourself, Lucas."

"You, too," Lucas replied. "And give your wife and little girl a kiss for me."

"Here, where do you get off kissing my wife?" Dan teased.

Lucas left the boat, then looked back to see Dan standing at the railing. They waved to each other, then Lucas walked away.

Lucas hurried home. He had not seen his parents in over four years, and he could just imagine the joy he would see on his mother's face.

When he reached the street where he lived, he stopped to look at the house. He had grown up in this house. It was a nice house, with three bedrooms, befitting someone like his father, whose job was that of a port master for river boats. He looked up and down the street, remembering all the times during his internment in Andersonville that he had pictured this very thing — him standing on the street where he had lived.

He hurried up to the house. "Ma, Pa, I'm

home!" he shouted as soon as he stepped inside.

He got no response to his happy shout, so he started through the house. He saw his dad sitting in a rocking chair in the parlor, rocking back and forth.

"Pa!" Lucas said happily. "I'm home! Where's Ma?"

Lucas's father looked up at him, not with the expression of joy Lucas had expected, but with a sad, almost challenging look on his face.

"We sent you letters, and you didn't write back. Why didn't you write back? Your mother was very hurt that you didn't answer her mail."

"Pa, I was in a prisoner of war camp. We got no mail, and we couldn't send any mail out." Lucas looked around. "Where's ma? Why hasn't she come to greet me?"

"Your mother died six months ago," another voice said.

The words hit Lucas like a blow to the stomach. "Aunt Tillie," he said. "I . . . I didn't know. I was in a Rebel prison camp, and we got no mail." He reached out to brace himself on the fireplace mantel.

"I've come here to live with Fred, so's that I can take care of him," his Aunt Tillie said.

"What about Uncle Clyde?"

Tillie shook her head, sadly. "Clyde died a few months before Irene did."

"I'm sorry, I didn't know," Lucas said again. He looked at his father for a long moment, fighting against the tears that were forming in his eyes.

"I hope you don't mind my staying here," Aunt Tillie said. "I sold my house right after Clyde died, and I don't have a place to go."

"Of course, you can stay here as long as you like," Lucas said. "You're family. What about Stanley and Lydia?"

"Stanley was killed at Chancellorsville and Lydia married Leonard Barth. He took her out to Oregon just so as he didn't have to fight. Last I heard she's got a couple of kids, but that's been a while back."

Lucas looked back toward his father. "Pa, are you still working?"

"No, the military took over managing all the river traffic."

"But the war's over now. I'm sure you could get your job back, if you wanted it."

"I don't want it," Lucas's father said, with no emotion in his voice. "With you gone to war and not knowing where you were, and me losing my job, it was just too hard on your mother. Without her, I have no reason to work."

"Are you hungry?" Tillie asked.

"Not really," Lucas said, surprising himself by his answer, since he had been in a constant state of hunger almost from the first day he had been taken prisoner.

Lucas walked out onto the front porch, and when the door was closed, he made no effort to stop the tears.

After a while, he went back into the house. "I'm sorry, Aunt Tillie, I'll eat whatever you have prepared."

"I've got fried chicken left from dinner, and I suppose I can heat up some gravy to go with the biscuits."

Lucas managed a smile. "Sounds great."

"Do you have any money?" Tillie asked when Lucas was finishing his food.

Lucas shook his head. "I don't have a penny to my name, but I'll get a job as soon as I can. Thank you, for taking care of Pa like you're doing."

"Well, it's like I told you, after Clyde died, I didn't have but a few dollars and no place to go, so I come here and Fred took me in."

With Dan Lindell

Janet had greeted Dan's return, happily, but their daughter, Lottie, who had been two years old when Dan had left for the war, couldn't remember him. She had no idea who this strange man was who had suddenly appeared in their house.

When Dan went to the St. Louis Department of Road Building and Maintenance, he was told his job as a supervisor was long gone.

"A lot of changes had to be made while you boys were gone to war," Mayor Thomas said. "You can't expect to get your old job back."

"I don't have to be the supervisor," Dan said. "I just need a job to support my family."

"I'm sorry, Dan, all my positions are filled," the mayor said. "I'm afraid there aren't any available jobs working for the city. Everyone who is anyone has a son or a brother or a friend who's looking for work, and unfortunately, those are the people who got the jobs."

The next two weeks were very difficult for Dan. Not only was he unable to find employment, his daughter still didn't want anything to do with him. Then, one afternoon after a fruitless morning of job hunting, Dan returned home. He couldn't go in and tell Janet that once again he had found nothing. He sat down on an old bench on the front porch. He lost track of time as he watched the traffic going back and forth on Gravois, a street the paving of which he had supervised.

"Dan, honey, what's wrong?" Janet asked, coming out onto the front porch.

"How have you and Lottie lived while I was gone? I certainly couldn't send you any money while I was in prison."

"We made it," Janet said. "I took a few jobs here and there, and Papa helped us out. Why do you ask?"

"I haven't been able to find a job anywhere."

Janet walked over and put her hand on his shoulder.

"I'm not worried, something will come up," she said. "You're too good a man not to have a job, somewhere, and more than just a job, you'll get on as a supervisor. I just know you will."

Lottie came out onto the front porch then, and she stood there for a moment, watching her mother and father. Then she walked over, and climbed up on the bench and then into Dan's lap.

"Don't be sad, Daddy. It'll be all right," she said.

Except for answering his questions in as few words as possible, this was the first time Lottie had ever initiated any conversation with him. He leaned forward and gave her a gentle kiss on the top of her head. He was glad she was looking away from him, because he didn't think it would be good for her to see him cry.

"Yes, sweetheart, everything is going to be just fine."

Two weeks later, Dan managed to get a good-paying job with the Missouri Pacific Railroad. He had reason to believe that there would be a considerable improvement in his prospects for the future.

Cape Girardeau

Lucas's prospects for employment had been as bleak as Dan's initial efforts. He had been offered jobs working in a livery stable or clerking in a store. Because of his dad's connections, he wound up getting the job of load master, supervising the loading and unloading of freight onto and off the boats at the river front.

"Just because your old man was port manager, don't think you're going to get any special treatment here," Pat Nickens, one of the workers said.

Nickens, who felt that he should have been the load master, became a thorn in Lucas's side. He complained about everything, and began bossing the other stevedores around, as if he were in charge.

Lucas put up with Nickens for about a

year, until it finally reached the point to where Lucas found it necessary to fire him.

After that, various items began disappearing from the shipments. Lucas was pretty sure he knew who the culprit was, so one night when a hundred dollars' worth of fifty-pound crates of coffee had come up from New Orleans, he realized that this would be a tempting target.

Armed with a pistol, Lucas waited in the dark until midnight when he heard a buckboard approaching the docks. There were two men in the buckboard, but because of the darkness, he couldn't see them well enough to identify either of them.

He waited until they started loading the coffee, then with pistol in hand, he challenged them.

"Nickens," he said, recognizing him. "I might have known you were behind the shortages. I don't know who your friend is."

"What the hell are you doing here?" Nickens asked.

"Well, it would appear that I'm protecting the cargo I'm responsible for. Come along with me, boys, we're going down to the police station."

"And what if we don't?" Nickens asked.

"If you don't, I'll shoot you and then take you down there."

"You really expect me to believe you'll shoot?" Nickens challenged.

"Well, I shot a lot of men during the war, and they were probably good men, not low-down thieving bastards like you two. So, what will it be?"

"I'll put 'em in jail for now," the night-desk sergeant said when Lucas turned them in at the police station. "But tomorrow, you need to come see the Chief so you can make out charges against them."

"I've got the charge-paper made out," Grady Cornwell, the chief of police told Lucas the next day. "All you have to do is sign it, and Mr. Nickens will go before the judge for theft."

"What about the other man, the one who was with Nickens?" Lucas asked.

The chief smiled. "Oh, that gentleman is Tuck Yarborough. He's already got paper out on him, so we'll just add this charge to it. Oh, and by bringing Yarborough in, you've earned yourself two hundred-fifty dollars."

"What?"

"That's right. There's a two-hundred-fifty-dollar reward for his capture."

"How about that?" Lucas said, with a broad smile.

"By the way, Mr. Cain, we have an opening for a police officer. If you're interested, I think you'd make a pretty good one."

"What does it pay?" Lucas asked.

"Nothing."

"What?"

Cornwell chuckled. "You won't be salaried, because policemen don't get a salary, but it all works out, because you'll receive fees for specific actions like when you serve a delinquent summons, or when you make an arrest. Also, because you don't receive a salary, you'll be able to collect rewards such as the one you'll be getting for bringin' in Yarborough. So, what about it?"

"Give me a day to think about it," Lucas said.

"All right, I'll hold the job open for a day. But after tomorrow, I'll have to look for someone else."

Lucas would have taken the job in a minute, but first he wanted to talk it over with his father.

"How are you going to make a living with a job that doesn't pay a salary?" Fred Cain asked.

"They don't pay a salary, so we can collect rewards," Lucas said. "Pop, I think I could wind up making more money than

I'm making down at the dock, and to be honest with you, I would much rather be a policeman than load and unload river boats."

Lucas's father let out a sigh. "You have to live your own life, son. I can't live it for you. I'd like to see you stay on the river, but you do whatever you think is best."

5

Within his first couple of weeks, Lucas made two arrests, receiving a reward for each of the two men he brought in. The rewards, plus the fees he received, gave him an income that was significantly higher than what he had been making as a load master.

This income continued for the next six months, so that his dad not only accepted his change of occupation, but became an enthusiastic supporter.

Then one day out of the blue, the local newspaper, the *Cape Girardeau Weekly Argus*, decided to do an article about the Confederate prison at Andersonville. Upon learning that Lucas had been a prisoner there, the paper sent someone to interview him. Lucas was at his desk, when one of the other policemen came to speak to him.

"Lucas, there's somebody here from the *Argus* that wants to talk to you about bein' a prisoner at Andersonville," Elliot

Poppell said.

"I've had enough of Andersonville. Send him away."

Poppell smiled. "I will if you want me to, but if it was me, I'd talk to her."

"Her?"

"Yeah, her, 'n she's a pretty thing, too."

More from curiosity than anything else, Lucas agreed to talk to her. And when he met with her, what he saw was a young woman about five feet eight, thin, but with well-rounded curves, blonde hair and blue eyes. She had a light, barely perceptible spray of freckles across well-defined cheeks, and a pert nose.

Lucas agreed with Poppell that she was quite attractive.

"Mr. Cain, my name is Rosie Compton. Thank you for agreeing to see me."

"Well, as far as seeing you, I must say that you are considerably easier to look at than most newspaper people I've had the occasion to meet."

Rosie blushed. "I, uh, thank you. But the *Argus* has sent me here to talk to you if you will cooperate."

"All right," Lucas said, "but there's nothing pleasant I can say about Andersonville."

"Given what I have read of it, I can certainly understand that."

The interview not only produced a story, but Lucas and Rosie also began a relationship. After they had supper together a few times, Lucas asked her to come meet his father. He had already told his father and his aunt about her, so when he brought her to the house, his aunt Tillie had gone all out to prepare a meal worthy of a Sunday dinner.

After they were finished eating, Rosie offered to help Tillie with the dishes, and though Tillie said that wasn't necessary, Rosie insisted.

"Boy," Lucas's father said, when the women were out of earshot, "don't let that one get away."

"I don't intend to," Lucas replied.

Two weeks later, their romance almost came to a tragic end. For some time now, Rosie had been asking Lucas to let her go with him on one of his police jobs. Lucas finally agreed, saying that she could go when he served a summons. It was one of the routine jobs, for which Lucas would receive seven dollars and fifty cents. He was to serve a summons for disturbance of the peace, and there was nothing dangerous about it.

Or, so Lucas thought.

The subject of the summons, Gus Myles,

worked as a hostler for the Southeast Missouri Stagecoach Line, but Lucas didn't want to serve him at work. He thought that would keep Myles from being embarrassed in front of those who worked with him.

"You stay close to me," Lucas said when he pulled the police surrey to a stop in front of the small cabin where Myles lived.

Lucas and Rosie started up toward the cabin when, without any warning, Myles stepped out of the cabin with pistol in hand. He took a shot, and Lucas could hear the bullet snapping by at head height.

"Get behind me!" Lucas shouted, as he pushed Rosie behind him. He dropped the summons and drew his pistol in one quick movement.

Lucas got off a shot before Myles could shoot a second time, and Lucas's bullet hit Myles in the center of his chest. Myles dropped his pistol, then slapped his hands over the bullet wound.

"You . . . you done killed me," he said.

And so Lucas had.

It later developed that Myles had resisted the minor summons because he was actually wanted for murder up in Hannibal, Missouri. The reward for him was one thousand dollars, dead or alive.

A few weeks later, Lucas made arrangements to take a boat ride down the river to the town of Commerce, and he invited Rosie to go with him.

"It'll take a whole day," he said. "We'll go down on a Memphis boat, and then we'll come back on a boat bound for St. Louis."

"You'll never believe this," Rosie said, "but even though I've lived in Cape Girardeau my whole life, I've never been on a river boat."

"Well, then it's time we fixed that."

It took them just over an hour to go down river to the small river-town. There, they bought a small loaf of hot bread and some roast pork from one of the general stores. They took the food to a bench on a bluff overlooking the river. Lucas tore the bread into two pieces and handed one to Rosie.

"You don't expect me to eat this whole thing, do you?" Rosie protested.

"Eat whatever you want," Lucas said, "but we're going to need a lot of energy."

They sat on the bench for well over an hour just watching the river traffic. Some were small boats flitting back and forth from the Illinois side of the river while others were large paddle-wheelers beating their way against the strong current of the Mississippi.

"All right," Lucas said, "let's do some

exploring."

Rosie was impressed and surprised with the fine homes that had been built in the little town. Also, there were more businesses than she would have expected. After a very pleasant afternoon, they made their way back to the river just in time to watch the St. Louis bound river boat coming into sight. The port master put up a flag indicating to the captain that there would be passengers or freight waiting to board the boat.

"This has been one of the most enjoyable days I've ever had," Rosie said, as she and Lucas stood on the deck looking at the sunset. "Sometimes it's good to just do nothing."

"I hope I can make the day even more wonderful," Lucas said.

"How could it possibly be more wonderful than this?"

"If you would agree to marry me," Lucas said.

Rosie gasped. "Oh, Lucas, are you asking me to marry you?"

"Yes, I am," Lucas said as he took her hands in his. "Rosie Compton, will you marry me?"

"Yes, oh, yes, I will marry you!" Rosie replied.

Lucas pulled her into his arms and they

kissed. The river pilot, who knew Lucas from his days as the load master, pulled the lanyard to blow the horn.

Dan was going through the mail, and saw a letter from Lucas Cain. Although they hadn't seen one another since Lucas left the boat at Cape Girardeau, they had kept in contact, so receiving the letter wasn't a surprise. What was in the letter was a surprise, however.

"Janet!" Dan called out. "You are going to get to meet my friend, Lucas."

"You mean Lucas is coming to St. Louis?"

"No," Dan said with a big smile. "We're going to meet him in Cape Girardeau. Lucas is getting married, and I'm to be his best man."

"Oh, that's wonderful!" Janet said. "You've spoken so highly of him; I was hoping I would meet him someday."

Two weeks later, Dan, Janet, and Lottie took a seven-hour boat trip down river to Cape Girardeau. Lucas and Rosie met them as they came down the gangplank.

There were introductions all around, then Rosie noticed that Lottie was feeling left out of the happy reunion. She bent over to speak to her.

"Lottie, I'm having a big problem, and

I'm hoping you can help me," she said.

"How can I help you?" Lottie asked.

"I'm going to need someone to be a flower girl in my wedding. Would you be willing to do that for me?"

"Yes!" she said happily. Then she looked toward her mother. "Would it be all right?"

"Of course, sweetheart. You'll be the best flower girl Miss Rosie could ever have," Janet said.

Rosie took Lottie's hand and the two walked off the landing ahead of the others.

Lucas thought he had never seen Rosie happier, and he could just imagine her as the mother of their child.

Lucas and Rosie were married the very next day. Dan was Lucas's best man, and Lottie, with a proud smile on her face, walked up the aisle, spreading flowers.

Abigail Sinclair, Rosie's best friend since childhood, was Rosie's maid of honor. A pianist and a cello played *Pachelbel's Canon in D,* as Rosie, escorted by her father, came walking up the aisle.

Rosie was popular, not only because of her work at the newspaper, but also because she had grown up in Cape Girardeau and the family had many friends. As a result, the First Presbyterian Church on Broadway was filled with well-wishers.

For their honeymoon, Lucas had arranged a trip down to New Orleans.

"Ha, after the *Sultana,* I wouldn't think you would ever want to get on a riverboat again," Dan said.

"Think about it, Dan," Lucas replied with a wide smile, "sitting out on the hurricane deck with you and 2400 other unwashed, uncouth men, or being in a private stateroom with a beautiful young woman who is my wife. Do you really see any comparison?"

Dan laughed. "Enjoy the trip, my friend."

It took the *Delta Mist* three days to go to New Orleans. After a week in New Orleans, enjoying all the city had to offer, they returned to Cape Girardeau on board the *Mississippi Queen,* this trip taking four days. Lucas could truly say that it was the most wonderful two weeks of his entire life.

By the time they were married, Rosie had become good friends with Tillie and had earned Fred's respect. Fred and Tillie had no problem accepting Rosie as part of their family. And, with Lucas's blessings, she continued to work at the *Argus.*

One night, a couple of months after they were married, Lucas and Rosie were sitting on the porch settee. Lucas had his arm around Rosie.

"You're awfully quiet tonight," she said. "What are you thinking?"

"I'm thinking of what my life was like during the war and then when I was in Andersonville, and now what it's like. I've never been so happy in my whole life." He pulled her closer to him, and when he did, she looked up at him and then kissed him.

"I love you, Lucas, more than I ever thought I could love anyone."

In spring of 1868, Fred Cain became ill with some undiagnosed malady. He lost all consciousness and lay in his bed for three days without saying a word. Then, at a little past seven in the evening of the twelfth of April, he suddenly sat up in bed, smiled broadly, and held out his arms.

"Oh, there's my dear love, Irene. Come to me, sweetheart!"

Tillie and Rosie had been by his bedside then, and Tillie called out to him. "Fred? Can you hear me? Rosie and I are right here with you."

Fred fell back upon his pillow, and drew his last breath. He was fifty-eight years, two months, and seven days old at the time.

Fred was buried ncxt to his wife, Irene. Because Fred Cain had been well known as the port master, several of Cape Girardeau's leading citizens had attended his funeral.

As Fred's body was being lowered into his grave, Lucas put his arm around Rosie's shoulder and drew her to him. "I was gone when he needed me the most."

"That may be, but at least he didn't have to go through his final days alone," Rosie said.

"Your father is with Irene now," Tillie said. "We know that, because she came to him, just before he died."

6

As late as 1869, Missouri was plagued by several outlaw gangs, the most infamous of those being Jesse James, his brother, Frank, and Cole, Jim, and Ely Younger. But there were many lesser known, though just as deadly outlaws. Most of the Missouri outlaws had fought for the Confederacy, Missouri having been a state with divided loyalties during the war.

One such gang, led by Quince Deckert, operated in Southeast Missouri. Deckert claimed to have fought for the Confederacy, though in truth he had been the head of a gang of outlaws who had used the Confederate flag, not to advance the cause of the South, but to enrich themselves during the war. The war ended, but Deckert's criminal activities didn't. He robbed banks, stage coaches, money couriers, and even a couple of trains.

There were two other men with Deckert,

and when they robbed a store in the Mississippi river town of Commerce, they killed the store clerk and a woman customer. A reward of fifteen hundred dollars was placed on Deckert, and seven hundred fifty dollars each for Gabe Owens and Murray Lane, the two men who rode with him. The total reward of three thousand dollars was enough to put Lucas on their trail.

"Lucas, I wish you wouldn't go," Rosie said. "These are very dangerous men."

"Now, Rosie, you know why I do this. The reward money will go a long way, especially with a baby coming."

"But I'm still working for the paper," Rosie said. "We can get by without you having to go after these men."

"I know," Lucas said, "but the time is fast coming when you can no longer work. We need to prepare for that. And even after the baby is born, you'll still have to stay home to take care of him."

Rosie smiled. "How do you know it will be a him?"

"Because that's what I want it to be."

"Oh, and that's what counts, huh?"

"Pretty much," Lucas said, with a smile. "Anyway, the reward, if I bring in all three of them, will be three thousand dollars. We can't turn our backs on that."

"All right, but, Lucas, please be careful. I don't know what I'd do, if I lost you."

"I'll be careful," Lucas promised.

Because the robbery and double murder had taken place in Commerce, Lucas informed the chief that he would take this case, then started out for the little river town of Commerce. The store that had been robbed was called Boatman's Market, on the corner of Water and St. Mary Streets, and Lucas went into the store to talk to Ernest Delaney, the owner.

"They got two hunnert 'n seventy-nine dollars," Delaney said. "They kilt my clerk, Cleve Raferty, 'n Betty Teasdale while they was a doin' it. Miz Teasdale was a good woman, 'n she warn't doin' nothin' but buyin' a packet of sewin' needles at the time."

"Do you have any idea where they went?"

"I got me a purty good idee, yeah. I've know'd Quince Deckert since he was a boy, 'n he warn't no count then, neither. He took over his pa's cabin that's in the Big Swamp, down aroun' Sikeston."

"Thanks, Mr. Delaney, you've been a big help," Lucas said.

The next day, Lucas was lying on his stomach on Sikeston Ridge, looking down at a cabin in the adjacent swamp land. There were three horses tied up in a lean-to shelter alongside the cabin, and Lucas was certain it was the three men he had been looking for. Smoke was coming from the chimney, and that gave him an idea as to how he would handle this situation.

Coming down from the ridge, making only stealthy movements, and going from tree to tree, he managed to get to the side of the cabin that had no windows. Once there, he climbed a tree, then dropped to the roof of the little cabin. Stripping out of his shirt, he stuffed it into the small, round chimney. The shirt did what he wanted it to do; it stopped the smoke.

Lucas pulled his pistol, then lay down just behind the peak of the roof, and waited. Less than a minute later, three men came out coughing and wheezing.

"Damn, Murray, you didn't check the chimney?" Deckert said.

"Chimney was just fine last time we was here," Lane said. "Hell, you two was with me, we didn't have no smoke then."

"Maybe it's a bird built a nest or somethin'," Owens suggested.

"That sure as hell ain't no bird," Deckert said.

Lucas stood up. "I'm afraid Deckert's right. That wasn't a bird that caused all that smoke. You men are under arrest."

"The hell we are!" Deckert shouted, and when he started back into the cabin, the other two went in with him.

Lucas knew they wouldn't be able to remain in the smoke-filled cabin, so he dropped down from the roof, then hurried out to stand about twenty feet in front of the door. A few seconds later, just as Lucas knew they would do, the three men came rushing back out of the cabin, but this time all three were carrying pistols.

"Shoot 'im!" Deckert shouted. "Shoot the son of a bitch!"

The three fired a couple of shots each, toward the roof, then realized that their adversary wasn't there anymore.

"I'm back here, gentlemen," Lucas said.

The three men spun around and began shooting, but their shots were hurried and wild. All missed.

Lucas shot three times, and didn't miss.

Seven months later, Rosie went into labor with what would be their first child.

"This is a good day, Rosie, our son is about to be born," Lucas said happily.

Doctor Brandt's office was within a block

of the house, so Lucas hurried down to get him. Then, as the doctor attended Rosie, Lucas paced back and forth in the living room. When he heard Rosie cry out in pain, he started toward the bedroom, but Tillie held up her hand to stop him.

"Let the doctor do his job, Lucas," she said. "You'd just be in the way."

"All right, but it sure seems to me like it's taking an awfully long time. Shouldn't the baby be here by now?"

"All we can do is wait," Tillie said.

They waited another hour, and as Rosie's cries became less and less, it became obvious that even Tillie was beginning to worry.

"What's wrong, Aunt Tillie? Does it normally take this long?"

"I don't know, I don't think so," Tillie admitted.

"If I haven't heard anything within the next five minutes, I'm going to go in there and see what —"

Lucas's comment was interrupted by the appearance of Dr. Brandt. Lucas became even more concerned when he saw the expression on Dr. Brandt's face.

"Doc, what is it?" he asked.

"I'm sorry, Lucas," Dr. Brandt said, with a sad shake of his head.

"You're sorry? What is it? What happened?" This time Lucas shouted the question.

"Childbed fever."

"What? What do you mean?"

"I'm afraid we lost her, Lucas. Rosie died during childbirth."

"No! My God, no!" Lucas shouted. He rushed by the doctor, into the bedroom where he saw Rosie lying on the bed, her legs spread upon a sheet stained with blood and the afterbirth. Her eyes were open, and unseeing.

"Rosie!" Lucas said, kneeling beside the bed and grasping her hand.

"The baby?" Tillie asked.

"A girl. She was stillborn," Dr. Brandt said in a voice that was quiet, and heavy with sorrow and regret.

Rosie's funeral was attended by many people. Most of the attendees were family and friends, but because she had worked at the paper, she was known by everyone in town, and many of these acquaintances joined family and friends.

The funeral was held in the Welch Funeral Home, and Lucas stood at the open casket, looking down at the woman he had loved. She was wearing her best dress, and the baby, wearing a white gown, had been put in her arm as if Rosie had just gone to sleep, holding her.

Lucas made no effort to wipe away the tears that were flowing silently down his cheeks.

The funeral cortege proceeded from the funeral home to the Lorimier Cemetery, where the grave had already been opened. The casket, containing the bodies of Rosie, and her baby, which Lucas had named Irene, after his own mother, was lowered into the grave. Gus Tuttle, the First Presbyterian Church minister, gave the committal prayer.

"We thank you this day for Jesus, for his precious gift of eternal life, and for the comfort of the Holy Spirit.

"In the midst of our natural sorrow, we thank you for your supernatural grace.

"In facing death, we thank you for the promise of life everlasting.

"And in the face of separation, we thank you for the assurance of eternal reunion.

"We thank you for Rosie Cain's life here on this earth, and we recognize that the body before us is not Rosie, but is the house, the tabernacle, in which she lived.

"We acknowledge that Rosie and her child are with you now, rejoicing in your presence and enjoying the blessings of heaven.

"Father, we now commit the bodies of Rosie and baby Irene Cain to this earth, and we rejoice that their spirits are with you even now.

"We look forward to that day, when we can all rejoice together, and we thank you that we are not without hope or comfort at this time.

"We thank you for making your presence very real to each family member, and that you will especially strengthen and sustain Lucas in the days, weeks, and months to come.

"In Jesus Name, Amen."

Those who were present for the committal repeated "Amen," then Lucas stepped over to the open grave, holding a handful of dirt.

"We therefore commit this body to the ground, earth to earth, ashes to ashes, dust to dust; in sure and certain hope of the Resurrection to eternal life," Tuttle said.

Lucas turned his hand to drop the dirt into the grave. The sound of the dirt hitting the coffin was like a hammer blow to his heart.

"Aunt Tillie, I'll be leaving Cape Girardeau," Lucas said, a few days after the funeral.

"Leaving? What do you mean you'll be leaving? Where will you go?"

"I don't know," Lucas said. "I'm thinking I'll go out West somewhere. I hate to desert you like this but . . ." He was quiet for a moment, then he let out an audible sigh. "I just can't stay here any longer."

"Well, I understand but I'll hate to see you go. I'll miss you."

"Without Rosie, there's nothing to hold me here. It just hurts too much."

"Lucas, in a way, you never came back after the war, at least not to the home you knew. Your mother was dead and then you lost your father. And now Rosie is no longer here for you, and the child she bore was never with us. Yes," Tillie said, nodding her head, "I can understand how hard it would be for you to stay here."

"I'm glad you can see that." Lucas took a sheet of paper from his pocket, and handed it to his aunt. "I want you to have this."

"What is it?"

"It's the deed to this house. The house is yours now."

"Oh, Lucas, no, you don't have to do that."

Lucas smiled. "I know I didn't have to. But doesn't that make the gift even better? I mean, if I don't have to give it to you?"

"Oh, Lucas, I don't know how to thank you," Tillie said. She wiped tears away from her eyes. "You were such a sweet boy when you were young, and I'm glad to see that you are as sweet now as you were then."

"I was a sweet boy? So, does that mean you've forgotten the time I dropped the cat down the well?"

Tillie laughed. "Well, there was that, but all's well that ended well, because we did get him back, mad and wet, but none the worse for it."

"Yeah, but as I recall, I still got a whippin' for it."

"As well you should have," Tillie said. She laughed, then again grew melancholy. "I'm going to miss you, Lucas Cain. Promise me you'll write to your old aunt now and then, just to let me know how you're doing."

"I promise," Lucas said, as he stepped into his aunt's open arms.

By now, Lucas had saved up more than three thousand dollars, and he gave two thousand of it to his Aunt Tillie.

"This should hold you for a while, and I'll send you more from time to time," Lucas promised. "At least enough to keep you going."

"Oh, Lucas, I'm going to worry about you," Aunt Tillie said as, with tears streaming down her cheeks, she gave Lucas an affectionate embrace.

After a leisurely, three-day ride to St. Louis, he called on Dan Lindell and his family, where he was given a warm welcome.

"Rosie didn't come with you?" Janet asked.

Lucas was silent for a long moment, and Janet read the expression on his face.

"Oh, Lucas, no," she said quietly.

"She died in childbirth," Lucas said somberly. "The baby died as well."

"Oh, Lucas," Janet said, embracing him.

"She died?" Lottie asked. "Mrs. Cain died?"

"Yes," Lucas said quietly.

Lottie, with tears flowing down her face, joined Janet in embracing Lucas.

"Lucas!" Dan said happily, arriving home then. "So you've come to see me at last. Are you a papa yet?"

"Dan," Janet said in a quiet, solemn voice. She shook her head.

"What is it?" Dan asked, his face now showing concern.

"Rosie and her baby died during childbirth," Janet said.

Dan stared at Lucas for a moment, then like Janet and Lottie had earlier, he embraced his friend.

Lucas spent three days with Dan and after the melancholy passed, he very much enjoyed his time with his old friend. Then, as he prepared to leave, Dan asked him where he was going.

"To be honest, Dan, I don't have the slightest idea. I'm just going to start exploring the west."

"Well, you don't have to start here," Dan said. "Why don't you take a train west, then start from there?"

"What would I do with my horse?"

"That's no problem. I'll get you a first-class ticket on a train that has a stock car. You can take your horse with you."

"First class?"

Dan smiled. "What's the good of me working with the railroad, if I can't do a favor for my friend?"

"All right, if you can get Charley and me on the same train, I say let's do it."

"Come down to the depot with me, and I'll introduce you to Tom Allen."

"All right, who's Tom Allen?"

"He's president of the Missouri Pacific Railroad," Dan said.

Two days later, with Charley occupying a stall in the stock car, Lucas took first class passage to Kansas City. After detraining in Kansas City, he began a long ride west, with no specific destination in mind.

7

Arriving in Topeka, Kansas, Lucas looked around and decided Topeka was as good a place as any to stay for awhile. He went first to the sheriff's office to apply for a job.

"I do need another deputy," Sheriff Moore said. "What makes you think you can handle a job like this?"

"Until about six weeks ago, I was a police officer in Cape Girardeau, Missouri," Lucas said. "It's a small town on the Mississippi River."

"Well, Topeka, Kansas, is a far cry from a quiet little river town in Missouri. You had to have some reason for leaving. I'd like to know — are you in trouble with the law?"

"No, sir, my . . ." Lucas paused for a long moment, then with an expulsion of breath, he said, "my wife died. I didn't want to stay there any longer."

Sheriff Moore nodded his head. "That I can understand."

"Thank you."

"Now if I take you on, I won't be able to pay much."

"I don't want any salary at all," Lucas said.

"You want to work for no salary?"

Harkening back to his days in Cape Girardeau, Lucas explained to the sheriff how he would rather depend on rewards.

"Good Lord, you mean you want to be a bounty hunter?"

"No, not as such," Lucas said. "I'll still do all the things that you would expect a deputy to do. It's just that as an unpaid deputy, I'll be free to accept rewards, and I'll have the authority that goes with having a badge."

Sheriff Moore smiled.

"Mr. Cain, this is one of the easiest hires I've ever made." Opening the middle drawer of his desk, the sheriff pulled out a deputy's star and handed it to Lucas. "You are now one of us. Welcome to Topeka."

Lucas smiled, then pinned the badge to his vest.

It was two weeks after Lucas took the job as deputy, that he had his first test. He was walking down Mill Street, when he heard a gunshot. Half a block in front of him, he saw two men backing out of Hinckley's jewelry store, both holding pistols, and one carrying a bag.

Lucas drew his pistol.

"You men drop your guns!" he shouted.

Both men turned toward Lucas, and both men shot at him.

Even as Lucas heard the cracking sound of the bullets whirring past him, he pulled the trigger twice. Both of the would-be robbers went down.

Lucas hurried to the two men. One was dead and the other was moaning because of the bullet in his stomach.

Lucas took the bag and both guns from the men, and then stepped into the jewelry store. One man was lying on the floor and another was kneeling beside him.

"What happened here?" Lucas asked as he moved toward the two men.

"It was awful, Deputy. John Potter here was my customer when two men came in and just started shooting. Then they took everything they could grab."

"Are you Mr. Hinckley?" Lucas asked.

"Yes, Vince Hinckley. Who's going to tell Mary Elizabeth about poor John? I'm afraid he's dead."

Lucas knelt beside the body, and after checking for a pulse, he determined that the man was indeed dead. "Is Mary Elizabeth his wife?"

"Oh no, not yet," Hinckley said as he picked up a ring that had slid across the floor. "This was to be her wedding ring. Poor thing."

Lucas felt instant empathy for the woman. "I'll ask the sheriff if he can tell her." He felt guilty that he wouldn't be telling her himself, but Rosie's death was too fresh in his mind.

"Oh, I think this belongs to you," Lucas said, as he retrieved the bag of loot he had taken from the robbers.

Hinckley let out a loud sigh. "With John being shot, I hadn't thought about what was taken. You have to know, in a frontier town like Topeka, a jeweler isn't the best place to make a good living. Not that I can complain, but if they had gotten away with my stock, I would more than likely have had to close my doors."

"Then I'm glad I could recover your stock," Lucas said. "I'll tell the sheriff about Mr. Potter."

By now, several townsmen had gathered around the two men Lucas had shot, so he stepped back outside to check on things.

"Did you shoot 'em, Deputy?" one man asked.

"I did."

"Well, this here 'n is still alive."

"Then I'd like for someone to go get the doctor," Lucas said.

"Jimmy Lee's already done it," the man said.

"Yeah, here he comes now," another added.

The two men Lucas had shot were Ike Hudson and Al Martel. Hudson was killed on the scene, but Martel survived, to be tried for the murder of John Potter.

The prosecuting attorney was Lamar Fawcett. Fawcett called Vince Hinckley as his first witness.

Hinckley explained how John Potter was buying a wedding ring for Mary Elizabeth Bentley.

"They came into the store, and while one of them held a gun on me, the other one started filling a cloth bag with all the items I had in my case. Rings, necklaces, broaches — but mainly watches."

"Which of the two men was holding the gun?"

Hinckley pointed to Martel. "He was."

When Lucas took the witness stand, he told how he just happened to be walking down Mill Street when he heard the shot, and saw Martel and Hudson backing out of the jewelry store, each holding a pistol.

Mary Elizabeth was the next witness.

"Your Honor, I object!" Jason Dither, the court-appointed defense attorney said. "The prosecutor is obviously using this poor young lady for dramatic effect."

"Your Honor, as Miss Bentley was directly impacted by the heinous crime, the court believes she should be heard," Fawcett responded.

"Objection overruled. The witness may testify," the judge said.

Mary Elizabeth testified as to how she and John Potter had planned for the wedding. She extolled all of John's virtues, and told how much she loved him. Mary Elizabeth's testimony was given around tears of sorrow.

Lucas was the final witness for the prosecution.

Al Martel demanded to be allowed to testify on his own account.

"Here's the thing, Judge," Martel began. "I ain't the one what shot 'im. That was Hudson, what shot him."

"Your witness, Mr. Fawcett," the judge said.

"There is really no need for cross examination, Your Honor. Martel has just confessed to the murder."

"What?" Martel blurted out. "I didn't do

no such thing. What I said was, that it was Hudson what shot 'im."

"How do you know that Hudson shot Mr. Potter?"

"On account of I was there, 'n I seen it," Martel said.

Fawcett smiled. "And therein, gentlemen of the jury, is Mr. Martel's confession. By Mr. Martel's own admission, he was a participant in the felony which resulted in the death Mr. Potter. The law is quite clear. If someone dies during the commission of a felony, it makes no difference whose bullet actually killed him. Mr. Martel is guilty of murder because he took part in the felony that got John Potter killed," the prosecutor said.

The jury was convinced by Fawcett's argument, and they found Al Martel guilty of murder in the first degree.

Judge Abernathy P. Richter sentenced Martel to death by hanging.

The day after Martel was hanged, Sheriff Moore showed Lucas two reward flyers.

"Well, Lucas, seems like your idea of giving up your salary is working for you. Turns out there was a reward of seven hundred fifty dollars on both Hudson and Martel. That amounts to fifteen hundred dollars

101

which goes to you," the sheriff said. "You know that'd be more 'n two years pay if you took a salary."

"Well, well," Lucas said, as a smile crossed his face.

Over the next several weeks, Lucas made himself known to the citizens of Topeka. He had already earned a reputation of being someone who could handle himself in just about any situation, but there was more to him than that.

Lucas was also a man who would go out of his way to help someone in need. One day he was in the mercantile when he saw an old lady buy two cans of beans, but when it came time to pay for it, she didn't have enough money, so she asked the store keeper, Mr. Hanlon, to put one of the cans back.

Lucas watched as the old lady shuffled out of the store with a look of despair on her face.

"Ed, who was that lady?" Lucas asked.

"That was Mrs. McVey."

"What do you know about her?"

"Well, she's a widow woman whose husband died about a year ago. It's a sad thing, too, because they once owned a pretty decent farm. But it turns out that Jim was a gambling man, and not a very good one at that. He kept getting deeper and deeper into debt, until he lost the farm. Then he killed himself, leaving Earline destitute."

"Where does she live? How does she get by?" Lucas asked.

"She lives in a little one-room cabin in the alley behind the apothecary. She earns money by taking in washing, though, as she is in competition with Wang Chu's Laundry, she's barely hanging on."

"I want you to do me a favor."

"What's that?"

Lucas told Hanlon what he had in mind.

Over the next couple of months, the people of Topeka noticed a marked difference in Earline McVey. She no longer sulked about town, but now walked around with a smile on her face, greeting old friends. She became a regular attendee at church, and volunteered to help others who were in need. Her business grew from merely taking in a wash, to actually establishing a laundry with helpers.

All of this came about because Earline's husband had left a five-hundred-dollar credit with Ed Hanlon that he had just discovered. Only Hanlon knew where the money had actually come from, and Lucas had sworn him to secrecy.

Six months later, the citizens of Topeka, as well as all of Kansas, were shocked and incensed over the rape and murder of twelve-year-old Lucy Carmichael.

Lucy was taken from her home by Silas Coombs, a field hand who sometimes did part-time labor for her father, Millard Carmichael. Three days later, after an intense search, Lucy's body had been found in an old, abandoned cabin, twelve miles from where she had been taken. The state of Kansas issued a reward for Silas Coombs of five thousand dollars, dead or alive.

Lucas took a leave of absence from his duties as deputy sheriff in Topeka, and started a state-wide search for Coombs. Sheriff Moore and Judge Richter both agreed that it would be a judicious use of Lucas's time and talent.

Two months later, Lucas traced the fugitive to the little town of Blue Hill, Kansas. There was only one watering hole in town, the Double Down Saloon, and when Lucas stepped inside, he saw the man he was looking for standing at the opposite end of the bar. The man caught Lucas's attention and he began studying him.

There was a drawing of Coombs on the

wanted poster, but what had caught Lucas's attention was the description of the man.

Coombs is five-feet ten inches tall with a scar that runs from his forehead and through his eye, down to his left cheek.

The man standing at the bar fit that description, and Lucas continued to study him. Lucas's intense scrutiny caught the man's attention.

"Hey, you," the man said, "just what the hell are you a' lookin' at?"

"Well, right now I would say I'm looking at one of the ugliest men I've ever seen," Lucas replied. "But you aren't just ugly outside, you're ugly inside."

Coombs's response was a derisive laugh. "Well, then, if you're that much purtier than me, does that mean you want me to buy you a drink, liken I do for the whores?"

"No, but if you behave yourself when I take you down to the jail, I might give you a cup of coffee," Lucas said.

"What are you a' plannin' on takin' me to jail for? For not bein' purty?" Coombs laughed a mocking, evil laugh.

"I have my reasons."

"Mister, you ain't likely to see the sun set tonight," Coombs said.

"Oh, I'll see it. You may not."

"Why won't I?"

"It looks to me like you're thinking about drawing on me, and if you do, that would be a big mistake because I'll have to kill you," Lucas said, speaking as calmly as if ordering another beer.

"Mister, I ain't got the time to be messin' with you, so why don't you just go away and leave me alone."

Coombs turned back to the bar as if dismissing Lucas.

"I'll let you finish your beer before I take you to jail," Lucas said.

Suddenly, and with a loud yell of defiance, Coombs swung back toward Lucas, making a grab for his pistol.

Coombs had the advantage of drawing first, and it wasn't until after he had already started his draw that Lucas reacted, making a lightning-fast draw of his own pistol and firing. Coombs was slammed back against the bar before sliding down. He sat there, leaning back against the bar, his gun hand empty and the unfired gun lying on the floor beside him.

"Damn, I drawed first 'n you still beat me," Coombs said. He hacked a blood-spewing cough.

"Before you die, Coombs, I want you to think about someone."

Coombs coughed up some blood before

he replied. "What do you mean you want me to think about someone?"

"Lucy Carmichael."

Coombs coughed again, more blood this time than before.

"Yeah, I remember Lucy. She was a purty little thing."

"She was twelve years old."

"Twelve years old. Yeah, that might be right. I 'member she didn't hardly have no titties at all."

"That didn't stop you from raping her though, did it?"

"Hell, I spec' she even likened it."

Lucas reached down and stuck his finger in the bullet hole.

"Ow! What the hell did you do that for?"

"I wanted to give you a little more pain before you died," Lucas said.

"What the hell's your name?" Coombs asked.

"Lucas Cain. I want you to know who killed you."

"I tell you what, Lucas Cain. Me 'n you's goin to be meetin' again someday, 'cause I'm goin' to be holdin' open a place for you in hell," Coombs said in a racking voice. He tried to laugh. "I'll get a poker game up, 'n me 'n the devil will hold a seat for you."

There was a rattling sound deep in

Coombs's throat, then his head fell to one side as his eyes, still open, glazed over.

"Is that right, Mister?" one of saloon patrons asked. "Did he really rape a little twelve-year-old girl?"

"Yeah," Lucas said. "He raped and killed her."

"Dyin' is too good for the son of a bitch."

The others in the saloon voiced their own agreement.

The town marshal came into the saloon then. "What was all the shootin' about?"

Lucas pointed to the body. "Marshal, that's Silas Coombs."

"Silas Coombs? Damn, there's quite a reward out on that fella," the marshal said.

"I'll be staying here in the hotel. I'll give you ten percent if you collect the reward for me so I can get back to Topeka."

The marshal smiled. "Yes, sir! I'll have that money for you in no time!"

8

Rock Ridge, Colorado

George Rogers and two others had made camp about three miles from the Denver Pike Emporium. The name was much grander than the store itself. The store was fifteen miles from Running Creek, but it was that remote location that enabled the store to not only survive, but actually do a brisk business. The Denver Pike Emporium was the most convenient store for the four ranches and six farms of Douglas County.

"Hey, Rogers, how much money you think they got 'n that store?" Duncan asked.

"Oh, I'd say four or five hunnert dollars, at least," Rogers said.

"That ain't that much money," Peters said.

"Yeah? How much money you got now?" Duncan asked.

"I ain't got none now."

Duncan chuckled. "You hear that, Rogers?" he asked. "Peters ain't got no money a' tall, but he says five hunnert dollars ain't enough."

"Well, Peters, you don't have to take none of it," Rogers said. "Me 'n Duncan will just keep it all, 'n you can wait 'till our next job, 'n see if we can get more money for you."

"No, now wait," Peters said. "They ain't no need of doin' nothin' like that. I'll take my share of whatever we get."

"Yeah, I thought you might," Rogers said. He swallowed the rest of his coffee, then put the cup and the pot back in his saddle bags. "All right, boys, it's time for us to make a little money this morning. Let's go shoppin' at the Denver Pike Emporium."

Fifteen minutes later, they approached the small store. There were no horses or wagons outside, giving the illusion of the store being completely abandoned.

"There ain't nobody here," Peters said.

"Good," Rogers said. "That means nobody will get in the way of our business."

"Yeah," Peters said, smiling. "Yeah, that's right, ain't it?"

The three men rode up to the store, then dismounted and walked inside. There was only one person inside, a rather small, gray-haired man, who was wearing thick glasses.

"Welcome, boys," the store clerk said. "I'll

just bet I have exactly what you're lookin' for."

"And just what would that be?" Rogers asked.

The man smiled, and held up a finger. "I just got in a case of whiskey. I'm thinkin' you boys might want a bottle."

"How much?"

"Two dollars a bottle."

"Sounds good," Rogers said. "We'll take a bottle."

They waited for the store clerk to pull down a bottle, then Rogers held out a ten dollar bill. "Sorry, a ten is all I have."

"That's no problem, I can make change," the clerk said, opening his cash drawer. "That'll be eight dollars change."

"No, that'll be ever'thin' you got in that drawer," Rogers said.

"What?" The clerk looked up in fear and surprise. "What are you talking about?"

"I'm talkin' about robbin' ya, you old fool. Let me have ever'thin' you got." Rogers augmented his demand with a wave of his pistol.

While shaking in fear, the old man emptied his cash drawer and handed all the money to Rogers.

"Thank you," Rogers said, just before he pulled the trigger.

The clerk went down with a hole his forehead.

"Ha!" Peters said. "Looked to me like that old son of a bitch might a' pissed in his pants."

"How much did we get?" Duncan asked.

"I'll count it after," Rogers replied.

"After what?"

"After this."

Rogers turned his gun on Peters and Duncan, and fired twice. Both men went down.

Rogers left the store, mounted his horse, then rode away, leaving the other two horses behind.

9

Topeka, Kansas

Rosie had died two years ago on this very day. Lucas thought he was over it, but the pain of her death had never left him. He was just able to keep it buried most of the time. Today, being the anniversary of her death, the pain returned.

Lucas knew what he was going to do. Leaving the hotel where he had lived since he had arrived, he walked down to the sheriff's office. Without saying a word, he walked up to Sheriff Moore's desk and surrendered his deputy badge.

"What's this about?" Moore asked. "Why are you givin' up your badge?"

"I'm ready to move on," Lucas said.

Moore stared at him for a moment, then sighed.

"I'm going to hate to lose you, Lucas, but I know you're doing what you feel you have to do." Moore stuck his hand across the desk. "Good luck to you, my friend, but if you ever want to come back, you'll always have a job as long as I'm the sheriff."

"Thank you," Lucas said. "I'll keep that in mind."

Leaving the sheriff's office, Lucas walked down to the Mud Slide Saloon. Seeing him approach, the bartender drew a beer and put it on the bar before him.

"I'll need a whiskey, Amos," Lucas said.

"A whiskey? You?"

"Yeah."

Amos reached for the beer, but Lucas stopped him from taking the mug away.

"I'll have both," Lucas said.

Amos got a concerned look on his face, then poured a whiskey and set that before Lucas. Lucas lifted the shot glass, and poured the contents into his beer.

"I've been in this business long enough to know when a man wants to be left alone," Amos said. "Just call out to me, if you need me."

"Leave the bottle, and I won't need you," Lucas said.

"All right." Amos's face showed that more than anything else, he wanted to find out what was troubling Lucas. But he knew that if Lucas wanted him to know, he would tell him.

Lucas finished the first drink, then poured himself another whiskey.

He didn't know how long he had been there, when Cindy came over to stand beside him. He was sure that Cindy wasn't her real name — none of the percentage girls used their real name.

"Are you all right?" Cindy asked.

"Why do you think I'm not all right?" Lucas replied, pouring himself another drink.

"Because I've never seen you drink like this."

"Amos?" Lucas called.

The bartender moved down to see what Lucas wanted.

"How much money does Cindy make for the saloon in one night?"

"Why do you ask?"

"How much?" Lucas repeated without answering Amos's question.

"About ten dollars."

Lucas took a twenty-dollar bill from his wallet, and handed it to Amos.

"Why did you do that?" Cindy asked, surprised and confused by Lucas's action.

Lucas gave Cindy a twenty-dollar bill. "I want you to change clothes, then come away from the saloon with me for tonight."

"Oh, Deputy Cain, it doesn't cost you that much."

"I don't want to do 'it'," Lucas said, with emphasis on the word it. "I want your company, that's all. Now, change from this . . ." Lucas made a motion with his hand to take in the revealing clothes Cindy was wearing, "into something you can wear in the restaurant."

Cindy smiled. "I'll be right back down."

When Cindy came back downstairs, she was wearing a dress that she could wear to church.

"You look very nice," Lucas said.

"Thank you," Cindy replied.

Lucas believed that he actually saw Cindy blush.

Lucas took her to the Rustic Rock, which was Cindy's first time ever to be in the nicest restaurant in town.

"They won't like for me to be in here," Cindy said.

"That's all right," Lucas said. "They'll like my money."

Cindy chuckled. "I suppose they will."

They were seated without any difficulty, but once they were at the table, Cindy whispered something to Lucas.

"There are three men in here who are glaring at me. They know who I am."

"Don't worry about it. If they give you any trouble, they'll answer to me."

Cindy chuckled. "I don't think they'll give me any trouble. All three of them are here with their wives."

"You want to go say hello to them?"

"What? No, I . . ." Cindy paused in mid-sentence when she saw that Lucas was grinning. "On the other hand, maybe I should," she said, laughing, and bringing laughter from Lucas.

"What's your name?" Lucas asked, over the steaks they were eating.

"Why, you know my name," Cindy said, surprised by the question.

"No, Cindy is the name you're using. What I want to know is, what's your real name."

"I never tell my real . . ." She paused for a second, then smiled at him. "It's Naomi Ragland."

"That's a pretty name. So, for this meal, I'll call you Naomi."

Lucas saw tears come to Naomi's eyes.

"I'm sorry," Lucas said. "Would you rather me not call you Naomi?"

"No, I . . ." Naomi wiped her eyes. "I'm sorry. It's just that, well, it feels good to have someone call me by my right name."

Lucas was enjoying the meal with Naomi — it helped him deal with the melancholy he was feeling.

■ ■ ■ ■

Once again, Lucas Cain found himself on the move, riding down a road with no specific destination in mind. On such rides, Lucas often allowed memories to play through his mind. He recalled his mother and dad, when he was a child. His childhood had been free of any stress.

Lucas had joined the army when the war started, and he remembered leaving Cape Girardeau with a flower stuck in the lapel of his uniform. The flower had been placed there by a very pretty young girl who had been his neighbor at the time. Her name was Ava, and Lucas had tried to look her up when he came back from the war, but learned that she had married and moved to St. Louis.

On the day he left for the war, a band played, and there had been cheers when his company marched south from Cape Girardeau. But the joy and excitement of going to war came to an end at a place called Pittsburgh Landing, on the Tennessee-Mississippi state line, near a small church called Shiloh.

More than forty percent of the men in Lucas's company fell in battle. Lucas lost a lot of boyhood friends and acquaintances in that battle, but he had also made a very good friend, Dan Lindell. Lucas and Dan had gone through the rest of the war together, and had become as close as brothers.

Lucas credited that friendship with allowing both of them to survive the hell of Andersonville.

Oddly enough, Lucas held the greatest anger, and absolute hatred, not for the Confederate guards, but for the group of fellow prisoners who called themselves "The Raiders" and especially Ben Brodie, who was the leader of The Raiders. Brodie had been on the *Sultana* when it blew up, and since Brodie stayed out of sight from most of the other prisoners who hated him, Lucas was sure he had died in the explosion. He was glad enough to think of Brodie's death. If anybody deserved to die, it was Ben Brodie.

After a gradual drift west, Lucas found himself in a small town that looked like a dozen others he had passed through. His first stop was the sheriff's office. When he went inside, he saw a man leaning back in his chair, with his feet up on the desk. His face was covered by the newspaper he was reading.

"So, what are they serving for dinner?" the man behind the newspaper asked.

"I don't know," Lucas replied.

At hearing the strange voice, the man lowered the paper. He had white hair, and a white handle-bar moustache.

"I'm sorry, I thought you were my deputy. What can I do for you?"

"What's the name of this town?" Lucas asked.

"Holiday."

"Holiday. That's a good name. Am I still in Kansas?"

The sheriff laughed. "You really are lost, ain't ya? Yes, you're still in Kansas."

"I just thought I'd check in with you, Sheriff," Lucas said. "My name's Lucas Cain."

"Howdy, Mr. Cain, I'm E. B. Bower. What brings you to Holiday?"

Cade laughed. "I guess it's like you said. I'm lost."

"Well, Holiday is always open to new people — that is if you're not runnin' from the law."

"In a way, I guess I am running from the law," Lucas said. "I've been everything from a police officer back in Missouri, to a deputy sheriff in Topeka, and in between those times, I've earned my keep as a bounty hunter."

"My, my, that's impressive." The sheriff tented his fingers. "Say, are you so tired of policing, that you wouldn't consider hirin' on here in Holiday?"

Lucas glanced at the sheriff with a puzzled look on his face. "Are you asking me to work for you?"

"That I am if you'd consider hirin' on. I had a deputy take to his bed last week and he's in pretty bad shape. There's little chance I'll ever get him back," Sheriff Bower said. "What do you say?"

"Well, I'm not actually looking for a job, but if you'd be willing, I'll offer you the same deal I had with Sheriff Moore, back in Topeka. You can telegraph him, to get his opinion of me."

"Oh? And what kind of deal was that?" Bower asked.

"I'll be your deputy in every way, making rounds at night, breaking up saloon fights, anything you want me to do. But I don't want to be paid."

"What? What do you mean you don't want to be paid? How do you propose to live?"

"By not accepting a salary, I'll be free to collect bounties."

"Well, hell, Cain, if you're going to do

that, why would you want to be a deputy in the first place?"

"I like the authority a badge would give me."

At that moment the front door opened, and a young man that Lucas decided must be in his early twenties, clean shaven, and with hair so short that it couldn't be seen under the hat he was wearing stepped into the office.

"I got ham sandwiches," he said, then stopping in mid-announcement, he looked at Lucas. "Who's this, Sheriff?"

"Jay, this is our new deputy, Lucas Cain. Lucas, this is deputy Jay Duhon. You two boys shake hands, because you're goin' to be workin' together."

Lucas smiled, realizing that Bower had just accepted his offer.

For the next several weeks, Lucas did routine deputy's work. He took his turns on the desk at night, made rounds, and arrested people who were drunk and disorderly. A few times he managed to bring in someone for whom a bounty was paid, but none of the bounties were very large. They were, however, large enough to provide him with an income that was significantly higher than what he would have made as a salaried deputy.

Lucas held the job in Holiday for about six months, but since there were few incidents of any significance, he was overtaken by wanderlust once again. Because the urge to move on was too strong for him to resist, he made the decision to leave. The morning after he came to that decision, he walked over to lay his badge on Sheriff Bower's desk.

"What's this?" Sheriff Bower asked.

"I've going to be moving on," Lucas said.

Sheriff Bower stroked his chin, stared at the badge for a moment, then looked up at Lucas. He shook his head, but the smile on his face showed that he wasn't that surprised.

"Well, truth is, Lucas, you've stayed with me longer than I thought you would. You've been a good deputy — I'll hate to lose you."

"Good, or cheap?"

Sheriff Bower laughed. "Well, I'll admit that it was good having you, without having to pay you. So why don't we say good, and cheap?"

"I'll accept that."

"Where will you go now?"

"To be honest with you, I don't have the slightest idea where I'll end up."

"Would you like a suggestion?"

"Sure."

"Adam Logan is the sheriff in Benton, Colorado. It so happens that he's also my cousin. If you'd be interested in stopping there for a while, I can give you a letter introducin' you."

"Thanks, Sheriff, I'd appreciate that."

It was a two-week, uneventful ride from Holiday to Benton. Benton could have been any town he had seen in the last year. It was located on the Missouri Pacific Railroad, with the main street running south from the railroad, at a right angle. There were three cross roads, but the businesses of the town were spread out on both sides of Holliday Street.

Lucas counted three saloons, a blacksmith shop, a livery, two mercantile stores, a drug store, a leather-goods store, a bank, a hotel, and the sheriff's office. He dismounted in front of the sheriff's office, tied Charley off at the rail, then stepped inside.

There was a man sitting behind a desk, sorting papers in piles. Both beard and hair were laced with gray. He was wearing glasses, but he looked up and took his glasses off when Lucas came in.

"Yes, sir, something I can do for you?" the man asked.

"Would you be Sheriff Logan?"

124

"I am. And who might you be?"

"My name is Lucas Cain, Sheriff, and I recently served as a deputy to Sheriff E.B. Bower. I believe he is a cousin of yours?"

Sheriff Logan smiled. "Yes, he is. How's old E.B. gettin' along?"

"I'd say he's doing quite well. He gave me a letter to give to you," Lucas said, removing the envelope from his shirt pocket.

Logan took it, then chuckled. "It's from E.B. all right. He asks me if I remember letting loose a bunch of frogs in the church. He's the only one who would know that."

"I was wondering what that was about."

"It was to let me know that this letter isn't something somebody forged." Sheriff Logan read the letter, then glanced up at Lucas. "Am I reading this right? You're willing to work for no pay?"

"Yes."

"Where are you staying?"

"I don't know, I just got into town."

"You can stay at Ma Rittenhouse's place. Show her the badge, and she'll take off twenty percent. Take your meals at Kirby's and he'll give you twenty percent off, too."

"What badge?" Lucas asked.

"This one." Logan took a deputy's badge from his desk. "Hold up your right hand."

Lucas did so.

"Do you swear to do a good job?"

Lucas chuckled. "Yeah, I do."

Lucas had been a deputy for three months, when the Ina Claire Walker incident happened.

Ina Claire was an attractive seventeen-year-old girl, the daughter of the owner of the Bank of Benton. Wild flowers were in bloom now, so she had gone down near the creek to pick some. She smiled, as she thought of the bouquet she would make for her mother.

Ina Claire saw a patch of yellow golden head intermingled with some white and purple yarrow. The flowers looked so pretty growing together, she happily began to pick them. She moved down closer to the creek bed as she continued to fill her basket. When she climbed back up to the top of the rise that formed the creek bank, she saw four men standing there. She didn't recognize any of them, and she had no idea why they were just standing there, but the sight of them frightened her.

"Uh, hello," she said, hesitantly.

One of the men had a strange look on his face. "Lookie here, boys, now ain't she purty?"

Ina Claire dropped her basket and began to run.

"Oh, no you don't," the man said as he quickly overtook her and knocked her down. "Why'd you have to go and do that? Now ya got your dress all dirty."

Ina Clair began struggling to get away.

"But ain't she a feisty one," the man said. "We'd better get her out of here 'fore someone comes up on us."

Only one man had spoken so far, and he might have been the ugliest man Ina Claire had ever seen. His eyes sat back under a heavy, overhanging forehead, his nose was flat, and what teeth he had were yellow and crooked. He pulled his gun from its holster, grabbed it by the barrel, then raised it up, preparatory to bringing it down on her head.

"No!" Ina Claire said, quickly. "I'll go with you."

The man grinned, but instead of easing the expression on his face, it made him appear even more sinister.

"Well, now, girlie, it could be that maybe you just ain't as dumb as I thought."

"What do you want with me? Where are you taking me?" Ina Claire asked in a squeaking, terrified voicc.

"You don't need to be worryin' none about that, little lady. You'll know when we get there."

They took her back to the road where a farm wagon was waiting. There, they tied her hands and feet, gagged her, then lifted her up into the back of the wagon and forced her to lie down. They pulled an old tarpaulin over her so that, even if someone was close enough to look into the bed of the wagon, they wouldn't see her.

Less than a minute later the wagon started moving. She had no idea who the men were, where they were taking her, or what they were going to do to her. She only knew that she had never been more frightened in her life.

10

Lyle Walker was the owner of the Bank of Benton, and when he came back from lunch, he saw an envelope on his desk. It was somewhat unusual, in that it hadn't come through the mail — it was just lying there with his name on the outside.

He picked it up, but before he opened it, he called out to one of his bank tellers.

"Arnold, how did this envelope get on my desk?"

"Some kid brought it in. He said he was getting ten cents to get it to you, so I put it on your desk."

"That's strange."

Lyle opened the envelope, then all the blood seemed to rush down from his head as he read it.

We got your daughter. If you want to see her alive again, leave $10,000 at the old way station on Salt Springs Road. Do not go to the sheriff or she dies.

He was still holding the note when his wife stepped into his office. There was a worried look on her face.

"Lyle, Ina Claire said she was going for a walk this morning, and she hasn't come back. This isn't like her, and I'm worried."

"Edna, I just got this note. I think you should read it." He handed the paper to her.

Edna read it, then gasped. "Oh, no! Our poor baby! What are we going to do?"

"I know someone who can help us."

"Oh, Lyle, you can't go to the sheriff. The note says Ina Claire will be killed, if you go to the sheriff."

"I'm not talking about the sheriff. I'm talking about his deputy."

"Tim Spivey? What are you thinking? That boy's not much older than Ina Claire herself."

"Not him, the new one. From what I've heard, he technically isn't even a real deputy. The sheriff tells me he's not getting paid, he just wears the badge."

"You can't be serious," Edna said. "You'd use a pretend deputy to rescue our daughter? Why would you do such a thing?"

"For two reasons. One, he isn't the sheriff, and two, from what Adam has told me

130

about him, he may be the only one in town who has a chance of finding Ina Claire."

After a ride of what seemed like hours to Ina Claire, the farm wagon was abandoned and a waiting man held four horses.

"Damn it, Chubby, couldn't ya grab five horses?" the man who had done all the talking asked.

"I done what ya said. Ya said get us some horses," Chubby said.

"Never mind. Get the girl."

Ina Claire had never been more frightened in her life. She had been put on a horse behind a rider who was not much bigger than she was. A rope tied the two together so that she couldn't jump down. That arrangement put her face so close to the back of the rider, that she could smell the stench of the unwashed body in front of her. She didn't know where they were, or even how far they had come, when they reached a mountain cabin in the woods.

"All right, girly, this is where we're goin," she was told.

Ina Claire knew now that the man who had done the talking was the leader of the four. After the rope was untied, he grabbed her and literally pulled her off the horse.

The rider started to dismount as well, but

the leader stopped him. "Gil, you go back to town and keep an eye on Walker. We need to make sure he don't do nothin' stupid."

"All right, I'll see you boys later. But don't you start havin' fun with the girl 'til I get back."

"There won't be any fun, unless I say so," the leader of the group said.

Lucas Cain was having a beer in the Ace High Saloon when he saw Lyle Walker come in. Walker looked around the saloon, then seeing Lucas, he came toward him.

"May I join you, Deputy Cain?" Walker asked.

Lucas didn't say anything, but he gave his assent with a slight wave of his hand toward the chair on the opposite side of the table from him.

"Mr. Cain, from what I've heard about you, I believe you might be the person who can help me."

"Help you with what?"

Walker reached into his pocket, took out a bound packet of twenty-dollar bills, and put it on the table between them.

"That's a thousand dollars, and it's yours, if you'll take on a job for me."

"You have a most interesting way of opening a conversation, Mr. Walker," Lucas said, as he took a swallow of his beer. "My first question is what do I have to do to earn that kind of money?"

Walker took out the note he had received, and showed it to Lucas. Lucas read it, then looked up toward the banker.

"Mr. Cain, if my daughter is still alive, I want you to find her and bring her home, safely. If she's dead, I want you to kill whoever took her."

Lucas drummed his fingers on the table for a moment.

"Please, Deputy, I beg of you. Find Ina Claire and bring her home to her mother and me. She's only seventeen years old. Who knows what they're doing to her?"

"Have you talked to Sheriff Bower about this?" Lucas asked.

Walker shook his head. "No, I'm afraid to. You read the note. If I get the law involved, they say they'll kill her. Is a thousand dollars not enough? Tell me what it will take for me to get my daughter back."

Lucas looked around, studying the others who were present. There were two percentage girls standing by the piano, though the piano player was absent. There were three men at one of the tables, engaged in a rather animated conversation; four at another table were playing cards. There was also a man who had come into the saloon a moment after Walker had. He was standing at the far end of the bar, and Lucas was sure he was watching Walker.

Lucas reached for the pile of money, counted off one hundred dollars, then shoved the rest of the money back to Walker. "I'll take a hundred dollars now, and when I get your daughter back, you can give me rest," Lucas said, speaking very quietly.

"This means you're going after her?"

"Yes."

Walker stuck his hand across the table to shake hands with Lucas.

"Thank you, Mr. Cain. Her mother and I are most grateful." He picked up the nine hundred dollars Lucas had left on the table.

"Tell me, Mr. Walker, why were you willing to pay so much money in advance? Don't you realize that an unscrupulous man could have taken your money and run away with it?"

Walker nodded. "I'm aware of that. But I was willing to take the chance, because I'll do anything to get my daughter back."

"All right, I'll get her back on one condition."

"What condition is that?"

"That you're willing to pay the ransom."

"What do you mean? I'm hiring you so I

don't have to do that," Walker said.

"No, you're hiring me so you can get your daughter back, alive and unharmed. The ten thousand dollars is bait. If all goes well, you'll get the money back when I bring your daughter back."

Walker was quiet for a moment, then he nodded. "All right. Come down to the bank, and I'll give you the money."

"No," Lucas said, interrupting. "I don't want to be seen leaving with you. You go to the bank now, and I'll be along later."

Lucas waited for a while during which time he made a quick study of everyone else who had been in the saloon during Walker's visit.

The man who Lucas believed had been studying Walker, left when Walker did.

That gave Lucas all the information he needed to know. The man following Walker was somehow involved with the kidnapping.

Gil Gentry had watched the conversation between Lyle Walker and the big man who was sitting at the table. He had no idea who the man was, but he knew it wasn't the sheriff. Then, he saw some money sliding back and forth between them. He also saw Walker show the note to the man. He knew then that the discussion had been about the

135

girl. It may be that Walker intended to use this man as the one who would deliver the money. He was going to keep an eye on the people going and coming from the bank. If this man was being chosen to deliver the money, he would have to come to the bank to get it.

About fifteen minutes after Walker left the saloon, Lucas walked down to the bank.

"Deputy Cain," Walker called to him. "About that loan we discussed. Come on into my office, and I'll have the money for you."

"Thank you."

Lucas was given the ten thousand dollars which was placed in a canvas bank transfer bag. He made no effort to hide the bag as he left the bank.

As soon as Gentry saw the man he had seen talking to Walker leave the bank, carrying a transfer bag, he knew Walker was going to respond to their demand. He mounted his horse and rode out of town, taking the Salt Springs Road and breaking into a gallop as soon as he was out of town.

11

Even before Lucas went into the bank, he had noticed that the man he had seen studying Walker in the saloon was now standing across the street, looking through the window of the leather-goods store. He gave no sign of being aware of the man, but saw him mount up and ride out of town.

Although the way station where he was supposed to deliver the money was on Salt Springs Road, Lucas decided it might not be smart to take the Salt Springs Road, so he took the Coffee Creek Road instead. The Coffee Creek Road didn't exactly parallel Salt Springs Road, but it did junction with a road that joined Salt Springs Road on the other side of the old abandoned way station. By going this way, he would approach the way station from the opposite direction he would be expected to.

Gentry had ridden for a little over half-an-hour when he reached the place that he had scouted out earlier this morning. Here, the road passed through a cut that would be an ideal location to set up an ambush. Just before the road passed through the cut, Gentry left it, then rode around to where he could keep his horse out of sight. Removing his rifle from the saddle sheath, he climbed up onto the top of the cut, lay down, and watched the road, waiting for the man who was carrying the ransom money. He cocked the rifle to put a round in the chamber. It would be an easy shot, then all he would have to do is take the money bag off the body.

Ina Claire Walker sat on the floor of the little cabin where she had been brought. Her hands and feet were tied and she was leaning back against the wall.

She was uncomfortable, hungry, and thirsty. The three men who were with her were eating. They hadn't offered to feed her, and she had made the decision that she wasn't going to ask for anything.

"Do you think Walker's goin' to come up with the money we're askin' for?" one of the men asked. Crawford was the one who had asked the question. By listening to them talk, Ina Claire had already learned all their names.

"He's got to, iffen he don't want to see his daughter kilt," Turner said.

"What if he don't?" Sellers asked. "If he don't come up with the money, are we actual goin' to kill her?"

"Yes, we'll absolutely kill her," Turner said.

"I don't know as I'd be for killin' her. Hell, I ain't never kilt a woman a'fore," Sellers said. "That is, lessen you count that Injun squaw I kilt here back a couple o' years ago."

"We got to kill her though, don't you see?" Turner explained. "Iffen we don't get the money 'n just let her go, well hell, we'd never be able to do this to anyone else 'n make it work. 'N even if we do get the money, we can't just let 'er go like as if nothin's happened."

"All right, I guess we can kill 'er iffen we have to. But I ain't goin' to be the one that does the killin'," Sellers said. "That'll be your job."

"On, don't you worry none 'bout that," Turner said, with a wide, evil grin. "I don't mind doin' the killin'."

As she listened to the men talking so cavalierly about killing her, her fear was so intense that it had the effect of numbing her. She knew she would be dead before the end of this very day, but in her strange, numbed-out state, it was as if she were already dead. She was already on the other side, listening to the conversations of the living.

She thought of her mother and dad. Was there any way she could visit them, now that she was already dead?

"I love you, Mama. I love you, Daddy."

Did they hear that? Surely, they did. But then, she didn't know if she had spoken the words aloud, or just thought them.

Because of the circuitous route Lucas had taken, the ride which normally would have taken just under an hour to reach the old way station, now took Lucas an hour and a half. When he reached the station, there was no one there, so he went inside and left the bank bag in plain view. Then he left the little building and took up a position where he could keep an eye on the station.

A mile down the road as Lucas knew he would be, Gentry was waiting at the cut intending on an ambush. But, because of the indirect path Lucas had taken, he didn't pass by.

"Where the hell are you?" Gentry asked, speaking to himself. "I seen you leave the bank with the money, so I know you're comin'."

Gentry waited half an hour longer, then with a sigh of disgust, he gave up his vigil and rode on to the way station.

Dismounting in front of the station, he went inside. That's when he saw the bank bag lying in the middle of the floor.

"What the hell?" Gentry said aloud. "Now, how 'n the hell did this get here?"

Gentry wondered if it was some sort of trick. Maybe there was no money in the bag.

Concerned that may be the case, he opened the bag and examined the contents.

"Son of a bitch!" he said in a happy shout. The bag was filled with bound packets of twenty-dollar bills.

Gentry gave a quick thought to grabbing the money and just taking off, but if he did that, he knew the other three would come after him. So, abandoning that thought, he closed the bag, then left the way station for the ride to the cabin where the others were waiting.

Lucas watched Gentry leave, then giving him some time, started after him. He stayed far enough behind Gentry that even if he was seen, Gentry wouldn't perceive any danger. Often, the normal curves in the road would mean that the two men had lost sight of each other. Lucas wasn't worried about that, because he was able to follow Gentry by the tracks his horse left. Actually, Lucas thought that might be better, because if he stayed out of sight, the man would have no knowledge of his presence.

Lucas had no idea where they were going, or how long it would take to get there. But the man he was following knew, and that was all that mattered.

Gentry saw the old, abandoned cabin with three horses tethered out front. Riding up to it, he dismounted, then taking the bag with him, he ran through the door. Crawford and Sellers were sitting at the little table, drinking coffee. Turner was sitting on the floor next to the girl.

Gentry held up the bank bag. "Boys, we got it!" he said excitedly. "The money's in this bag!"

"Let's divide up, now," Crawford said.

"Not yet," Turner said. "We've got somethin' else to do."

"What?" Gentry asked.

"Turner wants to kill the girl," Sellers said.

"Wait a minute, that's kind of a waste, ain't it?" Gentry asked.

142

"What do you mean, waste?" Turner asked.

"We got the money, we ain't in no hurry no more. Iffen we're gonna kill 'er, don't you think we should have a little fun with 'er, then we kill 'er?"

"Yeah, Turner, what do you say?" Crawford asked.

"All right, but not until we divide up the money, then I get her first."

"That's all right with me. I like to watch, anyway."

Ina Claire had a pretty good idea what they meant by saying they wanted to "have some fun with her," and that frightened her almost as much as the thought of getting killed. She thought of her mama and daddy, and how upset they were going to be. Her dad had raised the money to save her, but since they weren't going to let her go anyway, she wished now he hadn't paid them.

"Let's count out the money first," Crawford said. "I wanna feel it in my hands."

"Yeah," Sellers said. "That little ol' gal over there sure as hell ain't a' goin' nowhere."

"Damn, this was about the easiest way of raisin' money I ever done," Crawford said, as he watched all the money being dumped onto the table.

"It sure beats holdin' up a bank," Sellers said. "There ain't nobody a' shootin' at us."

"Hell, there ain't nobody what's ever even seen us," Turner said. "We could go right back into town tomorrow, have a few drinks 'n visit with some whores, 'n there won't nobody have any idea that we was the ones that took the girl."

As Turner and the others were divvying up their money, Lucas tied his horse off about fifty yards from the cabin, then with pistol in hand, he walked quietly up to the cabin, making certain he was not in position to be seen through the window. When he reached the cabin, he kicked the door open, thinking an explosive entrance would give him the advantage of shock effect, and it did. There were four men standing around a table, on which there was a pile of money, and they were clearly startled to see him.

"Get your hands up!"

"What the hell?" one of the men shouted.

"Shoot 'im, shoot 'im!" another man shouted, and all four of them made a grab for their guns.

Lucas didn't hesitate, he pulled the trigger four times, shooting so rapidly, that only two of the four men were able to draw their guns, and neither of them was able to get off a shot.

Lucas stood there for a moment, looking at the men, all of whom were now lying on the floor. As soon as he ascertained that they were all dead, he looked over toward the girl, who was sitting on the floor next to the wall. Her hands and feet were tied, and her eyes were open wide in shock and fear.

"Ina Claire," Lucas said, speaking calmly, and putting his pistol back in his holster. "Your dad sent me to take you back home."

"Daddy sent you? You're . . . you're taking me home?"

"I am indeed." Lucas cut the ropes that bound her. "Before the day is over, you'll be with your mother and father." Lucas smiled. "I'd say you probably need to get prepared for a lot of hugs and kisses."

"Oh!" Ina Claire said happily. "I'll be hugging and kissing them more than they can ever hug me."

"Hold on for just a moment or two. I'm going to be taking these men back also."

Lucas carried the four men outside, one at a time, then draped their bodies over their horses. He didn't know if he got the right man with the right horse, but under the circumstances, it didn't matter. Then, when he had all the bodies secured, he looked over at Ina Claire, who had been watching his every move.

Lucas mounted his horse, then held his hand down to her. "I'm going to scoot forward as much as I can, so you can get in the saddle behind me. It's going to be a tight fit, but it's better for the horse if you aren't sitting just over his flanks.

Ina Claire grabbed his hand, then was lifted up onto the horse. He had slid forward, leaving an open space in the saddle. And, as Lucas had said, it was a very tight fit.

As they rode back to town, she had her arms wrapped around Lucas, and pressed her body tightly against his. This man had saved her life. He was also a virile example of manhood, and though it was necessary for her to cling to him to keep from falling off, there was the residual effect of her enjoying a feeling unlike anything she had ever before experienced, by the closeness.

When they arrived, Ina Claire pointed out where she lived, and when they stopped out front, her mother came running out of the house with a big smile on her face and her arms spread wide.

Taking her hand, Lucas lowered her to the ground so her mother could greet her.

"Oh, sweetheart, sweetheart, sweetheart!" she shouted, gathering Ina Claire into her arms. She was crying with happiness.

After the hugs and kisses were taken care of, Mrs. Walker said that she wanted to take Ina Claire to the bank.

"I want your father to know that you're home safely," she said. "Is it all right if we go to the bank now?"

"Yes, I'll need to go to the bank anyway." He raised the bag of money. "This belongs there."

"If you'll wait a minute, we'll take the surrey," the girl's mother said.

Lucas smiled. "There's no need for hurry now. You've got your daughter back."

"I do indeed," she said, smiling as she gave Ina Claire another hug.

"I'll meet you there. I'll have to stop by the sheriff's office first," Lucas said.

"Yes, to be sure," Mrs. Walker replied. "And thank you again for rescuing my daughter."

"I'm just glad I had the opportunity," Lucas replied with a slight bow of his head.

As Lucas rode through town with the bodies of four men draped across four horses, he was the focus of everyone's attention. By the time he reached the sheriff's office, so many people had turned out to watch, that it was almost like a parade.

Sheriff Logan came out of the jailhouse to meet him.

"What have we got here?" the sheriff asked.

"These four men kidnapped Ina Claire Walker," Lucas answered.

"What? Good Lord, I hadn't heard? Is she all right?"

"Yes, I just dropped her off with her mother."

"I don't understand, how is it that you knew about this, and I didn't?"

"The ransom note was very specific. You weren't to be notified or they would kill her."

Sheriff Logan chuckled. "Well, that just shows how dumb these four bastards were. They didn't want me notified, but they weren't worried about you. Good job, Lucas, damn good job."

"I want to leave these four bodies with you." Lucas held up the bank bag. "I need to get this ransom money back to the bank."

Lucas arrived at the bank at the same time as Ina Claire and her mother. Dismounting, he helped the two ladies down from the surrey, then went into the bank with them.

"Daddy!" Ina Claire shouted as soon as they stepped into the bank, and with arms wide spread, she ran to him.

The effusive greeting was unexpected by the others in the bank, as the kidnapping of Ina Claire had been kept secret from everyone. As a result, they watched the reunion with curiosity.

"Come back to the office," Lyle invited, and Ina Claire, her mother, and Lucas followed him into the back of the bank.

"Oh, Daddy, it was awful! I was so afraid. Then, a knight in shining armor came to rescue me. Deputy Cain is a real hero!" she said, looking at him with approbation.

"Here's the ransom money," Lucas said, handing the canvas bag to Lyle.

"You've certainly earned your fee," Walker said as he counted out the nine hundred dollars that remained in the thousand that he had promised.

"I'd better get back to the sheriff's office," Lucas said. "I left four bodies with him."

"I'll come with you," Walker offered. "Just to make sure the sheriff understands the situation."

"Guess what?" Sheriff Logan asked as Lucas returned to the office. "I've checked it out, you'll be getting a two-hundred-fifty-dollar reward for each one of these men."

"Well, that's a pleasant surprise," Lucas

replied. That meant that as a result of the money paid him by Lyle Walker combined with the reward offered by the state of Colorado, he was two thousand dollars richer.

Later that afternoon, Lucas was sitting at his desk in the sheriff's office, writing out a full report of what had happened when Ina Claire came in to see him. She smiled shyly as she approached him.

"Mama and Daddy want you to come to dinner tonight," she said. "Will you?"

Lucas smiled. "Well, little lady, I'm not one to turn down a free meal."

When Lucas dismounted in front of the Walker house, a smiling Ina Claire hurried out to meet him. She was wearing a yellow gingham dress, and her hair was swept up in curls, in an attempt to make her look older than she really was.

"Come on, Mama and Daddy are waiting inside for you. I wanted to come out to meet you, because you're my hero."

Lyle and Edna Walker were waiting inside, and their greeting was very effusive. Their cook had prepared an excellent meal of roast beef, mashed potatoes and gravy, green beans, and rolls. Desert was black-berry and blueberry cobbler.

As much as he enjoyed the meal, he was made uncomfortable by Ina Claire's coquettish behavior. She was a very attractive young woman, even more so now that she was cleaned up after her kidnapping ordeal. But, and this was what discomfited him the most, he was almost twice her age.

When he left that evening, Ina Claire let him know that he would be welcome at any time.

A few days later, Lucas and Tim Spivey were making the rounds. "The whole town thinks you're quite the hero, rescuin' the banker's daughter like you done," Tim said.

"You would have done the same thing if you'd been in my shoes," Lucas said.

Tim laughed. "You went up against four of 'em. Yeah, I might've done the same thing all right, while I was peein' in my pants."

Lucas laughed as well. "Don't sell yourself short, Tim. You're a good man. You know what? I think you should meet Ina Claire. She's a very pretty young woman, and I think the two of you would get along very well."

"Hell, Lucas, she doesn't even know that I'm alive."

"Then we need to find out some way to let her meet you."

12

With Dan Lindell

Dan Lindell chuckled as he read the letter from Lucas Cain, in which he complained that some young seventeen-year-old girl was "after him."

"Lucas, you can't help it if you're such a ladies' man," Dan said, speaking to the letter.

They had not seen each other since Lucas had stopped in St. Louis, on his way west. And "west" was the only destination Lucas had given. Dan had, from time to time, however, gotten letters from Lucas, but never two letters from the same place. This letter was from some place called Holiday, Kansas. He'd have to look it up on the map to see where it was.

Dan put the letter away, and thought back to their time together during the war. Lucas Cain had become Dan's best friend, and there were no friendships stronger than those made during the time of war.

"Dan, Mr. Allen wants to see you," Dan's assistant said.

Dan was working for the Missouri Pacific Railroad. Though his office was in St. Louis, over the time since he had taken the job, he was often away from the city. His particular specialty was the construction of spur lines that would connect towns to the main line.

"You wanted to see me, Tom," Dan greeted. Tom Allen was the founder and president of the Missouri Pacific Line.

"Yes," Allen replied. "Do you have your bags packed?"

Dan laughed. "Where am I going this time?"

"Kansas. We need a spur line built from Sidney to Felix."

"How far is it between Sidney and Felix?"

"Twenty-five miles," Allen said.

Dan smiled. "I'll have it done in less than a month."

"I've no doubt about that," Allen said. "Dan, I'm not ignorant of the fact that building these spur lines from our trunk line to towns along the way was your idea. And I also recognize that the additional traffic we'll pick up will go a long way toward keeping this railroad solvent."

"It helps when these little towns can raise

part of the money to bring in the spur," Dan said. "I like my job, so I definitely want to see the railroad succeed."

"I've no doubt that the railroad will remain solvent, thanks, in no small part, to men like you."

When Dan got home that evening, he told Janet about his new assignment.

"How long will you be gone this time?" Janet asked.

"On, no more than a month I wouldn't think."

Janet sighed. "I know this is a good job, compared to some of the positions you've had to take. And you make good money, so I can't really complain. But I do hate it, when we're separated like this."

"I know. I don't like it either. But look at it this way. These separations are a lot shorter than the time we were separated during the war, and nobody's shooting at me now."

Janet smiled. "Yes, and I'm very happy about that," she said as she leaned over to give him a quick kiss.

It was another week before Dan was ready to go. The first thing he had to do was make certain that he had enough rails and cross-ties to enable construction to start. Then he had to make arrangements for the shipment of all the supplies he would need to keep the operation going once it was started.

"Do you think you'll be able to hire locals?" Tom Allen asked.

"Let me have four experienced men that I can use as section leaders," Dan said. "I think I'll be able to find men along the way who can do the job."

"Good. The construction always goes better, when we don't have to import labor."

One week later Dan left the train in Sidney, Kansas. He had brought his horse with him, and getting him from the stock car, he rode along the already surveyed path until he reached the town of Felix. The first place he went, was to the mayor's office.

"Are you Joe Cravens?" Dan asked.

"I am. What can I do for you, sir?"

"Mayor Cravens, I'm Dan Lindell, with the Missouri Pacific Railroad. As I'm sure you already know, we'll be building a spur line from here to Sidney, so that your town will be connected with the main line.

A broad smile spread across Mayor Cravens's face. "Yes, yes!" he said excitedly. "You've no idea how thrilled we are to be a part of that."

"And the railroad appreciates the money you were able to raise," Dan said. "Now, I

155

have another request. If it's possible, we like to use local labor when we build a connecting spur. Do you think you can find five men who would be willing to work hard for the next month?"

"We can absolutely get five men to work," Mayor Cravens said, "but do you think that's enough?"

"I've already made arrangements to hire a few from Sidney, so with those you can find for me, we'll have this line done in no time."

With Lucas, in Benton, Colorado
When the First Baptist Church of Benton held a box social, Lucas took Tim with him, arriving before anyone else.

"Here's one hundred dollars," Lucas said. "You make sure that you buy the box belonging to Ina Claire. No matter what anyone else bids. I'm sure nobody will top a hundred dollars."

"Then, if I get the box, what do I do?"

Lucas laughed. "Why, you meet Ina Claire, that's what you do. You both eat whatever she put in her box."

"But what about you? Won't she be expecting you to buy the box that she brings?"

"She might be, but if I'm out making rounds, I can't be there, now can I?"

Tim smiled. "No, I don't guess you can."

Lucas returned to the sheriff's office until it got dark, then he made his rounds. He looked at the Baptist Church from the street. There were more than a dozen wagons, coaches, and surreys parked out front, and lights were shining through the windows. He heard laughter coming from inside, and he hoped that Tim had been able to buy Ina Claire's box.

"She's beautiful!" Tim said the next morning. "And you know what? I asked if she would like to go riding with me, and she said yes!"

Lucas smiled. He didn't think he would ever have to worry about the young Ina Claire again.

Lucas pushed through the swinging doors to step into the Ace High Saloon. Out on the floor of the saloon, nearly all the tables were filled. A few card games were in progress, but most of the patrons were just drinking and talking. He stepped up to the bar.

"Yes, sir, Mr. Cain, your regular?" the bartender asked.

"Yeah, thanks."

As the bartender was drawing the beer, Lucas walked over to a jar that held several boiled eggs, preserved in vinegar. He had barely removed the egg, when he heard a shout from the front door.

"I finally found you, you son of a bitch! You killed my brother!" The shout was followed by a gun-shot, concurrent with the smashing of the jar. Vinegar and eggs tumbled out.

Lucas swung around, drawing even as he was turning. He saw someone pointing a gun at him, pulling the hammer back for a second shot.

Lucas fired before his attacker could pull the trigger the second time. As the smoke began to clear, Lucas's attacker stared through the white cloud. He dropped his gun, and slapped his hands over his belly wound.

"Who are you?" Lucas asked. "Why did you shoot at me?"

"You . . . killed my . . . bro . . . brother," the man gasped.

"Who was your brother?"

"You killed him, and you didn't even know his name? His name was Coombs, Silas Coombs." He barely got the words out before he collapsed. The closest man to him hurried over, then knelt beside him.

"He's dead," the man reported.

There were calls from outside, then the sound of people running. Several came into the saloon and stood under the rising cloud of gun smoke to stare in wonderment at the dead man on the floor. One of the new arrivals was Sheriff Logan.

"What happened here?" Sheriff Logan asked.

"This man said he was Silas Coombs's brother," Lucas said, pointing to the body, now lying face down on the floor.

"Who's Silas Coombs?"

"Don't you remember? I told you about him. He was a lowlife that I ran into, back in Kansas. He raped and killed a twelve-year-old girl."

"Oh, yeah, you did tell me about her. Lucy was her name?"

"Yes, Lucy Carmichael."

Near Eureka, Colorado

George Rogers was standing on a ridge looking down at a small house. There was a garden behind the house, a barn, and a corral. The house belonged to Chris Fowler, a farmer who lived there with his wife, Annabelle, and their thirteen-year-old daughter, Roxanne.

Mounting his horse, Rogers rode down the ridge and up to the cabin. Chris Fowler met him on the front porch.

"Welcome," Fowler said, "and what may

your name be?"

"The name's Rogers, but that don't mean anything. Right now, I'm just someone in need of a meal. It's about dinner time, and I can smell the cookin'. Do you suppose if I gave you five dollars, I could eat with you and your family?"

Fowler looked at him for a moment, then nodded.

"Come on in and join us. And keep your five dollars in your pocket. I don't feel it would be right to charge a hungry traveler for food."

"That's very nice of you, Mister . . ." Even though Rogers had been told the man's name, he paused in mid-sentence.

"Fowler, Chris Fowler," the farmer answered. "Come on in, the missus has just about got dinner ready."

When Rogers followed Fowler into the house, he saw Fowler's wife and daughter, who were busy setting the table.

"Put out another plate, Annabelle," Fowler said. "This here is a feller by the name of Rogers, 'n he's goin' to be our company for dinner."

"Well, Mr. Rogers, it's nice having you join us," Annabelle said with a friendly smile. "We're far enough from Eureka that we don't get a lot of folks comin' through here, so we always enjoy having someone at our table."

"I certainly appreciate your kindness. And who might you be, little lady?" Rogers asked the girl.

"My name's Roxanne," the girl replied with a slight blush.

"Well, you certainly are a pretty thing. I just imagine there are a lot of boys who come a' callin'."

Again, Roxanne blushed, but said nothing.

"I reckon that would be true if we were living in a town," Fowler said. "But we don't hardly never get no visitors out here, and that's just as well. Roxanne stays busy enough, helpin' her mother around the house, 'n learnin' her letters."

"So, you're going to school, are you?" Rogers asked.

"She went for three years, when we was livin' back in Wichita," Fowler said. "No school out here, so Annabelle's learnin' ever'thin' else she needs to know from her mama. Why, when we lived back in Kansas, Annabelle was a' teachin' school her ownself."

"Well, how lucky you are to have your own teacher," Rogers said.

"Except I don't never get to see anyone

my own age," Roxanne said.

"Don't ever, child, not don't never," Annabelle corrected. "That's a double negative, and remember what I told you about double negatives."

Roxanne smiled. "A double negative cancels itself out."

"Very good," Annabelle said with a proud smile.

"What do you do, Mr. Rogers?" Fowler asked.

"Oh, I sort of travel around some, doin' whatever work I can find. I've cowboyed some, I've drove a stagecoach, I've worked in a livery."

"It certainly sounds like you have enough experiences to get a job just about anywhere you might want one," Annabelle said with a friendly smile.

"Yes, right now I'm working for a railroad."

"Oh, that's too bad," Fowler said.

"Too bad? Why is that too bad?" Rogers asked. "Maybe there's something I can do for you."

"Not unless you can tell the railroad to go somewhere else to lay its track, rather than right through the middle of my farm."

Rogers chuckled. "Yes, I can see how that could be bad."

They carried on a friendly conversation for the rest of the meal, which was topped off by an apple pie that Annabelle removed from the pie safe.

"I can't tell you when I ever et a better meal," Rogers said as he pushed away the empty pie plate. "You are one fine cook, Mrs. Fowler."

"Why, thank you," Annabelle said. "But, to be truthful, I have to tell you that Roxanne made the pie."

"Did you now?" Rogers asked.

"Yes, sir," Roxanne answered with a blushing smile.

"Well now, that's quite something for a little girl as young as you are. It almost makes me feel bad that I have to do this," Rogers said.

"Do what?" Fowler asked, with a confused expression on his face.

"This," Rogers said, and pulling his pistol, he shot Fowler right between his eyes. Fowler fell forward, with his face smashing into his plate.

"No! What are —" That was as far as Annabelle's cry of shock and terror got, before Rogers shot her, his bullet going in through her nose, and blasting brain matter and blood from the exit wound. Like her husband, she flopped forward, onto the table.

Roxanne was too shocked and terrified to even make a sound. She stared at Rogers, with her brown eyes open wide in disbelief. When Rogers shot her, one of her eyes turned into a bloody hole, where the bullet entered.

A quick check assured Rogers that all three were dead. He cut himself another piece of the pie, and ate it as he sat at the table with the three dead members of the Fowler family.

Half an hour later he sat on his horse, looking back at the house. By now the structure was totally invested in flames, and he knew there would be nothing left.

He smiled as he rode away. He had just earned five hundred dollars, plus a good meal. And the apple pie was excellent.

With Dan Lindell

Dan Lindell was in Belfast, Kansas, where he visited the office of Gus Underhill. Underhill was the local lawyer who was arranging things for the railroad.

"Ah, yes, Mr. Lindell," Underhill said. "I received a telegram from Mr. Allen saying that I should look for you."

"And here I am," Dan said. "Do we have

all the clearances we will need?"

"Almost. We do have one holdout," Underhill said.

"Oh?"

"It's a man named Jim Barnes. His farm is right in the middle of our spur corridor, and so far at least, he has refused every reasonable offer to grant us access."

"Would it help if I spoke to him?"

"Oh, there's no question about it. If he doesn't grant us access, we'll have to abandon this spur altogether."

"Tell me what you know about him. Is he a hard person to get along with?"

"Well, no, not normally. Until the question of the access corridor for the rail spur came up, Jim was as affable as anyone in the county."

"I'll see what I can do."

Dan got detailed instructions as to how to find the Barneses' farm, so that by midafternoon on the following day, he approached a white, two-story house and a red barn. The farm looked very well-kept.

When he dismounted in front of the house, a woman came out onto the porch to greet them. The look on her face was one of total confusion.

"Uh, yes? Can I help you?"

"Mrs. Barnes?" Dan asked.

"Yes?"

"My name is Dan Lindell. I wonder if I might speak with Mr. Barnes. Is he around?"

"Jim stepped out to the machine shed, but I'm sure he'll be back as soon as he sees that someone's here. Come on in."

"Thank you," Dan said as he dismounted and followed Mrs. Barnes into the house.

"Have a seat," Mrs. Barnes invited when they stepped into the parlor. "Would you like a glass of lemonade? I just made some."

"That sounds like exactly what I would want," Dan replied.

"Oh, I see Jim is headed for the house now," Mrs. Barnes said as she poured a glass of lemonade and handed it to Dan.

When Jim Barnes came into the house, he had a puzzled look on his face. "Who are you?" he asked.

When Dan saw Jim Barnes, he looked shocked. "I know you," he said.

"What? What do you mean, you know me?"

"Were you a deckhand on the *Sultana*?"

"Yes, I was, but it's not something I like to remember. Were you on the *Sultana*?"

"Yes, I was, and I'm glad you were there too, because . . ."

Now, a big smile spread across Jim

Barnes's face. "Wait a minute! The chimney!" he said. "You were trapped under the fallen chimney, weren't you?"

"I was trapped, yes. But you and my friend saved my life. I've wondered all these years what happened to you, and I prayed that you survived. I'm very happy to see that you did."

The two men shared a happy handshake.

"How did you find me?" Barnes asked.

"I didn't find you. Well, I did, of course, but it was just a happy coincidence. I'm here for an entirely different reason."

"Oh?"

"Mr. Barnes, my name is Dan Lindell, and I work for the Missouri Pacific Railroad."

Barnes shook his head, then held up his hand, palm out. "No," he said. "I'm not interested in selling my farm."

"Oh, you don't understand. We don't want to buy your farm. All we want is a one-hundred-foot-wide easement across your property, and you can work with our surveyors to point out the path that would cause you the least trouble."

"An easement," Barnes said.

"Yes," Dan answered. "And you will be compensated."

"Compensated?"

"That means we will pay you for the right to lay tracks across your property. And, I think you would be quite pleased with just how much we will pay."

"How much?"

"What is the distance between the northern-most boundary of your land, to the southern-most boundary?"

"I'm not exactly sure, but I would guess that it is somewhere around two thousand feet."

Dan smiled. "We're willing to pay five dollars per foot. How would ten thousand dollars sound to you?"

"What?" Jim and his wife both shouted at the same time.

"And, as I said, that would only be for the easement. The farm would still belong to you to do with as you wish."

"What do you think, Carol Jean?" Jim Barnes asked his wife.

"Oh, sweetheart, yes, yes!" Carol Jean said excitedly. "Why, with ten thousand dollars, we would be completely out of debt, with money left over."

"Oh, I didn't tell you. We won't be buying that easement, we'll be leasing it, which means the ten thousand dollars will be paid annually."

"Wait a minute! Are you telling me we'll

be getting ten thousand dollars every year?"

"Yes, sir, every year for as long as the tracks are in use."

"Mr. Lindell?"

"It's Dan," Dan said.

"Dan," Jim corrected, with a huge smile. "You've got yourself a deal."

13

"I'll be leaving you now," Lucas said as he laid his deputy's star on Sheriff Logan's desk.

"You're leaving? Where are you going?" Sheriff Logan asked.

"I don't know."

"What the hell, Lucas? That don't hardly make no sense a' tall. What do you mean you're leavin', 'n you don't even know where you're goin'?"

"That's how I got here. I'm a drifter, Adam, you knew that when I got here."

"Yeah, I guess I did. But I sort of thought you might get to likin' this place so much that you'd be willin' to stop your wanderin' around."

"I don't know that I'll ever be willing to do that, but I do like some places more than others, and Benton has been a town I've appreciated."

"Well, there you go, then. That ought to

be reason enough for you to, uh," Logan paused for a long moment. "You're goin' anyway, aren't you?"

"Yeah, I am. I'm sorry, Adam, but it's just something I have to do."

Sheriff Logan sighed, then shook his head. "All right, I wish you would stay, but I know I can't talk you out of it, so," he extended his hand. "I hate to see you go, so let me just say, good luck to you."

Lucas took Sheriff Logan's hand. "Thank you. And make sure you keep Tim on. He's turned out to be a right good deputy."

Sheriff Logan nodded. "That he has. You've been a right good influence on that boy."

One week of travel brought Lucas to the little town of Carlin, Colorado. Wanting a supper that he hadn't cooked, and a beer to wash away the trail dust, he saw a sign advertising the Top Hand Saloon and figured he could take care of both wants with the same stop.

Although he had never been in this particular place, the bar running down the left side of the saloon, the brass foot rail, the mirror behind the bar, the piano in the back — all of this was so familiar that he felt at home. He stepped up to the bar.

A bartender with gray sideburns and matching moustache moved down to greet him.

"Haven't seen you before. You new to Carlin?"

"You might say that, though I'm just passing through."

"Where're you headed?"

"I don't know."

The bartender laughed. "Mister, that's what I'd call a free spirit. What can I get you?"

"I'd like a beer. Also, what do you have to eat?"

"Bacon and beans."

"That's good enough."

"I'll let you get started on your beer." The bartender turned to draw his beer, when Lucas heard a woman scream. When he looked around, he saw that a man was standing out in the middle of the floor, with his arm around a woman's neck. He was holding his pistol to her head, but he was talking to one of the men who was sitting at a card table.

"They's some cheatin' goin' on here, 'n this here woman has been helpin' you."

"What are you talking about? I haven't done anything!" the woman said, her voice breaking with fear.

"Now, all three of you get away from the table and leave the money on it. I aim to get back what I was cheated out of."

"Simmons, I don't know which one of us you're a' callin' a cheater, but I can tell you for a fact, that there ain't nary a' one of us a' cheatin'. You just ain't that good of a player is all, 'n you ain't never been."

"Simmons," one of the other bar girls said, "let Sally go. She ain't done nothin' but just watch for a while."

"Yeah, well if them three don't get up 'n leave all the money on the table, I'm goin' to blow this whore's brains out. Fact is, I may do it anyhow."

"Damn," the bartender said. "Simmons is just crazy enough to do it. He ain't worth a plug nickel. It's too bad nobody hasn't kilt him a long time ago."

"How about if I do it now?" Lucas said. Pulling his pistol and turning, he pointed it toward the man who was holding Sally.

Simmons saw Lucas turn away from the bar.

"Now, mister, just what the hell is it you're a' plannin' on doin'?" Simmons asked.

"Well, if you don't let go of the girl, I'm goin' to kill you," Lucas said.

"What do you mean, you're gonna kill me? Are you a blind fool? Don't you see I got a

173

gun pointed at this woman's head?"

"Yeah, that's just it. Your gun is pointed toward her, my gun is pointed toward you."

"Drop the gun, mister. Drop it now, or I'll kill the girl. This ain't your fight."

"Do you want to die?" Lucas asked.

"What are you talkin' about?"

"If you kill her, I'm goin' to kill you. Is that really what you want to happen?"

"Drop your gun, mister," Simmons said again, more nervously this time.

"No." Lucas held his arm out straight with the gun pointed at Simmons. He pulled the hammer back, the little click of the action clearly heard in the quiet saloon. "You can either let her go, then walk away, or you can kill her, then I'll kill you. It's your choice, mister."

Simmons's eyes grew wide in fear, and small beads of perspiration popped out on his forehead and his upper lip.

"I'll give you to the count of three to make up your mind," Lucas said. "One."

"You're crazy!"

"Two."

"No, no!" the man said. He dropped his gun and took his arm away from Sally's neck. Quickly, and with a little cry of relief, Sally darted away from him to join the other bargirls who, like everyone else in the saloon, had been drawn to the drama.

Two of the men who had been playing cards, jumped up to grab the now unarmed man.

Lucas put his pistol back into his holster, then turned to the bartender.

"I'll have that beer now."

"Yes, sir," the bartender said with emphasis. "And, Mister, the beer, and your supper is on the house."

Sally, the young woman Simmons had been holding, hurried over to Lucas and threw her arms around his neck.

"Oh, thank you, thank you, thank you," she said. "I've never seen you before, but whoever you are, you're my hero now!"

Lucas chuckled. "No, I'm not a hero. I'm just a fella who goes around rescuing beautiful young ladies in distress."

Sally laughed. "Well, for this lady in distress, you couldn't have come at a better time."

With George Rogers

George Rogers was enjoying a supper in the Pair O' Jacks Saloon in Hilton, Colorado. His dining companion for the evening was Rosco Minner.

"You did a good job getting the Fowler property cleared," Minner said. "Since the

Fowler family died in the fire, the land has become the property of the state and will be easy enough to acquire."

"That's what I like to hear, satisfied customers," Rogers said. "So, do you have another job for me?"

"As a matter of fact, I do have another job. One thousand dollars?"

Rogers smiled. "I enjoy doing business with you."

"Good," Minner said. He reached down to the floor beside his chair, then brought up a briefcase. Opening it, he took out a map and some papers, and spread them out on the table before them.

"Here is everything you'll need to know," he said.

Rock Slide, Colorado

Two weeks later, George Rogers was in the Two Gun Saloon having a drink with Russ Sage. It wasn't a casual drink or even a casual meeting. The two men had come together to discuss a business proposition.

"Roscoe Minner says that you're the man I want for a job I need done," Sage said.

"I believe he said something about a thousand dollars?" Rogers replied.

Sage laughed. "You get right to the point, don't you, Mr. Rogers?"

"It makes things a lot easier," Rogers said.

"I intend to build a spur line from here in Rock Slide, to connect with the Atchison, Topeka, and Santa Fe Railroad over in Timpas."

"But you need my help in persuading someone to let your spur line pass through their land," Rogers said.

"What? No, nothing of the sort. In fact, there are people competing for the right to have the railroad pass through their land."

"Then I don't understand. What do you need me for?"

"Marcus Danford," Sage said.

"Who's Marcus Danford?"

"He plans to put in a bid to the railroad to give him exclusive rights to build the spur. And if we wind up going head-to-head for the contract, I'm afraid Danford will win."

"Why do you think that?"

"He's built three other spur tracks, so as far as the railroad is concerned, he's a proven commodity."

"If you go head-to-head, you'll lose out?" Rogers said.

"I'm afraid so."

Rogers chuckled. "What if he didn't even have a head?"

Sage laughed out loud. "I see that you

understand what's expected of you."

"It won't be my first time to do a, uh, special job for someone," Rogers said.

"No, I guess not. Like I said, Minner told me you would be the man that would get the job done."

"I'll get started right away," Rogers said as he pushed back from the table.

"Oh, there's one thing I should warn you about," Sage said.

"What?"

"Actually, it's more of a who, than a what. Ashly Pardeen."

"And who's Ashly Pardeen?"

"Pardeen is a gunfighter that Danford has hired to protect his interest."

"That won't be a problem," Rogers said.

"I don't know, they say he's fast with a gun."

"Like I say, he won't be a problem."

"Are you . . . are you that fast?" Sage asked.

Rogers laughed. "Being fast has nothing to do with it. I don't plan to get in a gunfight with him. All I plan to do is kill him."

Sage laughed. "You really are a man who gets right to the point, aren't you? All right, Mr. Rogers. The job is yours."

■ ■ ■ ■

Marcus Danford had an office in Iron Springs, Colorado, identified by the large sign that hung on the front of the building.

MARCUS DANFORD
Danford Railroads Incorporated

When Rogers stepped inside, he saw a very thin man, with a prominent Adam's apple, sitting at the front desk. The man greeted Rogers.

"Yes, sir, is there something I can do for you?"

"Are you Danford?"

"Oh, heavens no, sir," the man replied with a nervous laugh. "I'm Mr. Truax. I work for Mr. Danford."

"I'd like to talk to Danford."

"All right, if you'd just wait here, I'll see if Mr. Danford can meet with you."

Rogers walked over to the wall to study some large photographs. There were three photographs of railroad locomotives, and each locomotive bore the name, "Danford Rail." Each photograph also had a small sign bcncath the pictures, identifying which specific spur the engine represented.

Truax came out a moment later.

179

"Mr. Danford will meet with you now."

Without replying, Rogers stepped into Danford's office.

Danford was a very fat man, with puffy cheeks, several chins, and a large, soft frame. Rogers figured that he had to be well over three hundred pounds.

There was another man standing by the wall. He was wearing a tied-down holster, and there was no restraint on the pistol. This man was tall and willowy, with a small moustache over thin lips that appeared to be set in a scowl. Rogers figured that this would be Ashly Pardeen.

"Mr. Truax said that you wanted to speak with me," Danford said, wheezing as he spoke.

"Yeah, I hear you're plannin' on buildin' a spur railroad from here to Carlin," Rogers said.

"Yes, I am. Are you seeking employment?"

"No, I'm here to tell you not to do it."

"What? Why, I've already invested rather heavily in the survey, and have even gathered some of the equipment I'll need. Why shouldn't I do it?"

"Russ Sage has hired me to see to it that you don't build the spur," Rogers said.

The tall, willowy man that Rogers knew to be the gunfighter chuckled. "Well, you're goin' to have a problem with that, Mister. Because Mr. Danford has hired me to see that nobody gets in the way."

"And just who are you?" Rogers asked.

"The name's Pardeen. Ashley Pardeen," the gunfighter said with a sinister smile. "I expect you've heard of me."

"Can't say as I have," Rogers said. He turned his attention back to Danford. "Mister, have this office closed and stop any buildin' o' the railroad that you might be doin'."

"Just who the hell are you, to come give me orders like that?" Danford said, angrily.

"The name is George Rogers, and I'm the one who's going to stop you from building this railroad."

Rogers left the office then, without another word. Once he was outside, he stepped around the corner of the building, then pulled his pistol and waited. A moment later, as he knew he would, Pardeen came barreling out of the building. He stood there for a moment, looking around as if trying to locate Rogers.

"I'm over here, Pardeen," Rogers said.

Startled, Pardeen turned toward him, drawing his gun as he did so. Pardeen got his gun out of the holster, but Rogers fired before Pardeen could bring the gun up level.

With an expression of shock on his face, Pardeen dropped the gun and slapped his hand over the entry wound, then looked down as blood began oozing through his spread fingers.

Even before Pardeen fell, Rogers went back into the office.

"Did you take care of him?" Danford called.

Rogers stepped through the door into Danford's office.

"Yeah, I did," he said, shooting Danford.

Rogers shot Truax as he left the building.

That same day, Rogers, one thousand dollars richer, left Iron Springs. Within a week the spur line was under construction, the operation handled by Sage Enterprises.

14

With Lucas Cain

When Lucas rode into the town of Robinson, he saw a train stopped under the water tower. The fireman was standing on the tender, controlling the water spout as he put water into the tank. As he rode by the locomotive, he saw the engineer looking out through the window with a bored expression on his face.

Lucas had never been to Robinson before, and it hadn't been his intention to visit it this time. It just happened to be in his path of wandering through the West with no specific destination in mind.

Although the sign at the entrance of the town read "Robinson" it could have read anything, because there was very little difference between Robinson and just about any other small town he had ridden through. The main street ran parallel with the railroad, with three cross streets. The houses were on the cross streets, and all the town businesses were on either side of the main street. There were three saloons in town, two on the south side of the street and one on the north side.

Lucas chose the one on the north side, and tying his horse off at the hitching rail, he stepped into the Bucking Horse Saloon.

"Two beers," he said when he reached the bar.

"Two?" the bartender replied.

"Yeah. One for thirst, and one to enjoy."

The bartender chuckled. "All right, mister, two beers it is."

A moment later the two beers were placed in front of Lucas, and picking up the first one, he drank the whole thing in just a few gulps. Then, pushing the empty mug aside, he picked up the second beer and drank it much more slowly to, as he had explained to the bartender, enjoy the taste.

"Hey you, saddle bum. When's the last time you've had a bath," someone called out to him.

Lucas made no response.

"Mister, when I'm talkin' to you, you damn well better quit starin' into your beer and pay attention to me."

The harshness of the young man's voice caused the other customers in the saloon to interrupt their own conversations so that they might follow what was developing.

Luca looked over toward him. What he saw was a young man with an arrogant expression on his face, dressed all in black, and with a pistol worn low with the holster strapped down.

"All right, I'm looking at you," Lucas said. "If you're trying to get me to buy you a drink, I'm sorry, but you just aren't pretty enough."

The saloon customers, and even the percentage girls laughed at Lucas's comment.

Lucas's comment, and the resultant laugh of the others in the saloon, made the young man very angry.

"Don't you ever take a bath?" the young man asked.

"Yeah, I bathe from time to time. I had a bath last year, or maybe the year before, I don't rightly remember."

"You can't even remember the last time you had a bath?"

"Mister, I don't know why you're so interested in when the last time I took a bath, but I have to tell you, if you're looking to take a bath with me, you're going to have to look somewhere else, because I'm not interested."

At this comment the saloon patrons laughed again, louder this time than they had before.

"Mister, I'm just goin' to have to kill you," the young man said, his face distorted by his rage.

"Can I give you a little advice?" Lucas asked.

"What? Advice? What do you mean, advice?"

"Well, you look pretty angry right now. And nobody is at their best when they're as mad as you are."

"I don't need any advice, mister, and I sure as hell don't need it from you. Do you know who I am?"

"No, who are you?"

"My name's Amon Chance. I reckon you've heard of me," he said with a twisted smile.

"Well, Amon, my name's Lucas Cain. I'm pleased to meet you. I'm always glad to make new friends." He held his hand out to offer a handshake.

"I'm not your friend, you old fool!" Amon said, even angrier than before. "I'm goin' to kill you. Draw!"

Lucas's gun appeared in his hand so suddenly that most who were watching didn't even see him draw.

Amon, who had started his own draw, stopped and stared at the gun in Lucas's hand in shock and fear.

"There, do you see what I told you? When you're as angry as you are, you can't do your best," Lucas said, smiling at the surprised young man.

"I . . . I," Amon said.

"I tell you what, I'll give you another chance," Lucas said, returning his pistol to his holster. He held his hands out. "Go ahead, try again. You go first."

Amon reached for his pistol, but before his hand even touched the handle, Lucas again, had his gun in his hand.

"See there, you still aren't doing it right," Lucas said. "I tell you what, Amon, why don't you just let me buy you a drink, and we can be friends." Lucas returned his pistol, then held up his finger. "But, I'm still not going to get naked in a bath tub with you."

Again, the others in the saloon laughed, and this time Amon laughed with them.

"All right, Clay, I'll have a whiskey," he said to the bartender.

"How about buying me a drink, mister?" a very pretty and scantily dressed young woman asked, as with a seductive smile, she sidled up beside Lucas.

187

"Why sure, darlin', I'd be glad to. What's your name?"

"I'm Lila. And, Lucas, you don't have to tell me your name, I heard it a moment ago when you told Amon."

"Well, then, there you go, Lila, we're already friends," Lucas said as he paid for the drink Clay set in front of Lila.

"Why don't we sit at a table?" Lila invited.

"That would nice," Lucas said, picking up his beer and following her to an empty table.

The two visited for a while, with Lila getting more and more provocative with her comments.

Finally, Lucas stood and smiled down at the young woman. "Lila, I just stopped in town for a beer and a few minutes of rest, but I have to be going now."

"You don't have to go right now do you?" Lila asked. "You could come up to my room, where we could get better acquainted."

"I appreciate the invitation, darlin', but I really do have to go."

"Where're you goin' that you can't stay even an hour longer?" Lila asked, putting even more invitation in her voice.

Lucas chuckled. "That's just it, I don't know where I'm going."

"What? Why, that makes no sense at all,"

Lila said. "How is it that you don't know where you're going?"

"Well, how can I know until I get there?" Lucas gave Lila a friendly nod, then with nearly everyone in the saloon staring at him, he left, got mounted, then urged Charley on down the street, exiting the other end of town, then continuing on with no particular destination, nor purpose, in mind.

Higbee, Colorado

"Twenty-five hundred dollars?" Rogers said. "Are you saying you'll give me twenty-five hundred dollars to take care of this problem for you?"

"Believe me, if I can get Pauline Foley to sell her ranch to me, it'll be well worth the twenty-five hundred dollars."

"All right," Rogers said. "I'll do it."

Rogers knew people who knew people, and that led him to the two men he hired to take care of the job for him. They were evil enough to do what needed to be done, and dumb enough to be totally unaware of the actual value of the job.

Rogers met with Lem Proctor and Eli Boyle at the Hog Lot Saloon.

"A hunnert dollars?" Proctor asked.

"Yes."

"That's a hunnert dollars apiece, ain't it?"

189

Proctor asked, putting his hand to his chin and staring shrewdly at Rogers.

Rogers sighed. "You boys are driving a hard bargain," he said, "but, yes, it'll be a hundred dollars apiece, once the job's done."

"All right," Proctor said. "Get your money ready, 'cause me 'n Boyle is goin' to get the job done."

"I'm sure you will," Rogers said.

With Pauline Foley

Pauline Foley was sixty-five years old. She had buried her husband, William, a year earlier. A widow now, Pauline continued to operate Hillside, the ranch William had built. At five thousand acres, Hillside was one of the larger ranches in Bent County. But even though the ranch was quite large, they were actually using only about a thousand acres, so that she, her daughter, and one hired hand were all that was required to run it.

Over the last few months, Pauline had received several offers to buy her ranch, but both her daughter, Sue Ellen, and Swayne Evans, her hired hand, supported her decision not to sell. Swayne Evans had been with the ranch almost from the time William had started it.

This morning Pauline planned to go into Higbee to get groceries and a few more items that she needed for the house. When she walked out to the barn, she saw that Swayne had already attached the team of mules to the wagon.

"Duchess didn't want to get in harness this morning," Swayne said.

"Oh? What was wrong with her?"

"Nothin', other than that she's a female, 'n there ain't nothin' that's got no harder head in the world, than a female or a mule, 'n when you put them two things together, why then you got yourself a thing to behold."

"Why, Swayne Evans, are you saying I've got a hard head?"

"You do at that, but in your case it's a good thing. It's your bein' hard headed that's savin' the ranch from bein' took over by whoever it is that's a' wantin' it.

"By the way, we're missin' another five cows," Swayne said. "You know what that's about, don't you? Whoever it is that's a' tryin' to buy this ranch, is doin' things like snatchin' up a few cows here 'n there to cause you trouble."

"Yes," Pauline replied, "and at fifty dollars a head, losing five cows is more than just a little trouble."

"I know you're gettin' a lot of pressure to sell, but I hope you don't. Exceptin' for when I was a kid, I ain't never really had no home like what I got here."

"Well, you don't have to worry about it, because I don't have any intention of selling, no matter how much pressure is put on me."

"You're a good woman, Miz Foley. Bill done just real good when he married you."

Pauline smiled. "Hush, Swayne, you're making me blush. Go on, now, I've got to get on into town. I want to be back before dinner."

"Yes, ma'am. Let me help you into the wagon."

Pauline didn't really need any help, but she knew that Swayne enjoyed helping her, so she offered no resistance.

Swayne or Sue Ellen could have made this trip to Higbee, but Pauline enjoyed coming to town where she could visit with a few friends. Also, she enjoyed the time being in the open air, just driving down the road.

Her wagon was pulled by a team of mules, Homer and Duchess. Pauline had a special affection for Duchess, because she was the first mule that Bill bought when they moved to Colorado.

"Duchess, old girl, you 'n I have been

through it all together, haven't we?" Pauline said, speaking to her mule. "You were with us during droughts, floods, and blizzards. Why, we couldn't even see the road then, but you got Bill and me back. Bill had no intention of ever getting rid of you, and neither do I."

Duchess nodded her head, and though Pauline knew it was no more than a normal action, she chose to believe that Duchess was telling her that she was happy to be a part of Hillside.

Half way between Hillside Ranch and Higbee, Lem Proctor and Eli Boyle were camped just off the side of the road. "How damn long are we a' goin' to have to stay here?" Boyle asked. "Hell, we been camped out here for three days now, not doin' nothin' but just sittin' out here."

"Yeah, well, we're gettin' a hunnert dollars apiece by doin' nothin' but just sittin' here," Proctor said. "Besides, it cain't be much longer. It's been a little over a week since the last time she come inter town, 'n she comes inter town near 'bout ever' week, so I 'spect she'll be comin' up the road anytime now."

"Yeah, and then it's a hunnert dollars," Boyle said.

"You come up with any way o' spendin' it yet?" Proctor asked.

Boyle laughed. "Hell, what's there to come up with, other 'n whiskey 'n a woman?"

"Well, I'm glad to see you've got that all figured out. Oh, wait a minute. Yeah, good, it looks like our waitin' is over, 'cause they's a wagon comin' up the road now," Proctor said.

"How do you know it's the right one?"

"It has to be the right one, 'cause it's bein' pulled by a team of mules, 'n it's bein' drove by a woman."

"We stop it now?"

"No, we'll wait 'til she starts back. If she's got some groceries we can mess with, it'll be easier. Just let 'er ride on by."

It was only about half an hour ride from Hillside Ranch into Higbee. While in town, she planned to get a hat for Sue Ellen. She also wanted to visit with Lucile, who was a good friend.

A bell, attached to the door, jingled as she pushed it open. Lucile was in the back of the store, and she came up to greet her customer.

"Pauline, since we spoke last week, I've got just the hat for Sue Ellen. I put it away, come back here and I'll show it to you."

What she showed Pauline was a wide-brimmed straw hat with pink silk flowers and white ribbons.

"Oh, Lucile, yes, this will be just perfect for Sue Ellen, if I can ever get her to wear it. She prefers shirt and pants to a dress, but maybe this will tempt her. Thank you, you found just what I wanted."

The ladies visited for a while, then Pauline went down to the general store where she began stocking up on groceries to last her for the next week.

"You still gettin' all them offers for your ranch?" Cephas Brown asked as he loaded the wagon for her.

"I am, but I'm not paying any attention to them," Pauline said. "I'm not going to sell."

"Well, on the one hand, I'd say why not sell? I mean, runnin' a ranch is hard work, and if you got enough for it, it might be wise for you to do so. But on the other hand, you're a good customer and a good friend, so I'd hate to see you sell it, then pull up stakes and go somewhere else."

"You don't have to worry about that, Cephas. I'm not planning on going anywhere."

As they were loading the wagon, a young boy of about twelve years old came up to them.

"Miz Foley?"

"Yes, Johnny?" Pauline replied.

"Mr. Garrett, he seen you down here, 'n he sent me to ask you if you would come see him before you left."

"All right, Johnny, thank you."

David Garrett was the lawyer that Bill Foley had used to write his will. Ironically, within a month of making out his will, Bill died of pneumonia.

Pauline drove the wagon down to the front of Garrett's office, set the brake, then walked into his office.

"Hello, David," she said, greeting him by his first name.

"Hello, Pauline," Garrett said. "Please, have a seat."

"Johnny said you wanted to see me?"

"Yes, I've been authorized to make you a new offer for Hillside."

"David, we've been through this a dozen times, and my answer has always been, and will continue to be, I'm not interested in selling."

"I know you've said that, but I think you might want to reconsider. With the money you're being offered, you could retire and live in comfort for the rest of your life."

"And where would that leave Sue Ellen and Swayne?"

"I'm sure that, with your recommendation, Swayne could get on just about anywhere he wanted," Garrett said.

"I don't want Swayne going anywhere else. I'm quite comfortable with him right where he is. David, who is it that keeps making these offers for the ranch?"

"Now, Pauline, you know I can't tell you that. There's such a thing as lawyer, client confidentiality. It would be a violation of legal ethics were I to tell you."

"How ethical is it to steal cattle and burn pasture land?" Pauline asked.

Garrett looked shocked. "Is that happening?"

"Yes, and it's happening more and more often — at least once a week two or three cows wind up missing or else dead."

"Well, I'm sorry to hear that. I can assure you, that it isn't my client doing such a thing."

"But, I don't understand. Why would anyone do such a thing? What is it that makes my land so valuable that there is such a demand for it?"

"I don't know the answer to that question, Pauline. I'm just a small-town lawyer, trying to make a living. And if I didn't think it would be good for you to sell Hillside, I wouldn't even tender the offer."

"I understand, David, and I also know that you feel it would be more beneficial for me to sell, than to hold on to the property. But if you value my friendship, please understand — I have no desire to sell."

"I do, indeed, value your friendship, Pauline, and I will inform my client that you are adamant in your decision not to sell."

"Thank you, David. I certainly value your friendship as well." She stood then. "And now, if we have no further business, I must go. I have a wagon full of supplies and I must get home."

"Yes, by all means. If you won't reconsider, I guess we're finished here." He got up and walked her to the door. As she was getting into the wagon, he called out, "Have a safe trip home."

Pauline waved as she started down the street.

15

With Lucas Cain

Lucas's western odyssey continued, and he was getting butt-sore and trail weary from the continuous non-specific drift.

Lucas reckoned himself to be thirty years old. He wasn't certain that he was thirty yet, because other than knowing that it was the summer of 1872, he had no specific concept of the date. His birthday was June seventeenth, so if he wasn't thirty yet, he soon would be. And to be honest, he didn't really care whether he was thirty or not. He was, he reasoned, what he was, and there was nothing he could do about it.

"I tell you what, Charley," he said, "how about we stop for a while in the next town we come to? I'd like to take a few days off to drink some beer and eat food that I haven't shot or pulled from my saddle bag."

Because Lucas was alone so much, he often talked to his horse, believing that it was better than talking to himself. "And I'll put you up in a livery where there are bound to be a few good-looking mares that you can flirt with. As long as it's only flirting," he added with a little chuckle. "I don't want you to be getting into any trouble, now."

He figured that by stopping in the next town, he would be able to establish both his location and the current date. Lucas chuckled as he considered it. It was only a matter of curiosity that would cause him to inquire as to time and place, because the truth was, the way his life was now, neither date nor location was important to him.

"It's you and me, Charley, just the two of us," Lucas said to his horse, and he reached down to pat his hand against Charley's neck.

Lucas wasn't the only one on Higbee Road traveling alone and speaking aloud. Pauline Foley was on the road less than half a mile before him, and as she was driving the grocery-laden wagon back home, she gave voice to her own thoughts, in her case, speaking to Duchess.

"Oh, Duchess, how I wish Bill was here to handle this. I don't want to sell Hillside. I know how much it meant to him . . . to us, really. But I'm getting so much pressure to sell, and the thing is, I don't even know who's trying to buy the place. David Garrett is making the offer for someone, but he says he can't tell me who's making the offer. It might make a difference if I knew who I was selling to."

Homer, the other mule, snorted, and Pauline chuckled. "You just don't worry about anything, Homer. Duchess and I are talking, woman to woman."

"How much longer do we have to stay here?" Boyle asked. "I'm gettin' tard of waitin."

"We'll stay here 'till she —" He paused in mid-sentence. "Wait a minute, there she comes now. You see 'er?"

"Yeah, I see 'er."

"And lookie there, her wagon is loaded with groceries 'n such, just like I told you it would be. Get mounted, we'll go out in the road and stop her."

"Yeah, 'n she's all alone, too. This is goin' to be the easiest money we ever made."

"Ha, why don't we go inter business?" Boyle said. "We can put us up a sign that says, 'Fer a hunnert dollars, we'll stop old ladies in the road'."

Proctor laughed. "That's a good 'n."

The two men road out into the road, then stopped facing back toward the approaching wagon.

"Better get dismounted now," Boyle said. "That way, you can mess with the wagon, while I'll keep her from runnin' off."

Pauline saw two men on the road in front of her. Normally that wouldn't be a cause for concern as she often met riders on the road, but these two men weren't riding. They were just stopped right in the middle of the road, and the way they were positioned would prevent her from passing. One was mounted, while the other one was just standing there holding the reins of his horse.

"Now, look up there, Duchess. Just what in the world do you think those two are doing? Surely, they're going to move over to let us pass."

But they didn't, and she had to stop when she approached them.

"Would you two gentlemen please move aside, so that I might pass?" she asked.

"Ha, Boyle, did you hear that?" the man on the ground asked. "She called us gentlemen. There ain't nobody that's ever called us gentlemen before."

"Well, hell, Proctor, who wants to be a gentleman anyhow?" Boyle replied.

The tone of the voices of the two men was a little frightening.

"Very well, if you won't move, I'll just go around you," Pauline said. She lifted the reins preparatory to snapping them against her team.

"Lady, you ain't a'goin' nowhere lessen we say you can," the man on the ground said, and pulling his pistol, he shot one of the two mules that were pulling the wagon.

"Duchess!" Pauline shouted in shock as Duchess collapsed while still in harness. "Oh my God! You shot Duchess! Why did you shoot my mule?"

"I shot her to keep you from goin' any-where," the man who had shot Duchess said.

"Proctor, do a good deed, and unload her groceries for her," Boyle said.

"All right," Proctor said. "I'll unload your groceries for you. Oh, wait, you ain't back at your house, are you? Well, that's all right, I'll just unload 'em here, 'n you can come back 'n get 'em," he added with a cackling laugh as he began to toss the groceries onto the road.

"Who are you people? Why are you doing this?" Pauline asked. "Why did you kill Duchess?" Pauline began to weep, not from fear, but from sorrow over losing a creature that was so dear to her.

"You wanna know why? To get your attention, that's why. Iffen you would sell your ranch, why, you wouldn't have to put up with anything like this," Boyle said.

"You kill my Duchess to get me to sell my ranch? Do you really think something like this is going to make me change my mind?"

"I'm cold," Boyle said. "Proctor, don't you think Miz Foley might be a little cold?"

"She might be," Proctor said.

Boyle handed a can down to Proctor. "Why don't you build a little fahr 'n warm her up?"

"Yeah," Proctor said. "That's a good idea."

Proctor began pouring the liquid from the can onto the wagon. Pauline could tell by the smell that it was kerosene.

"No!" she shouted. "What are you doing?"

Proctor struck a match and tossed it onto the splash of kerosene. Flames leaped up from the side of the wagon.

"Are you insane?" Pauline shouted as, quickly, she climbed down from the burning wagon.

Lucas saw a wagon on fire in the road ahead. A woman, obviously distressed, was standing beside the wagon, and there were two men there as well, one mounted, and the other, standing alongside. Lucas's initial thought was that the men were helping her.

As he drew closer though, he realized that, instead of helping her, they were tormenting her. Because he and the wagon had been coming toward each other, his approach was unseen by the two men.

"Please, go away and leave me alone," he heard the woman say in a frightened voice.

Neither of the men, nor the woman, had yet seen him.

"Hey, you know what, Boyle? They's some flour 'n sugar amongst the groceries here. Why, what with the fire 'n all, I'll just bet that Miz Foley could bake us a cake."

Lucas saw the man rip open a sack, then dump the flour, much of which was carried away by the wind, as a white cloud.

"Please," the woman begged again. "Leave me alone!"

"We'll leave you alone when you do what we tell you to do," the dismounted man said. He was pointing his pistol at the woman, who, Lucas now saw, was a somewhat older woman.

Lucas pulled his rifle, raised it to his shoulder and fired. The man holding the pistol let out a yelp of pain as the bullet carried his gun away.

"What the hell?" the mounted man shouted. Turning toward Lucas, he started to reach for his pistol.

"That's not a good idea, friend," Lucas called out. He was holding his rifle in such a way as to be able to cover both of them as he closed the distance to the buckboard. That was when he saw that one of the two mules that had been pulling the wagon now lay dead, though still in harness.

"What's going on here?" Lucas asked.

"That's between us 'n Miz Foley here. You ain't got no business buttin' in," the mounted man replied.

"Mrs. Foley, do I have your permission to 'butt in'?" Lucas asked.

"Yes, yes, please, make them put out the fire!"

"You heard the lady," Lucas said. "Get some dirt and put out that fire."

"Mister, this here ain't none of your concern," the mounted man said.

Lucas drew his pistol, then shot the hat off the mounted man. "I just made it my concern," he said. "My next shot will be six inches lower."

"Proctor, what the hell? You just gonna stand there 'n do nothin'?" Boyle asked.

"I am doin' something, I'm puttin' this fahr out. Now get down here 'n help me, Boyle, I cain't do it all by my ownself." Proctor was using his hat to carry dirt over to the wagon, then he dumped it on the flames.

Boyle dismounted, then stepped back to help Proctor throw dirt on the burning part of the wagon. Within a couple of minutes, the flames were extinguished, and an examination convinced Lucas that, except for some charred wood, the wagon was still serviceable.

"We're all done here, now," one of the two men said.

"Not quite."

"What do you mean we ain't quite done? You asked us to put out the fahr, 'n that's what we done."

Lucas pointed to the groceries that were scattered across the ground.

"Put her groceries back in the wagon."

The two men began picking up the scattered groceries.

"All right," Boyle said. "We put out the fahr, 'n we loaded up her wagon, so we're goin' now."

"You've got a little more to do," Lucas said. "I want you to disconnect this dead mule, and pull it out of the way."

Proctor pulled a knife, and started to cut through the harness that was around the dead mule.

"No, don't do that. We'll need the harness

when we connect the horse."

"What horse?"

Lucas pointed to the two horses that were standing by.

"Oh, either one of those will do. I'll let you pick the horse."

"What?"

"We'll use one of your horses, you can select which one it will be."

"You mean you're stealin' one of our horses?" Proctor asked.

"Well, I wouldn't call it stealing. After we get Mrs. Foley and her groceries home, I'll take the horse into the next town and leave it at the livery. You won't have any trouble getting it back. Now, get this dead mule moved out of here, and get one of those two horses in harness."

The two men did as they were told, though they didn't do it without complaint. Then, when they had the new horse in harness, they stepped away from the wagon.

"What now?" one of them asked.

"I would suggest that you two get on back to where ever it is that you came from."

"How we goin' to do that? They's only one horse, 'n they's two of us."

"Well, if you're good enough friends, you can double up on your horse. If that doesn't work, one of you can ride, and one of you can walk."

"What about my tack?"

"If you can hold on to it, you can take it with you. Otherwise, you can just leave it here, and I'll return it when I bring the horse to the next town," Lucas said.

The man with the wounded hand re-mounted. The other man stared up at him.

"Boyle?" he said.

Boyle let out an audible sigh. "All right, you can climb up, but you're leavin' your saddle here. There ain't no way I'm goin' to have that pokin' into my back." He held a stirrup out, allowing Proctor to get mounted.

Boyle looked back at Lucas. "You ain't heard the last of this, Mister."

"Oh, I'm sure I haven't," Lucas said.

Lucas watched the two men ride away on one horse, then he looked over at Mrs. Foley, who was looking down at the dead mule.

"Are you all right, ma'am?" Lucas asked.

"Duchess was such a dear, sweet mule. I've had her for over twenty years. My husband bought her right after we came to Colorado. She didn't deserve to die like this."

"I'm sorry."

"You have nothing to be sorry for. If it

209

hadn't been for you, I'd be standing out here all by myself, with a burnt wagon and a dead mule . . . that is if I was still alive."

"Mrs. Foley, my name is Lucas Cain. If you don't mind, I think I'd like to ride along with you until you get home. I don't want there to be any chance that those two . . . gentlemen . . . would look you up again."

"Believe me, Mr. Cain, Boyle and Proctor weren't gentlemen," Mrs. Foley said, "and I would very much appreciate your company. Actually, if you would, I'd like it if you'd tie your horse off to the back of the wagon, and ride with me." She patted the seat beside her.

"I will, provided you let me drive," Lucas replied with a smile. "I don't exactly know how it will be with a mixed team of a mule and a horse."

Mrs. Foley's eyes clouded. "I don't know how Homer will make out without Duchess." She wiped a tear away. "I don't know what I'll do without Duchess. Such a shame to see her lying dead by the side of the road."

"Would you like me to bury her?" Lucas asked.

"No, she deserves to be buried at Hillside. I'll have Swayne come drag her home."

"Is Swayne your husband?"

"No, he's my hand," Mrs. Foley said. "My husband died sometime back."

After tying Charley to the back of the buckboard, and throwing the tack from the "borrowed" horse into the buckboard, Lucas came around front and climbed in. The conveyance dipped with his weight as he did so.

Once he was in the seat, Lucas snapped the reins against the team, and the buckboard started forward. Mrs. Foley looked over at the dead mule as the wagon rolled by.

"Oh, the poor thing," she said quietly.

"Did those men rob you?" Lucas asked.

"No."

"Then, I don't understand. What was this all about?"

"I think they're just a couple of very evil young men," Mrs. Foley said.

Lucas was certain there had to be more to the story than that. The two men didn't rob Mrs. Foley, nor did he think her life was ever in actual danger. And yet he was totally convinced that there was, indeed, a reason for the harassment.

16

"Turn here," Pauline said, after a drive of about twenty minutes. Where she pointed, was more of a lane than a road, and it ran at right angles to the road itself.

Within five minutes after leaving the main road, Lucas saw a white, two-story house with a covered front porch. In addition to the house, there was a barn, and another smaller house. As he pulled up in front of the house a young woman stepped out onto the front porch. Lucas guessed her age to be in the early to mid-twenties. She might have been pretty, but she had a scowl on her face, she was wearing men's clothing, and she was holding a rifle in her hand.

"Who are you?" the young woman asked. Then she noticed the fire-charred side of the wagon. "Mama, where's Duchess? What happened to the wagon?"

"Sue Ellen, this is Mr. Cain," Pauline said. "He was very helpful to me on the road.

This is my daughter, Sue Ellen."

"Pleased to meet you, Miss Foley," Lucas said.

"What happened?" Sue Ellen asked again, ignoring Lucas's greeting.

"I encountered two men on the way home from shopping. They shot and killed poor Duchess and set fire to the wagon. Then, Mr. Cain came along and had them put out the fire before it had done too much damage." Pauline smiled. "He also arranged for them to lend me a horse."

"Why, who would do such a thing?" Sue Ellen asked, lowering the rifle.

"I've never seen them before, but I heard them call their names. Boyle and Proctor."

"Let me help you unload your purchases, then I'll put the wagon away for you, and . . . what's this mule's name?" Lucas asked.

"Homer," Pauline replied.

"All right, I'll put Homer away for you, too."

"What will we do with Proctor's horse?" Pauline asked.

"When I leave, I'll take him to the livery. What is the nearest town, anyway?"

"Higbee," Pauline said.

After emptying the wagon, Lucas drove it out to the barn, where he was met by an older, rather scruffy looking man with white hair and beard stubble.

"Who are you?" the man asked. "What are you doin' with Miz Foley's wagon, 'n where's Duchess?"

"The name is Lucas Cain, and I'm driving Mrs. Foley's wagon because I came to her assistance out on the road. And that's where Duchess is, lying dead alongside the road."

"Damn, what happened to her? Duchess was a good mule, 'n she warn't sick or nothin'."

"A couple of men stopped Mrs. Foley out on the road, had some words with her, then shot one of her mules."

"Any son of a bitch that would shoot a mule, especially one like Duchess, don't deserve to live. I hope you kilt the bastard what done it."

"No, I didn't kill anyone, I just sent both of them on their way, then helped Mrs. Foley get home safely. But before I sent them away, I arranged to borrow one of their horses to take Duchess's place."

The old man laughed. "Damn, I sure as hell would 'a like to have seen that. Oh, by the way, my name's Swayne Evans." Swayne extended his hand. "I work for Miz Foley, 'n I also worked for Mr. Foley a' fore he died."

"It's a pleasure meeting you, Mr. Evans."

"No, please, call me Swayne. I don't reckon there's never been nobody what's ever called me Mr. Evans. Even Sue Ellen ain't never called me nothin' but Swayne from the time she warn't nothin' but a little nipper."

"All right, I'll call you Swayne, and please call me Lucas. But now, tell me, do you have any idea why a couple of men would jump an old lady and start harassing her the way they did?"

"You mean Miz Foley didn't tell you?"

"No, as you can imagine, she was pretty shaken up, so I didn't want to cause her any more problem than she already had."

"Yeah, that was prob'ly a pretty good idea. Well, here's the thing. It seems like there's somebody what's wantin' her to sell Hillside. I don't know who it is, but they keep askin', 'n she keeps sayin' no. We've had more 'n just a few cows turned up stoled, or dead. I wouldn't be surprised if whoever is behind the problems we been havin' 'round here, wouldn't be the same ones what sent them two men to bother her. Who was they, by the way? Did you happen to get their names?"

"No first names, but one was called Boyle and the other was Proctor."

"Oh, yeah, I know who them two are. They ain't friends or nothin', but I know who they are, 'n they're 'bout the meanest sons of bitches you'll find anywhere around here."

"Do you think they were bothering Mrs. Foley so they could buy the ranch?"

"No, not for themselves." Swayne laughed, a scoffing laugh. "Most o' the time, them two ain't hardly got enough money betwixt 'em to even buy a drink. No, sir, what it more 'n likely is that them two no account polecats was paid to stop Miz Foley 'n to do what they done to her, that's for sure 'n certain."

The two of them unhooked the wagon team, put Homer in the barn, then tied off Proctor's horse.

"What are you going to do with him?" Swayne asked, pointing at the spare horse.

"I'll take him into town and leave him at the livery. I told the two men that's what I would do."

"Hell, if it was up to me, I'd just let 'im go," Swayne said.

"Well, I told them I would leave him at the livery, and I intend to do just that. You said somebody wants her to sell. Who is it?

216

Who's trying to buy the ranch?"

"That's just it, there don't nobody know who it is, 'n that's one o' the problems. They's some lawyer in Higbee what's makin' the offer, but he won't tell nobody who it is that's actual wantin' Miz Foley to sell. He says that, 'cause he's a lawyer, he don't have to tell who his client is."

"I suppose he's claiming lawyer, client privilege," Lucas said.

"Yeah, somethin' like that. You know about that, do you? How come you to know? Are you a lawyer?"

"No, but I've been a police officer, a deputy sheriff, and a deputy marshal. So, I've got a little background in the business."

"You don't say? Well, anyhow, like I told you, all these things keep on a' happenin' to the ranch, but this is the first time anybody's ever actual tried to hurt Miz Foley though."

"Tell me what you know about the two men who attacked her, Boyle and Proctor. You said you knew who they were. Do you have any idea who they might be working for?"

Swayne made a sarcastic snort. "Hell, them two no-count sons of bitches don't work for nobody regular. They're in jail 'bout as much time as they're out 'a jail. They's prob'ly just somebody that's hired 'em to do this one thing for 'im. They're just the kind that would attack an old woman out on the road, if somebody paid 'em to do it. 'N since they don't neither one of 'em work for anyone in particular, well, it wouldn't be very hard to get them to do somethin' like that."

"It might be a good idea to find out who hired them," Lucas suggested.

"What do you mean somebody came up and stopped you?" Rogers asked.

"It's just like I said," Proctor replied. "Things was goin' real good, why we had that ole' lady half scairt to death, 'n she would 'a done anything we told her to do, then this fella come ridin' up, 'n stopped us."

"There were two of you," Rogers said. "Are you tellin' me just one man got the better of the two of you?"

"Yeah, well, he kind 'a snuck up on us," Boyle said. "We was payin' attention to the old woman, like we was supposed to do, 'n the next thing you know, he come up from behind, a' shootin' at us. We didn't have no choice but to ride away when he told us to, or more 'n likely he would 'a shot us both."

"But, me 'n Ely put some kind o' scare in Miz Foley, so, like as not she's goin' to want to sell that ranch anyhow, no matter that someone come up shootin' at us when we wasn't expectin' no one," Proctor added.

"Yeah, so I think you should go ahead 'n give us that hunnert dollars," Boyle said.

"The deal was to pay you after she sold the ranch," Rogers said.

"Well, there ain't no doubt in my mind but what she's goin' to do it," Proctor said. "So, how 'bout half now, 'n the rest of it after she sells the ranch?"

"That wasn't the bargain," Rogers said. "The bargain was you would get paid, *after* she sold the ranch."

17

"Mr. Cain, I wonder if you would like to eat a bite with us," Pauline asked, when Lucas walked back up to the house.

"Oh, Mrs. Foley, I wouldn't want to put you out any," Lucas replied.

"Don't be foolish. After what you did for me, feeding you is the least I can do."

Lucas chuckled. "Well now, if you mean that, after all the campfire meals I've had, there's no way I'm going to turn down a home-cooked meal, so I'll just take you up on your offer. It's bound to be better than the beef jerky I was going to have."

When Lucas sat down to the table a few minutes later, he saw again the young woman who had met them on the porch. As he examined her more closely, he saw a slender young creature with an erect carriage and a woman's shape that couldn't be hidden by the man's shirt she was wearing. She had blonde hair and eyes the color of a blue sky. He realized that she was actually quite attractive.

"You already met my daughter, Sue Ellen," Pauline said.

"Oh yes, ma'am," Lucas said with a smile. "She's the one who wanted to shoot me."

"Please believe me, Mr. Cain, if I had wanted to shoot you, I would have."

Lucas was amused that she didn't react to his comment in the way of a woman who would be shocked by his charge. Rather she made the comment in a matter-of-fact tone of voice.

He chuckled. "You know, Miss, I just believe you would have."

"You met Swayne?" Sue Ellen asked. "He will be in to eat shortly. As he is our only hand, he takes his meals with us."

"Swayne said you had been getting offers for your ranch," Lucas said.

"Yes, we have."

"Miz Pauline?" Swayne called from just outside the kitchen door.

"Yes, Swayne, come on in, dinner's just about on the table," Pauline replied.

"Thank ye, ma'am."

Swayne came in and took a seat.

"Sorry to hear about Duchess," Swayne said. "She was as good a mule as I've ever know'd."

"Which reminds me, I want you to take Homer and try to bring Duchess home. She deserves to be buried here."

"Yes, ma'am," Swayne said.

"Mrs. Foley, I can't thank you enough for inviting me to eat with you. This is delicious," Lucas said, trying to change the subject.

"You can thank Sue Ellen for that," Pauline said.

"Thank you, Miss Foley," Lucas said. "I must say that this is an improvement over being met with a rifle in your hand."

"I apologize for that," Sue Ellen said, self-consciously. "It's just that since these offers to buy our ranch, we haven't always been treated well."

Pauline then told the story of how she and her husband William had come to Colorado from Tennessee by way of a wagon train, some twenty-five years ago. Shortly after they arrived, Bill Foley met Swayne Evans. Swayne came to work for them, even before Sue Ellen had been born.

"It was my husband's dream to build something for Sue Ellen and me," Pauline continued. "That's exactly what he did, and I have no intention of selling this ranch during my lifetime."

After the meal was finished, Lucas told all

goodbye, then astride Charley and leading the extra now-saddled horse, he rode on into Higbee, which, he was told, was six miles south of Hillside Ranch. Just as he came into town, he saw the Boots and Saddles Saloon, and thinking that a beer would taste good after a long, hot ride, he figured to stop there after turning the horse in at the livery.

When he dismounted in front of the Mitchell Livery, he was greeted by a man who had gray hair and a gray beard.

"Wantin' to board them two horses are you?"

"Are you Mr. Mitchell?"

"Zeke Mitchell."

"No, Mr. Mitchell, just this one," Lucas said, dismounting and handing the reins of the led horse over to him.

"All right, what's the name?"

"Lucas Cain."

"And the horse's name?"

"I don't know."

"You don't know? Well, pardon me, Mister, but you ain't makin' no sense. I ain't never heard of no one what didn't know the name of his own horse before."

"Yes, well, that's the problem," Lucas said. "This isn't my horse, it belongs to a man named Proctor."

"Lem Proctor. Yeah, I know him. Don't care much for him, but I know him. How'd you come by his horse?"

Lucas told of his encounter on the road with Boyle and Proctor, and how they had killed one of Mrs. Foley's mules.

"Which one did they kill? Homer or Duchess?"

"Duchess."

"Damn, they killed Duchess? That's awful, Bill Foley set quite a store by that mule, 'n I know that Mrs. Foley did, too."

"Yes, Mrs. Foley did take it pretty hard."

"You can see why she would. Hell, Duchess was more liken a child to her, than a mule."

"I sort of gathered that. So anyway, after they killed Duchess, I just took one of their horses to form a team to bring the wagon in, and I told them I would leave the horse with you. So, I reckon one of them will be seeing you soon."

"Who'll be paying?"

"Boyle or Proctor, I suppose."

"What if they don't pay?"

"Do you have reason to believe that they won't pay?"

"I know both them boys, 'n they ain't neither one of 'em worth a plug nickel."

"Well, then, Mr. Mitchell, in that case, I

guess you'll just have yourself a horse."

Mitchell chuckled. "Yeah, I reckon I will."

"Where's a good place to get a beer?" Lucas asked.

"We got a couple places, the Hog Lot and the Boots and Saddles. But in my mind, the best place would be at the Boots and Saddles Saloon. It's just across the street, then that a way down the street a few buildings." Mitchell pointed. "You can't miss it."

Lucas laughed. "Mr. Mitchell, I've been all over the West. And the one thing I've learned for sure is how to find a saloon."

At that precise moment, Proctor and Boyle were sitting at a table in the Boots and Saddles.

"Who the hell was that son of a bitch anyway?" Boyle asked.

"I don't know, but he damn sure ain't from around here. There ain't nobody from aroun' here would dare come at us like that."

"He come up behind us, too. If we would 'a seen the son of a bitch, he wouldn't have never gotten away with it," Boyle said.

"You got that right," Proctor insisted.

18

When his business with Mitchell was concluded, Lucas rode back down to the Boots and Saddles Saloon, and after tying Charley off at the hitching rail, he stepped inside.

There were three men standing at the bar, and several more sitting at a couple of tables out on the floor. There were four percentage girls, wearing face paint and dresses that displayed their feminine charms, moving around, flirting with the men and often drinking with them.

"What'll it be?" the bartender asked.

"A beer would be good, thank you."

The bartender filled a mug from the beer barrel, then set it on the bar in front of him, gold, with a white head.

"I don't believe I've seen you in here before."

Lucas smiled as he put a half-dime on the bar. "Well, not likely since I haven't been in here before."

"Welcome to Higbee."

"Thanks."

"Hey, Eli, look over there," Proctor said quietly, nodding toward the bar.

"What?"

"Just look, damnit," Proctor hissed.

"Damn, that's the son of a bitch that stopped us out on the road, ain't it?"

"Yeah. Tell you what, I'm goin' upstairs," Boyle said.

"Upstairs?" Proctor replied, surprised by the announcement. "I thought we was goin' to take care of this guy the next time we seen him. Well, there he is."

"Yeah, we're goin' to. Once I get up there, I'll step up to the railin'. When you see me standin' there with my gun in my hand, you stand up and call him out."

"What do mean? You want me to call him out all by myself?"

"No, didn't you hear what I said? You call him out, 'n then soon's he turns around, I'll shoot 'im, before he even sees me."

Proctor chuckled. "Yeah, that's a good idea. All right," he said, "let's do it."

As Lucas started drinking his beer, he looked in the mirror and recognized Proctor and Boyle sitting at one of the tables. As he

227

was studying them, the one he knew as Boyle got up from the table and went upstairs. Assuming that he had gone up to visit with one of the soiled doves, Lucas thought nothing of it.

He took another swallow of his beer then, but in the mirror, he saw Proctor stand. He was holding his pistol at waist high, and he was pointing it in Lucas's general direction.

"You stole my horse, you son of a bitch!" Proctor shouted. One of the bar girls was just passing between them and hearing Proctor's challenge, moved quickly out of the way.

Boyle's shout interrupted everyone's conversation and they all looked to see who the subject of the yelling was. They saw the stranger at the bar turn to face the man. The bartender moved hastily to get out of the way, as did everyone else who was standing at the bar.

"Hello, Proctor," Lucas said in a calm voice.

"What? How the hell do you know my name?"

"Oh, we met before, out on the road, remember?" Lucas said with a mocking smile.

"What's your name, you horse stealin' son of a bitch?"

"My name is Lucas Cain, and I didn't steal your horse, Mr. Proctor. I just borrowed him for a while in order to get Mrs. Foley home, after you killed her mule."

"You killed one of Mrs. Foley's mules?" one of the saloon patrons asked. "She put great store in them mules, especially the one she called Duchess."

"Duchess is the one he killed," Lucas said.

"Damn, Proctor, why the hell would you do somethin' like that?"

"Why I done it ain't nobody's business," Proctor said. "The thing is, this son of a bitch come bustin' in where he didn't have no right to be doin' it, 'n he stole my horse."

"Like I said, Proctor, I didn't steal your horse, I just borrowed him. You'll find your horse down at the Mitchell Livery."

"If he is, he ain't got no business bein' there, 'n I aim to settle up with you. Pull your gun, you son of a bitch!"

"Well now, that wouldn't be fair, would it? You're already holding your gun."

"I said draw your gun!"

Lucas was pretty sure that, even with his pistol already in his hand, Proctor wouldn't challenge him without some additional edge, and he had a good idea he knew what that edge was. Glancing upstairs, Lucas saw Boyle standing at the railing pointing his

229

pistol at him.

"You not only already have a gun in your hand, your friend is up on the balcony pointing a gun at me."

"Shoot 'im!" Proctor shouted.

Lucas made a lightning draw then fired, not at Proctor, but at Boyle who was standing at the upstairs railing. A shocked Boyle dropped his pistol, slapped his hands against the hole in his chest, and as blood spilled through his fingers he fell over the railing, turned one-half flip, and landed on his back on a table below.

Even as Boyle was falling, Lucas whirled toward Proctor and fired, his shot almost concurrent with Proctor's shot. The bullet energized by Lucas's pistol struck Proctor in the middle of his forehead, and a mist of blood sprayed out from the resulting hole as Proctor fell backwards.

But Lucas hadn't gotten away unscathed, because even as he was pulling the trigger for his second shot, he felt the blow of a bullet plunging into his left shoulder.

Lucas returned his pistol to its holster, then put his hand over the shoulder wound. He leaned up against the bar.

One of the bar girls came over to him. "Here," she said, "let me take care of that for you."

The girl grabbed one of the bar towels, then held it against the wound to stop the bleeding.

"Thanks," Lucas said.

By now, nearly all of the other customers in the saloon were gathered around either one or the other, of the two bodies that lay on the floor.

"My name's Molly," the girl said. "Go over to that table and hold this to your wound, and I'll bring your beer over to you."

"To be honest, now I think I might need something a little stronger."

"Here you go, Molly, a whiskey for Mr. Cain," the bartender said. "On the house," he added. "There will be folks comin' in here for the next several weeks, just to see where one man took on them two fellers at the same time, 'n kilt both of 'em. I'll be makin' plenty enough to pay for this drink."

Molly carried the whiskey over to Lucas and he tossed it down in one swallow.

"What happened here?" a loud voice demanded, and Lucas looked toward the door. The man who had called out was a big man, over six feet tall, and well-muscled. There was a city marshal's star pinned to his vest.

"Boyle 'n Proctor both throwed down on this man," the bartender said, pointing toward Lucas. " 'N here's the thing, marshal, they both already had their guns drawed, but this here feller was able to kill both of 'em. Onliest thing is, this here man was shot, too."

"What's your name?" the marshal asked.

"Cain. Lucas Cain."

"Cain, is it? Well, if that's your right name, I ain't aware of no posters out for you. Did you know these two men?"

"I met them for the first time today."

"Do you have any idea why they tried to kill you?"

"Marshal, this man's wound is bleeding quite heavily," Molly said. "Why don't you take him down to the doctor and talk to him there?"

The marshal nodded. "All right, I can do that. Come on, Cain, the doctor's office is just down the street. You think you're good to walk?"

"Yeah, I can walk," Lucas said, and holding the towel to his wound, he followed the marshal outside. "What about my horse?"

"Which one is it?" the marshal asked.

"The black on the end," Lucas said.

"I'll take him down to Mitchell's for you. I'm Terry Forsyth, the marshal in these parts."

Lucas didn't answer but stumbled a bit.

232

"You feelin' woozy or anything? The doctor's office is just a little farther."

"I'm all right," Lucas said, seeing a sign that read, *Duane Conway, M.D.*

"Dr. Conway, we got a man shot out here," Marshal Forsyth called out when the two of them reached the doctor's office.

"If you can walk, come on over here," Conway said, nodding his head toward an examining table.

"Here, let me get your shirt off," Conway said.

Dr. Conway removed Lucas's shirt, then looked at the wound. "There's no exit wound, so the bullet's still in there. I'm going to have to take it out, but I suppose you know it's going to hurt some."

"It can't hurt as much coming out as it did going in, can it?"

"I don't know. Could be it might hurt just a little more."

Lucas chuckled. "Damn, Doc. It might do you well to do a little work on your bedside manner."

Dr. Conway laughed as a woman walked into the room. "It's good that you've got a sense of humor. Kind of hold him still if you will, Mary."

The woman put one hand on Lucas's bare shoulder, and another on his arm as Dr.

Conway began probing the wound with a long, narrow rod. Lucas winced, and sucked in his breath.

"Here it is," Conway said a moment later, holding up the blood-soaked, dark slug.

"I'm glad that's over," Lucas said.

"It's not entirely over," Dr. Conway said. He cleaned the wound, then the woman poured a generous application of a disinfectant onto the wound, which, Lucas thought, was more painful than the actual removal of the bullet.

"See what I mean? Sorry 'bout that, but we don't want the wound to get infected," Dr. Conway said. "Now I need to sew you up."

As Dr. Conway was treating Lucas's wound, over in the Hog Lot Saloon, Jonathan Northcutt was sitting at a table in the farthest corner. He stood out from the others in the saloon, not only because he was sitting alone, but also because he was wearing a black jacket, a white shirt and cravat, and a red vest with a gold watch fob chain. He was nursing a beer and playing solitaire when Sam Foster approached his table.

"What is it, Foster?" Northcutt asked, not looking up as he placed a red ten on a black jack.

"Boyle 'n Proctor was just kilt over to the Boots and Saddles. Both of 'em."

"Who killed them?" Northcutt asked in the same tone of voice he might use in inquiring about the time.

"It was some fella they run into when they stopped the Foley woman."

"What do you mean they stopped the Foley woman?"

"Boyle 'n Proctor stopped Miz Foley out on the road, 'n they shot one of her mules," Foster explained.

"Why in the world would they do something like that?"

"I don't know. I just know that they done it, is all."

"What's the name of the man who shot them?"

"I think I heard his name was Cain, or something like that. I don't know for sure."

"I'm sure we'll find out, soon enough," Northcutt said.

"What about Boyle 'n Proctor?" Foster asked.

"What about them?" Northcutt put a red queen on a black king.

"Well, I mean, aren't you goin' to do somethin' about it? I mean, they was both kilt."

"So you said."

"But you're the prosecuting attorney."

"So I am."

"Yeah, 'n they was kilt."

"So they were."

"I just, uh, well, I thought you should know."

"And now I know, so if there's nothing else, step up to the bar, have a drink on me. Otherwise, leave me alone."

"Yes, sir. Uh, thanks for the drink."

Northcutt made a dismissive wave with his hand. For the entire time Foster had been there, Northcutt had not looked up from his cards.

"Now that the doc's got you fixed up, do you feel like talking a bit?" Marshal Forsyth asked as he had stepped into the doctor's office.

"Yeah," Lucas answered. "I don't see why not."

"Why'd them fellers try to kill you?"

"They seemed to take issue with me stopping them from causing trouble for Mrs. Foley."

"What do you mean, causing trouble?"

Lucas told Marshal Forsyth about coming up on the two men after they had killed one of Mrs. Foley's mules and set fire to her wagon.

"If you talk to the people in the saloon, you might hear that Proctor accused me of stealing his horse."

"And did you steal his horse?"

"Not exactly."

"Mr. Cain, what does 'not exactly' mean? Either you stole the man's horse, or you didn't."

"In a manner of speaking, I suppose you could say that I stole it, but all I really did was borrow it, however, I did borrow it without permission. I used it to replace the mule they had shot, so we could get the wagon back to Hillside. As soon as I got Mrs. Foley safely home, I brought his tack and the horse to town with me. He's in the livery now."

"Did you tell Boyle that his horse was in the livery?" Marshal Forsyth asked.

Lucas nodded. "Yeah, I told him, but it didn't seem to make any difference to him. He and Proctor started shooting anyway."

"And this was the result," Dr. Conway said, pointing to the bullet he had dropped into a little pan of water a bit earlier. A narrow stream of tiny red bubbles climbed up from the bullet, as it lay in the bottom of the pan of water.

With the bullet removed, the wound cleaned and sewed shut, the doctor applied a bandage.

"Doc, I'd like to take him out to the Foley ranch so I can talk to him and Mrs. Foley at the same time. Do you think he's all right to ride?"

"I think so. The bullet didn't hit a bone or anything. It should heal back good as new, as long as he keeps the wound clean so infection doesn't set in."

"I'll do that," Lucas promised.

"Mr. Cain, do you have any objections to riding along with me so I can get Mrs. Foley's side of the story of what happened out on the road?"

"I'll be glad to, Marshal."

19

"What the hell? Do you mean he killed both of 'em?" George Rogers asked.

"He sure as hell did. Slick as a whistle, it was. I mean Proctor and Boyle already had their guns drawn. 'N get this, Proctor warn't even down on the floor. He was up on the upstairs landin', looking over the railin', a fixin' to shoot, but this here feller turned, 'n shot him first, then he shot Boyle."

"Who was this fast gunman?" Rogers asked.

"I don't know who it is," the man who was telling the story replied.

"I've heard his name spoke," another man said. He was one of several who were present in the Hog Lot Saloon gathered around to hear more about the shooting that took place over in the Boots and Saddles. "They say he's a feller called Lucas Cain. But he ain't from here, so there don't nobody really know him."

"Is he still in town, or has he ridden on?" Rogers asked.

"Oh he's still here, all right. He's took 'im a room at the Parker Hotel."

As the others continued to talk about the shooting that had taken place at the Boots and Saddles Saloon, Rogers left them to sit at another table, all alone.

LeRoy Mullins was in the Hog Lot saloon. The talk of the town was about the shoot-out that had taken place over at the Boots and Saddle saloon.

"Hey, Mullins," one of the other said. "Did you hear about the shootin' over in the Boots and Saddles?"

"Yeah, I heard about it," Mullins said, his voice dripping with anger. "Lem 'n Eli was my two friends, 'n that son of a bitch just shot 'em down liken he was a' butcherin' hogs or somethin'."

"No, it warn't nothin' like that. They drawed on him first."

"I don't care who drawed first. Lem 'n Eli was both real good friends o' mine. We rode for the same brand together, 'n that son of a bitch kilt 'em."

While this discussion was going on in the Hog Lot, Lucas was with Marshal Forsyth as they rode out of town.

"Where do you come from?" Marshal Forsyth asked.

"Cape Girardeau. It's a town in Missouri, about a hundred miles south of St. Louis, on the Mississippi River."

"Damn, you're a long way from home. Were you a river boatman?"

Lucas chuckled. "No, to be honest, I was in your line of work. I was a police officer."

"A police officer, huh? What made you give up the noble profession?"

Lucas thought about Rosie's death, and he knew that was what put him on his endless western trek, but that wasn't something he wanted to share with Marshal Forsyth.

"I don't know, I guess I just got itchy feet," Lucas said.

Forsyth laughed. "I've always thought I'd like to do something like that, but just never could get up the gumption to do it. I sort of envy you. What brings you to Higbee?"

"Nothing in particular. Truth is, I was planning on giving my horse a few days' rest, and eating food that I didn't cook. But then I ran across Mrs. Foley being set upon by those two men. And, well you know what happened, so I guess I'm going to stick around for a while."

"Yes, I'm glad you're doing it willingly."

"Marshal, someone is trying to buy the Foley land, and Mrs. Foley doesn't want to sell," Lucas said. "Apparently, the reason Proctor and Boyle stopped her was because they were trying to nudge her into selling."

"Yeah, I've heard that someone was after Hillside," Marshal Forsyth said.

"Do you know who it might be? I'm pretty sure it wasn't Proctor or Boyle. I'm sure they were just acting for someone else."

"No, I don't have any idea who it might be. She's got neighbors on three sides of her. I know that Duke Richards has said he would be willing to buy her out, but I don't think he's been putting any pressure on her."

"Is there something on her land that someone else might want? Water, for example?"

"Well, the Las Animus runs across her land."

"Las Animus?"

"Yes, it's a narrow river, but that can't be the reason someone is after her ranch, because the Las Animus serves all three of her neighbors."

"Why else would this man, Duke something, try to buy the ranch?"

"Duke Richards. And truth to tell, I think he was just offering to buy the place to take it off Mrs. Foley's hands after Bill died. Duke and Bill Foley were good friends, and I don't think he would bother Pauline like that."

"Swayne Evans said this wasn't the first problem they've had."

"So you met Swayne Evans, did you?" Marshal Forsyth asked. He chuckled. "Swayne's quite a character. I've got no proof, but I'm pretty sure old Swayne used to ride the owl hoot trail. Bill Foley found him with a dead horse and half frozen to death. He brought him home, nursed him back to health, and Swayne hasn't left since. He was loyal to Bill, and now he's just as loyal to Pauline."

"I thought it might be something like that."

"How's your shoulder doin'? Hurtin' you any?"

"I'm doing fine, thanks."

"Well, here we are," Forsyth said, as they reached the lane that turned off the main road.

A minute later, when Lucas and Marshal Forsyth stopped in front of the Foley house, Sue Ellen was standing on the front porch, and once again, she was holding a rifle.

"Hello, Sue Ellen," Forsyth said as he and Lucas dismounted.

"I saw you coming up the lane," Sue Ellen said. "I wasn't sure who it was. Thought it might 'a been the same two men that stopped Mama out on the road. You can't be too safe."

"It is a good rule to live by," the marshal agreed.

"Mr. Cain, your shoulder!" Sue Ellen said, noticing the bandage for the first time. "What happened?"

"He got shot," Forsyth said.

"Shot? Who shot you, and why?"

"Is your mother here?" Forsyth asked. "She needs to be a part of this conversation."

"Yes, she's in the house," Sue Ellen said. "Come on in."

"Mama, Mr. Cain got shot," Sue Ellen said as they stepped inside.

"Oh, heavens, I hope it isn't too bad," Pauline said.

"The doctor says it won't give me any trouble," Lucas said.

"Hello, Marshal Forsyth, what brings you here?" Pauline asked.

"I'd like to talk to you about what happened out on the road," Forsyth said.

"Certainly, come on into the parlor and have a seat. I've got coffee," Pauline said.

"Thank you, that's very kind of you."

Pauline poured coffee for Lucas and the marshal, then a cup for herself. Sue Ellen also took a cup of coffee and sat down to listen.

"Before you start talking, I want to know who shot Mr. Cain, and why?" Pauline said.

"Well, that's part of the reason why we're here," Marshal Forsyth said. "He was shot by Lem Proctor."

"Ah, so it did have something to do with what happened to me," Pauline said.

"Apparently so. Please, if you would, tell me just what did happen to you."

Pauline told the story, starting from the moment she was stopped and how Duchess was shot, and then her wagon set afire. She continued on until she told about being rescued by Lucas.

Marshal Forsyth nodded toward Lucas when Pauline was finished. "Well, that matches the story Mr. Cain told, and now, as to how Mr. Cain was shot. It seems that when Mr. Cain went into town, he stopped in the Boots and Saddles, and while there, he was shot at by both Ely Boyle and Lem Proctor. He returned fire and killed them both, but as you can see, he was hit in the shoulder."

"And the doctor said it isn't serious?" Sue Ellen asked.

"The doctor said it shouldn't cause him any trouble."

"That's good to know," Sue Ellen said.

"Is there anything I can do for you, Lucas?" Pauline asked. "After all, you would have never been shot if it hadn't been for you stopping to help me out."

"I'll be fine," Lucas said. He smiled. "And you've already helped me. By confirming the story I told, I feel certain that the marshal believes me. You do, don't you, Marshal Forsyth?"

"Yes, but it doesn't matter whether I believe you or not. I think the prosecutor will still think he has to bring charges against you."

"What?" Pauline said. "How can that be?"

"I think it's a matter of policy. But I feel certain that it will be found to be justifiable homicide."

"Oh, Mr. Cain, I'm so sorry I got you involved in this," Pauline said.

Lucas chuckled. "Actually, Mrs. Foley, I believe you could say that I got myself involved."

"Mama, if Mr. Cain hadn't come along, why there's no telling what those men might have done to you," Sue Ellen said.

"Well, that's true," Pauline said.

"Marshal, do you have any idea who those

two awful men were working for?" Pauline asked.

"Apparently, they were working for whoever it is that's wanting to buy your ranch. Do you have any idea yet who that could be?"

Pauline shook her head. "I'm afraid I don't have a clue, and David Garrett won't tell me anything."

"Duke Richards, perhaps?" Marshal Forsyth asked.

"Oh, no, Duke was one of Bill's very good friends. He would certainly not do anything like that. Shortly after Bill died, Duke offered to buy me out, but I'm certain he did that only because he thought it would be of benefit to me. When I told him I didn't want to sell, he said he understood, and he has made no further attempts to get me to sell."

"And Garrett hasn't told you who he represents?"

Pauline shook her head. "No, I've asked him, but he says he isn't permitted to tell me."

"Well, certainly someone wants it bad enough to cause you some grief over it. Please, if you will, Mrs. Foley, you tell me if anything else happens."

"Thank you, Marshal Forsyth, I'll do that."

Forsyth stood then, and so did Lucas. "I'd better get back to town. Thanks for the coffee."

Pauline shook her head. "That's nothing. What I want to say is thank you for your concern."

When Lucas and Marshal Forsyth walked back to their horses, Swayne was standing there waiting for them.

"What's wrong, Marshal, why are you out here?"

"Hello, Swayne," Forsyth said. "I just wanted to hear Mrs. Foley's account of what happened out on the road today."

"I'll tell you what happened. Them two sons of bitches tried to burn Miz Foley's wagon, 'n I wouldn't a' been surprised if they wouldn't have shot her, if Lucas here hadn't come along when he did. You goin' to put them two inter jail, are you?"

"No need to," Forsyth said. "They're both dead. Mr. Cain killed them."

"Damn!" Swayne said with a broad smile as he slapped his knee. "Good for you."

Lucas and Forsyth said their goodbyes and started back to town.

"It seems sort of funny that Swayne didn't ask anything about your wound," Forsyth said.

"He didn't need to. He heard that Boyle and Proctor were both dead, and nothing else was important to him," Lucas said.

Forsyth chuckled. "Yeah, I reckon you're right about that."

Doctor Conway had asked Lucas to stay in Higbee for a few days, just to make certain that infection didn't set in. In order to comply with the doctor's suggestion, Lucas took a room in the Parker Hotel.

"You're the fella that got into the shootin' scrape in the Boots and Saddles, ain't ya?" the hotel clerk asked.

"That would be me," Lucas said.

"Yeah, well, don't start nothin' like that here, in the hotel. We got only peaceful people stayin' here."

"I'll try not to," Lucas said with a sardonic smile.

"Room 203," the clerk said, handing him the key. "Sign the register."

Lucas accepted the key and signed the register.

"Does the hotel have a dining room?"

"No."

"Where's a good place to eat supper?"

"The Cattlemen's Restaurant is the biggest, but Waggy's is the closest. It's just two doors down the street."

"Waggy's?"

"Yeah, it's a lot smaller than the Cattlemen's. Waggy's belongs to a man named John Wagner, but ever' one calls him Waggy."

"All right, I'll give it a try," Lucas said.

Waggy's was relatively small, but then the town of Higbee was small, so he was certain that the restaurant was big enough. It had a dining room which was about the size of the parlor of a somewhat larger than medium sized house. As soon as he stepped in, though, he could smell the aromas from the kitchen, and they smelled good.

"Just sit anywhere you want," a woman said. The woman was overweight and had gray hair tied back in a bun.

"Thanks."

"You would be Mr. Cain?"

"Uh, yes," Lucas said, surprised that the woman knew his name.

"My husband John 'n me own this place. Our special today is fried chicken gizzards, fried potatoes, turnip greens, and cornbread."

"Wow, that sounds just like the kind of home cooking I used to get back in Missouri."

"John and I are from Mississippi. My name is Wanda."

Lucas smiled. "Then if you're from Mississippi, I know it will be good."

"This here meal will be on the house," Wanda said.

"What? Why?"

"Well, for two reasons, really. One is because you rid this town of a couple of vermin when you kilt them two no accounts. 'N the other reason is because if you think my meal's good enough, then you'll more 'n likely be takin' other meals here."

The food was good, and Lucas enjoyed his meal, even though he realized that he was the subject of half a dozen quiet conversations. When he was finished, he left a generous tip on the table, said goodbye to Wanda, then returned to the hotel.

20

It was a very warm night, so before Lucas went to bed he opened the window and the transom over the door. This allowed a slight breeze to pass through the room, making the Texas night more bearable.

Shortly after Lucas went to bed, Jeremy Mullins came into the hotel, then crossed the lobby to the front desk. The desk clerk was sitting in a chair with his head tilted forward and his eyes closed. He was snoring.

Ha, Mullins thought. *This is going to be easier than I thought.*

Mullins turned the registration book around, then began perusing the latest check-ins. It was easy to find Lucas Cain's name, because he was the only one who had checked in today.

As Lucas lay in bed, he found that the day had been too busy and his mind so crowded with thought that he was having difficulty in falling asleep.

The difficulty in sleeping may have saved his life, because he was awake enough to hear someone at his door. Because the hallway was well lit, when he looked toward the door, the glass in the transom reflected the presence of a man standing just outside. Because of the angle, he couldn't see the man's face, but he could see that he was holding a gun.

Lucas swung his legs over the side of the bed and reached for his gun. As he did so, the bed springs gave a loud squeak.

On the other side of the door, Mullins heard the bed springs squeak, then the sound of footfalls coming across the floor. Turning quickly, he ran down the hall and was around the corner before the door opened.

Lucas heard the sound of running in the hallway. He moved quickly to the door and looked outside, but whoever had been at his door was out of sight.

He was pretty sure that his night-time visitor had something to do with his helping Mrs. Foley. And if he could discover who was trying to buy her ranch, he might find out who was after him.

■ ■ ■ ■

"Damn," Marshal Forsyth said when Lucas went to see him the next morning. "You haven't been in town all that long and already two men have tried to kill you, and now a third may have wanted you out of the way. You don't make friends all that easy, do you?" Marshal Forsyth's smile indicated that the comment was in jest.

"I don't know, I've always rather thought I was a friendly enough guy," Lucas said, also smiling. "But maybe Higbee's not my kind of town."

"So, what are you going to do? Are you going to stay around, or are you going to leave town?"

"That sounds like you're trying to run me out of town. Are you?"

Forsyth laughed, and held up his hand. "No, actually, that might be out of my hands anyway. I'm pretty sure they'll be an indictment issued, and you'll have to stay in town."

Lucas had a scowl on his face. "How can that be? You know what happened and Mrs. Foley confirmed my account."

The marshal nodded his head.

"Then why the indictment?"

"What can I say? We have a very active prosecuting attorney. But if it's any consolation to you, I believe the story as you and Mrs. Foley have told it."

"Well, it's good to have the law on my side."

"As long as you stay on the side of the law," Forsyth said.

"Oh, I intend to do that. In fact, I'll take a step further and help the law out."

"What do you mean, help the law out?"

"I'm going to find out what's going on, who's after the Foley land, and why they want it so badly."

Forsyth stroked his chin. "You're going to have to be careful doing that. You have no authority to start any kind of an investigation."

"Let's just say that I'm satisfying my curiosity."

"Where do you plan to start?" Forsyth asked.

"What ranches are adjacent to Hillside?"

"Come over here, I can show you on the map."

Lucas followed the marshal over to a table, and there Forsyth picked up a map and unrolled it on the table, using a couple of paper weights on the corners to hold it flat.

"Here's Hillside," Forsyth pointed out. "And here are the three closest ranches to Hillside. First is the Rocking R, which belongs to Duke Richards. Then the Box Y, which belongs to Bertis Yancey, and here is the Circle P — it belongs to Amos Pogue." As Forsyth named each of the ranches, he pointed them out on the map.

"All three of the other ranchers have equal access to the water of Las Animas?" Lucas asked.

"Yes."

"Then access to the water isn't the problem, is it?"

"No, I wouldn't think so."

"I think I'll start by paying a visit to some of her neighbors," Lucas said.

"Mr. Cain?"

"Yes?"

"Don't cause any trouble."

"I'll try not to," Lucas said, "but if trouble comes to me, I'll not walk away from it. My first stop will be David Garrett's office."

"Why do you want to talk to a lawyer?"

"Didn't you say he's the one that made the offer to buy Hillside?"

"Yes, but it wasn't for himself, it was for some mysterious client, and he won't tell you anything."

"It won't hurt to try."

"Be my guest," Forsyth offered with a sweep of his hand.

Lucas had no problem finding Garrett's office. It was a small building with his shingle displayed in front.

DAVID GARRETT
Attorney at Law

There was a man sitting at a desk who Lucas figured to be in his mid-fifties. He was wearing a brown suit with a white shirt and string tie. His hair was brindled with gray, his complexion was florid, and he was wearing horn-rimmed glasses. He looked up as Lucas entered the office.

"Mr. Garrett?" Lucas said.

"I'm Garrett. Is there something I can do for you?" Garrett asked as he rose from his desk.

"Yes, I hope so, anyway. I'm Lucas Cain."

"I know who you are, Mr. Cain."

"Apparently everyone in town knows who I am," Lucas said. "I'm told that you're representing the person who wants to buy Hillside."

"I am."

"I wonder if you'd tell me who that might be."

"Sir, you just rode into town. I have to ask what business it is of yours."

"You know who I am because the two men I killed had attacked Mrs. Foley. I believe that attack was meant to intimidate her in hopes she would decide to sell her ranch."

"Mr. Cain, you have to know, if I can't tell Pauline Foley — a woman I've known for many years — I sure as hell can't tell you who my client is."

"Even though your client is breaking the law?"

"But we don't know that it is my client who is doing these things, now do we? And, as a matter of fact, I doubt very much this is my client's doing. You are aware that the offer to purchase Hillside is to be tendered by me."

"Very well, Mr. Garrett. Thank you for your time."

"I'm sure we will visit again," Garrett said.

"Oh, and why would that be? I mean, especially if you won't tell me who's trying to buy Hillside?"

"You'll need my services, and when you do, I'll be here for you," Garrett said mysteriously.

"I take it, you didn't get the job done," George Rogers said.

"No, the son of a bitch heard me outside the door, 'n he got out of bed 'n come for me," Mullins said.

"So what did you do?"

"I took off a' runnin', is what I done."

"I'm not paying you five hundred dollars to run from Lucas Cain."

"You ain't payin' to have no gunfight with him, neither. All you're payin' me for is to kill 'im. 'N that I can do without no gunfight."

"Don't wait too long before you do it," Rogers said.

"You don't have to worry none about that. I'm goin' to kill the son of a bitch as soon as I see 'im," Mullins insisted.

After leaving the lawyer's office, Lucas rode back out to Hillside Ranch. This time, when Sue Ellen met him she wasn't carrying a rifle, though she was still wearing jeans and a man's shirt.

"Well," Lucas said. "I'm making some progress. You don't seem all that ready to shoot me, now."

"The option is still there," Sue Ellen said with a wide smile. "It's nearly dinner time, so come on in and join us."

"I should say no, thank you, but I remember how good it was the last time. And, I suppose you could make a case that my perfect timing of arriving at dinner time was more than coincidence."

"I suppose you could say that," Sue Ellen replied as she held the door for Lucas.

"Mama, I've invited Mr. Cain to have dinner with us," Sue Ellen called to her mother.

"I spoke with Mr. Garrett this morning," Lucas said as they began eating.

"Goodness, you aren't in trouble for shooting those terrible men, are you? I thought Marshal Forsyth said he believed mama's story," Sue Ellen said.

"He did, but I guess it's not up to Marshal Forsyth," Lucas replied. "But the reason I spoke with Garrett is because I wanted to find out something about the efforts that are being made to buy your property."

"You've already been a big help, but there's no need for you to get any further involved. I mean, look what happened to you, just because you came to my defense out on the road," Pauline said. "Why, you were almost killed for helping, and I couldn't live with myself if anything happened to you, because of me."

"Mama, something has already happened," Sue Ellen said. "He was shot."

"All the more reason for him not to get further involved with our problems," Pauline said.

Lucas felt Pauline's eyes on him. Her glance was one of concern and compassion.

"I've been shot at before," Lucas said, with no further explanation.

There was no more discussion of what had happened on the road when Pauline was accosted by Proctor and Boyle, nor of the shoot-out that had taken place in the Boots and Saddles Saloon.

21

When Lucas returned to town, he once again visited the Boots and Saddles Saloon.

"Beer, Mr. Cain?" the bartender asked.

"Yes, thank you. Bartender, you know my name, what's your name?"

"My name's Manny Burns," the bartender said.

"Well, it's very good to meet you, Mr. Burns."

"Hey, Burns," someone called from the other end of the bar. "What for are you serving that murderer?"

"There's no call for that, Mullins. All Mr. Cain did was defend himself. Proctor and Boyle both drew first."

"And he kilt both of 'em," Mullins said. "Far as I'm concerned, that makes him a murderer."

Lucas turned to look at the man who was being hostile toward him. He was a young man, in his early twenties, with hair so light a brown that it nearly could be described as blond. "Mr. Mullins," Lucas said in a conciliatory tone, "may I buy you a drink?"

"Now just why the hell would I want to drink with a murderer?" Mullins asked.

"Well, I'm sorry you feel that way."

"Yeah, I just bet you are."

When Burns set the beer before Lucas, he spoke quietly. "Pay no attention to that one. Boyle and Proctor were his friends. Actually, he was about the only friend they had."

"Thanks," Lucas replied, just as quietly. Lucas glanced back toward Mullins, and couldn't help but wonder if this man was the one who had paid him a visit last night.

The next morning, Lucas stopped by the local newspaper. He had learned during all of his wanderings that there were very few secrets from the editor of a small-town newspaper.

The name of the paper, *Higbee Ledger,* was painted on the window in large red letters outlined in blue. When he opened the door, he saw a chest-high counter that separated the front of the office from the back. On the other side of the counter was a Washington Hand Press. The man standing beside it, oiling the platen assembly, looked up when Lucas stepped inside.

"Mr. Cain," he said with a broad smile.

Lucas chuckled. "This business of everyone knowing my name is going to take some getting used to."

"Well, such is the price of fame." He stuck his hand out. "I'm William Lightfoot, publisher of this journal. Now, what can I do for you?"

"Mr. Lightfoot, what do you know about the ranch, Hillside?"

"It was started by Bill Foley, who was a good man. But then Bill died," Lightfoot said. "I'm sure whoever is after Hillside expected that his widow, rather than continue to run the ranch, would sell it. But that hasn't happened," Lightfoot said.

"No, but that hasn't stopped the harassment," Lucas replied. "You haven't asked why Proctor and Boyle tried to kill me."

"No, because I'm sure you came in here to tell me."

"When I was on my way into town the other day, I came across Boyle and Proctor terrorizing Mrs. Foley." Lucas went into detail about what happened. "I put a stop to it, then escorted her on home."

"Well, I can't tell you who it is that wants to buy the ranch, but I can tell you for sure that it wasn't Lem Proctor or Ely Boyle. They barely had enough money to keep

264

themselves alive. I would say that it's a good bet they were doing it for someone else," Lightfoot said.

"Yes, that's what I've been led to believe. But the question is, of course, who hired them in the first place?"

"Well, I must say the solicitation efforts have been upped some. Oh, I know that a few cows have gone missing, but, as far as I know, this is the first time there has actually been any physical contact with either Pauline or Sue Ellen."

"Somebody must want that land awfully bad to be willing to attack an old woman, just to get control of the ranch. Is your paper going to look into this?"

Lightfoot shook his head. "This is a small town, and this is the only paper. Until I know where everyone stands, I fear I would wind up aggravating everyone, the innocent and guilty alike. That wouldn't accomplish much and, on a selfish note, it wouldn't be very good for the paper."

"I guess you're right. I hadn't thought about that."

Lightfoot smiled. "On the other hand, however, if you were to find out who's behind this, I would happily publish an exposé. And, if you believe we could have some sort of surreptitious arrangement, where my assistance, let us say, is kept very quiet, then perhaps we could work together."

Lucas smiled, then stuck out his hand. "It's a deal. Oh, there's one more thing that has happened. Last night, by a rather innocent happenstance, I saw someone standing just outside my door holding a gun. I've no doubt but that whoever is trying to get the ranch from Mrs. Foley, hired someone to kill me."

"Good Lord. And you saw him, you say?"

"Yes." Lucas explained how he saw the man in the transom. "Unfortunately, I was unable to see his face. But of course, I wouldn't have known him even if I did see him. I haven't been here long enough to meet but a few people."

"Hmm, this does add to the mystery, doesn't it?" Lightfoot said. He smiled. "And I do like a good mystery."

Leaving the newspaper office, Lucas started toward the Boots and Saddles, then decided it might be better to go to a saloon he hadn't visited yet. The Hog Lot was just across the street, so that's where he headed.

"Mr. Cain," the bartender greeted when he stepped inside, "I was wondering when you'd get around to visiting us."

Lucas chuckled, and shook his head. "I

just got into town yesterday, and already it would seem that everyone knows my name."

"When you come into a town as small as Higbee and shoot two of its citizens, you're going to become famous, or infamous, depending upon one's interpretation of the event."

"I hope everyone in town realizes that they shot at me first."

"Well, it does help your cause when you figure that Boyle and Proctor were a couple of low-lives that very few will miss."

"You say very few. Would Mullins be one?"

"Ah, so you have met Jerry Mullins, have you? Yes, he is one who would be of Proctor and Boyle's ilk. What'll you have?"

"A beer."

"First one for a new guy is free," the bartender said as he set the mug of beer before Lucas.

"No, I'd better pay for it, because this is the only one I'll have tonight."

"There's no need for Mr. Cain to pay for it," a man called from the back corner table. "I'll pay for it."

"Yes, sir, Mr. Northcutt," the bartender called.

"Who is Northcutt?" Lucas asked quietly.

"He's an attorney."

As Lucas drank the beer, he turned his

back to the bar so he could examine the other customers. He got a closer look at the man who had just bought his beer. Northcutt was wearing a dark suit, with a red vest, and a cravat. Lucas wanted to ask a few questions as to who might want Hillside badly enough to send a couple of brigands like Boyle and Proctor to attack Mrs. Foley. And he hoped that this man, Northcutt, might be able to answer those questions.

"Won't you join me, Mr. Cain?" Northcutt asked.

Lucas was curious about the invitation, so grabbing his beer, he picked his way through the customers until he reached Northcutt's table.

"Have a seat," Northcutt invited with a wave of his hand.

Lucas did so. "Thank you for the beer."

"You're quite welcome, Mr. Cain. My name is Jonathan Northcutt."

Lucas smiled. "Well, there's no need in me introducing myself. You already know my name."

"Indeed. But you must admit, Mr. Cain, that your arrival in our little town was quite, shall we say, dramatic?"

"I'll give you that," Lucas replied.

"If I may ask, what brings you to Higbee?

Our town is so small that it's seldom the intended destination of a traveler."

"Oh, Higbee wasn't my intended destination, Mr. Northcutt. I'm what you might call a rambling man. I have no specific reason for being here — I was just passing through."

"And yet you stayed here long enough to gun down two of our citizens. Admittedly, they were the dregs of our society, but local citizens none the less."

"I wouldn't say that I 'gunned them down.' The truth is, and I'm sure you must know, that I was acting in self-defense. They shot at me first."

"So you say."

"Are you saying that you don't believe me?" Lucas asked.

"I can make no comment as to whether or not I believe you. That would be an ethical violation of my position."

"Violation of your position?"

"Yes, I am a prosecuting attorney, and as it so happens, Judge Kramer's normal schedule is that he will be here tomorrow. Mr. Cain, it is my intention to take advantage of his presence, by bringing your case to trial. I would suggest that you secure an attorney to plead your case."

"Marshal Forsyth told me that I might be

269

indicted," Lucas said, "though, for the life of me, I don't know why that would be. Proctor and Boyle shot at me first. Hell, there were at least a dozen witnesses."

"Then wouldn't it be to your advantage to have this case adjudicated so that it is taken care of, once and for all?"

"I don't know. I hadn't thought of it in that way. I suppose there might be something to that."

"I think it is time for you to consult with your lawyer."

"I don't have a lawyer."

"David Garrett is the only other lawyer in town, so I suggest in the strongest possible terms, that you see him. And since the judge will be here tomorrow, you should see Garrett today."

"I've already met with Garrett," Lucas said.

"About defending you?"

"No, I —" Lucas paused in mid-sentence. Garrett had suggested that he might need a lawyer. "Yes, I guess maybe we did discuss it."

"I thought as much. Mr. Garrett and I have already had a preliminary discussion of your case, and he is already working for you. It was in response to his plea that I have agreed to release you on your own recognizance, rather than incarceration or a monetary bail."

"All right, I will go see him again," Lucas said as he stood. "I'll come back to tell you what he said."

"That wouldn't be appropriate at this time," Northcutt said. "I'll be prosecuting you, remember."

"Yes, well, thanks for the beer anyway."

Northcutt's reply was a nod of his head.

When Lucas returned to Garrett's office, he tied his horse off at the hitch rail, then stepped inside

"I thought I'd be seeing you again," Garrett said. "You've met with the prosecuting attorney?"

"Uh, yes, I suppose so."

"Mr. Cain, you are going to be tried for murder, and as I'm the only other lawyer in town, I think you might wish to employ me as your defense counsel."

"How much will that cost me?"

"My fee is fifty dollars."

"What if you lose the case?"

"I won't lose the case."

"Oh, well, in that case, you're hired."

Garrett smiled. "Good, but seeing as I'm the only lawyer in town, it isn't as if you have a choice now, is it?"

271

Lucas laughed. "No, I don't suppose I do."

"Tell me exactly what happened."

"I thought you said you already knew what happened."

"Yes, I do, but now I want to hear it in your own words, words that I can use to construct your defense."

Lucas started with him seeing Boyle and Proctor harassing Mrs. Foley. He skipped the part about visiting with the Foleys and meeting her daughter. He ended with the confrontation with Mullins in the saloon.

"Do you think Mrs. Foley would agree to be a witness?" Garrett asked.

"Oh, yes, I'm quite sure she would."

"Then, if you would, ride out to Hillside and ask her if she would appear in your defense. The trial will be held in the Boots and Saddles saloon at nine o'clock tomorrow morning."

22

After Lucas left Garrett's office, he rode out to Hillside Ranch to ask if Pauline Foley would be a witness for him in the trial that was coming up the next day.

Again, he was met by Sue Ellen, though this time she met him with a smile rather than a Winchester.

"Hello, Miss Foley."

"Mr. Cain, how good it is to see you again," she greeted.

"We're going to have to quit meeting like this," Lucas said with a smile.

Sue Ellen chuckled.

"And please, call me Lucas. That is, if I haven't worn out my welcome. I mean, this is my third time out here in the last two days."

"All right, Lucas, if you call me Sue Ellen. And after what you did for Mama, you are a very welcome visitor. Please, come in," she invited.

"It's not entirely a social call. I shall need to talk with your mother, if she is here."

"Oh, she's here all right, and Mama does love to talk."

"Mr. Cain," Pauline greeted warmly, "it's so nice to see you again."

"I have a favor to ask of you, Mrs. Foley."

"Well, you have certainly earned a favor," Pauline said.

"Tomorrow, at nine o'clock, I am to be tried for the murder of Boyle and Proctor. I wonder if I could count on you as a witness in my defense."

"What? They're calling it murder? Why, I can't believe that. Of course I will testify for you," Pauline said. "Why don't you eat with us, and then spend the night since we need to be in town so early. There's plenty of room in the bunkhouse, and Swayne would enjoy the company."

"Thank you, Mrs. Foley. I think I'll take you up on that." Lucas didn't comment, but he was thinking of the visitor who had stood outside his hotel room the previous evening.

"We have a couple of hours before supper, Lucas. Would you like to ride out and take a look around the property?" Sue Ellen asked.

"Why, thank you, Sue Ellen. I'd like that."

"I'll just get Dolly saddled," Sue Ellen said, starting for the door.

"Please, let me help."

Sue Ellen laughed. "Not on your life. Swayne has been saddling horses for me since I was four years old when I got my first pony. I'm afraid if I didn't let him do it this time, he would be very upset."

"Well, let's not get him upset, because I sure don't want to get on Swayne's bad side," Lucas teased.

"Smart move."

Lucas walked alongside Sue Ellen, leading Charley as they went out to the barn to get Sue Ellen's horse, Dolly. They were met by Swayne.

"Swayne, Lucas and I are going to take a ride around the ranch. Would you saddle Dolly for me?"

"Yes, ma'am. I'll get 'im saddled up, and right out here."

"Thanks."

"Him?" Lucas said.

"What?"

"Your horse's name is Dolly, but Swayne said he would 'get him' saddled. I thought Dolly would be a mare."

Sue Ellen laughed. "Dolly is a gelding. I got him when I was six years old, and Papa said I could name him anything I wanted so

I chose Dolly."

Lucas chuckled. "Well, if he's all right being called Dolly, who am I to complain?"

"I thought you might come around to it," Sue Ellen replied.

A couple of minutes later, Swayne returned with a beautiful palomino. "Here he is, Miss Sue Ellen."

"Thank you, Swayne."

Sue Ellen and Lucas mounted their horses, then rode off.

Sue Ellen was riding astride Dolly, and Lucas couldn't help but notice how graceful, agile, and athletic she was. Sue Ellen was as good a rider as any man Lucas had ever known.

"Hillside is a pretty good-sized ranch, but it isn't as large as our three neighbors," Sue Ellen said. "It makes you wonder, as large as all the other ranches are, why someone would particularly want ours enough to attack Mama like they did?"

"Yes, that's the mystery."

Sue Ellen took him to the bank of Las Animas River. Here, it broke into white water as it cascaded down flat steps of rocks.

"Oh, Lucas, have you ever seen anything so beautiful?" Sue Ellen asked.

Lucas was looking at Sue Ellen, and enjoying the view at this moment, more than any time previous. Sue Ellen was a very pretty young woman with a shape that couldn't be hidden by the man's shirt she was wearing. She had blonde hair, and eyes the color of a blue sky.

"No," Lucas said. "I don't think I have."

The way Lucas spoke the words got Sue Ellen's attention, and when she turned, she saw that he was staring at her, with a soft smile that gave her a warm feeling, and she felt her cheeks burning as she blushed.

"Sue Ellen, may I ask a question?"

"Of course."

"A pretty girl like you, why haven't you married?"

"I did get married," Sue Ellen replied.

"Oh?" Lucas asked, shocked by her response.

"His name was Steve Blackburn and we were married for six months before he . . ." Sue Ellen paused for a long moment. "Before he was thrown from a horse and broke his neck."

"Oh, I'm sorry," Lucas said. "I've been calling you Miss Foley."

Sue Ellen smiled. "That was six years ago, and since Steve wasn't from around here, everybody kept calling me Sue Ellen Foley anyway, so I had the judge change my name back to Foley. You needn't apologize because you had no way of knowing."

They continued to ride around the ranch. Lucas was hoping he would see some reason that would make the land so valuable to someone else, but there was nothing that stood out.

After about an hour, Sue Ellen reined Dolly to a stop. "I think we should probably go back now. Mama will be needing my help with supper."

"All right," Lucas said, his smile broadening.

Conversation around the table that evening was animated with tales of the Foleys' early arrival in Texas, as well as some of Lucas's exploits. He was reluctant to mention either Rosie or his time at Andersonville, both subjects still very raw for him.

Then after supper, Lucas went with Swayne to the bunkhouse, which as Pauline had said was large enough to accommodate six, but was occupied only by Swayne.

"What can you tell me about Sue Ellen?" Lucas asked Swayne that night when they were alone in the bunk house.

"What do you want to know about her?" Swayne replied. "I've know'd her since she was knee-high to a grasshopper."

"She said she had been married once?"

"Yes, to Steve Blackburn. He was a nice young man who rode in here one day and stole her heart. She was mighty shook up when he was throwed from that horse. Broke his neck. Poor Sue Ellen. She had that horse took out in the hills and shot."

"Does she have any, uh, male friends? What I'm asking is, is she spoken for?"

Swayne laughed. "I know'd it. Hell, I know'd it first time I seen you a' lookin' at her with them big cow eyes. You liken her, don't you?"

"I think she's a very pretty girl, and I find her . . . interesting."

"Well, she finds you interestin', too, on account of she was lookin' across the table at you tonight with the same kind of cow eyes you was a' lookin' at her with."

"I would like to think that's true," Lucas replied.

"Oh, it's true, you can believe me on that, but I wouldn't be gettin' my hopes up. She ain't took up with no man since Steve died."

"What about you, Swayne?"

"What do you mean, what about me?"

"I was told that Mr. Foley found you with a dead horse and you half frozen to death."

Swayne nodded his head. "You heared right, old Bill saved my life, 'n it warn't only 'cause he brought me here 'n kept me from

279

freezin' to death. They was other ways he saved me."

"Oh? And how was that?"

"He give me a job 'n that stopped me from wanderin' around. My wanderin' around seemed like it got me in enough trouble that they was always some folks lookin' for me. 'N thems that wanted me the most put out wanted posters on me. You could get a thousand dollars for turnin' me in, 'n Mr. Foley, why, he know'd that, but he brung me back here to work for 'im, anyway. Fact is, if it warn't for him, I'd more 'n likely be dead now. That's why I took it so hard.

"And it's too bad he died a'fore someone started tryin' to buy this ranch so much. He would 'a put a stop to it in a heartbeat, but now they seem to have it in mind that they can get Miz Pauline to sell to 'em."

"Are they right? Will she sell?"

"Not on your life. That woman's tough as granite."

"Who is it?" Lucas asked. "Who's trying to buy the ranch?"

"That's somethin' that don't nobody seem to know. Well, no, that ain't right. There's one person that knows, 'cause he's the one that's always tryin' to get Miz Pauline to sell."

"You're talking about David Garrett?"

"Yeah, he knows who wants to buy the ranch, but the son of a bitch won't tell us nothin'."

"To be fair, Swayne, he can't say who it is. If he's a fair and honest attorney, he can't tell who he represents, unless his client authorizes him to do it," Lucas said. "And I hope to God David Garrett is a fair and honest attorney, because he'll be the one representing me in my trial tomorrow."

"I forgot about that," Swayne said.

Lucas chuckled. "It isn't something I'm likely to forget."

"No, I reckon not. They's folks says he's a snake. You're a good man, Cain. Watch out for that one."

23

The next morning, Pauline and Sue Ellen went into town with Lucas. Pauline and Sue Ellen were in the buckboard, and Lucas rode alongside.

"I hope everything goes all right for you, Lucas," Pauline said.

"Me, too," Sue Ellen said. "Are you just a little scared?"

"Not really," Lucas replied. "I think, mostly, that this is just a clean-up trial. If there was really anything to it, Northcutt would not have given me bail, or at least he would have made me post bond, rather than releasing me on my own recognizance."

"Did you say the trial was to be held in the Boots and Saddles Saloon?" Sue Ellen asked.

"Yes, I'm sure Higbee is too small a town to have a courthouse."

Sue Ellen laughed. "This will be the first time I've ever been in that saloon."

"Well, I would certainly hope so, young lady," Pauline said.

"I wonder what it's like? Are there . . . uh . . . sporting girls in there?"

"Sue Ellen!" Pauline scolded.

"Well, I'm just curious is all."

"I'm sure you've heard what they say. Curiosity killed the cat," Pauline said.

"Well, thank goodness I'm not a cat," Sue Ellen replied with a slight chuckle.

When they entered the saloon cum courtroom, they saw that the bar was closed, and all but three of the tables were stacked up in the corner. One of the three remaining tables sat in front of several rows of chairs. This would act as the judicial bench. The other two tables, also in front of the gallery, were set on each side. These tables would be for counsel: prosecution to the right, defense to the left as one faced the bench.

In addition to the chairs of the gallery, there were twelve more chairs, in two rows of six that were in front of the gallery and arranged perpendicular to it. These chairs would be for the jury.

Some thirty-five remaining chairs were set up for the gallery, and many were already filled as there were citizens of the town present. The bar girls were present as well, but because they were wearing street clothes instead of their normal revealing garb, nobody would recognize them for who they were, unless they were frequent enough customers to have made the girls' acquaintance.

David Garrett met Lucas and the others as soon as they stepped inside.

"Mr. Cain, you will sit at the defense table with me. Mrs. Foley, you will be in the first row of seats, right behind me. Miss Foley, even though you aren't a witness, I reserved a seat for you, as well."

"Thank you, David," Pauline said.

When Lucas walked up to take his seat at the defense table, he saw Northcutt sitting over at the prosecution table. The twelve jurors were already seated.

Marshal Forsyth, who was acting as the bailiff, announced the arrival of the judge.

"All rise! This court is now in session, the honorable Jeremiah Kramer, presiding."

Everyone stood as Judge Kramer stepped out of the saloon store room, which was in the corner of the saloon that the gallery faced. Kramer was a short man, about five feet, three inches tall, bald headed, except for a white circle of hair just above his ears. He also had a paunch. He was wearing rimless glasses, and had an oversized nose perched above a thick, handlebar moustache.

The judge took his seat then rapped on the table. "This court is now in session. You may be seated."

There was a scrape of chairs as the men and women of the gallery took their seats.

"Bailiff, please tell us for what reason this court has been convened," Judge Kramer said.

"Your Honor, there comes now before this court, one Lucas Cain to be tried for murder," the bailiff said.

"Is counsel for defense present?" Judge Kramer asked.

Garrett stood. "David Garrett, Your Honor. I am defense counsel."

When Garrett sat, Northcutt rose. "Your Honor, Jonathan Northcutt for the prosecution."

"Very well, with counsels for defense and prosecution present, Mr. Northcutt, you may present your opening statement, sir."

"Your Honor, gentlemen of the jury, on the seventh of this month, Lem Proctor and Eli Boyle came into this very building, it at the time acting in its capacity as a saloon, to have a few drinks, and to engage in convivial conversation with their friends. Then, there entered this building, a man who had served time in a prison, and who had killed previously. His arrival changed the entire balance of the relaxed gathering of friends, because shortly after his arrival, an act of violence occurred that took the lives of Lem Proctor and Eli Boyle. Prosecution will prove that what was intended to be an afternoon of pleasant intercourse among friends became instead a killing ground, as these two men were murdered by Lucas Cain."

Northcutt took his seat.

"Opening statement, Mr. Garrett?" Judge Kramer asked.

Garrett stood.

"Your Honor, gentleman of the jury, I would like to enlighten you about Mr. Cain's time in prison. The esteemed prosecuting attorney is correct when he says that Lucas Cain served time in prison, but what he didn't tell you is what that prison was. Lucas Cain was a soldier in the recent war, and the prison in which he served time was the infamous Andersonville Prison. Mr. Cain was a prisoner of war in that accursed place. Mr. Northcutt is also correct in pointing out that the Boots and Saddles Saloon, this very building, did indeed become a killing ground. But it was not murder, as alleged by the prosecuting attorney — it was instead, and as we will prove, justifiable homicide by an act of self-defense."

Garrett returned to the defense table.

"Mr. Prosecutor, make your case," Judge Kramer said.

"Your Honor, prosecution calls to the stand Miss Dorothy Lestina."

The witness called by Northcutt was a young, attractive woman. Lucas recognized her as the bar girl who had been present on the day of the shooting. She approached the witness stand, then raised her right hand as she was sworn in.

"Miss Lestina, would you state your name, please?"

"Dotty, uh, that is, Dorothy Lestina."

"Miss Lestina, were you here, present, when the murder took place?" Northcutt asked.

"Objection, Your Honor," Garrett said. "Calls for conclusion. Murder has not been proven."

"Sustained."

"Let me rephrase the question, Miss Lestina. Were you here when the shooting took place?"

"Yeah, honey, I was."

The gallery laughed.

"Witness will show more decorum in her

responses," Judge Kramer said.

"More what?"

"Don't refer to the counselors as 'honey.' "

"Oh. All right, honey."

Again, Judge Kramer brought down his hammer. "Mr. Prosecutor, please manage your witness."

"Yes, Your Honor," Northcutt replied. "Now, Miss Lestina, if you will, tell the court what you saw. And please, show some restraint in your use of the language."

"Well, I was standin' pretty close to the table where Lem was sittin' when I heard 'im say, 'You stole my horse you . . . uh, here he said a bad word. Can I say what the word was, or will he get mad at me again?" she asked, nodding toward the judge.

"You can say it."

"He said, 'You stole my horse, you son of a bitch'. And then, that man," she pointed to Lucas, "got mad on account of Lem called him a son of a bitch, so he shot 'im. But here's the thing, he shot Eli Boyle a'fore he shot Lem Proctor."

"Who shot first?"

"From where I was standin', it looked like Mr. Cain shot first."

"Your witness, counselor," Northcutt said.

Garrett approached the witness. "You say you were present here, in the saloon, when

288

the shooting took place?"

"Yeah, I was."

"Why were you here?"

"On account of I work here."

"What sort of work do you do here?"

"I'm a hostess."

"A hostess? Isn't that just another way of saying you are a bar girl?"

"Objection, Your Honor, disparaging the witness."

"Sustained."

"Did you remain close to the table when the shooting started?"

"Uh, no, 'cause of the way they was talkin', I got a'scaired, 'n I run over there by the piano," Lestina said.

"And where was the defendant standing?"

"Over there, by the end of the bar."

"And where was Proctor?"

"Oh, he was there, in the middle of the room."

"Was he facing you?"

Lestina chuckled. "No, he wasn't facing me. He was facing Mr. Cain."

"Then I ask you this. If he wasn't facing you, how do you know that he didn't draw his gun first?"

"I . . . uh . . . don't know. But I know that Cain fired first."

"He fired at Proctor first?"

"No, he, uh, it was like I said, he shot Eli, who was standin' up there, first." Lestina pointed to the balcony.

Northcutt's next witness was a man named Jerry Mullins. Mullins was a big man, taller even than Lucas, and probably twenty pounds heavier. And it wasn't fat.

"Mr. Mullins, do you have anything to add to the testimony thus far given?" Northcutt asked.

"Cain stole Lem's horse, and when Lem called him out on it, 'n called him a son of a bitch, why Cain there, he just went sort of crazy, 'n pulled his gun 'n started shootin', 'n he shot Lem 'n Ely both."

"Do you think that Proctor or Boyle would have fired their guns if Cain hadn't shot first?" Northcutt asked.

"No way either one of 'em was actual fixin' to shoot. I know'd both them boys just real good, 'n what they was doin' was just sort of bluffing Cain, on account of because he stoled Lem's horse."

"No further witnesses, Your Honor," Northcutt said.

"Mr. Garrett?" Kramer said.

Garrett approached the witness, then stopped just in front of him. "Mr. Mullins, how well did you know the deceased?"

"Who?"

"The deceased, Mr. Mullins. Ely Boyle and Lem Proctor. How well did you know them?"

"Well, like I said, I knowed both of 'em real good. We all three of us rode for the Box Y."

"The Box Y. That would be Bertis Yancey?"

"Yeah, that's the one what owns it."

"Do you know if Mr. Yancey wants to buy Hillside?"

"Objection, Your Honor. Bertis Yancey is not on trial here," Northcutt called out.

"Your Honor, the question goes to the defense allegation that the first encounter between my client and Misters Boyle and Proctor had to do with the two men, now deceased, putting undo pressure on Mrs. Foley, in an attempt to force her to sell her ranch."

"Objection overruled, you may continue with this line of questioning," Judge Kramer ruled.

"Thank you, Your Honor. I repeat my question. Do you know whether or not Mr. Yancey has expressed an interest in buying Hillside?"

"I don't know. I ain't never heard him say nothin' about it one way or another."

"Were you aware of Proctor and Boyle's intention to confront Mrs. Foley?"

"Well, yeah, sort of."

"Explain to the court what you mean by sort of?"

"The mornin' that this happened, they said they was goin' to go out on the road 'n have a little fun," Mullins replied.

"What sort of fun?"

"Well, they said they was goin' to stop a woman that would be comin' into town."

"Did they tell you why?"

"No, I figured they was talkin' about . . . uh, you know, what men sometimes do with women, like what men do with Dotty . . . Miss Lestina."

There were a few ribald chuckles in the gallery.

"No further questions, Your Honor," Garrett said.

"Redirect, Mr. Northcutt?"

"No, redirect, Your Honor."

"Are there any more witnesses for the prosecution?" Judge Kramer asked.

"No more witnesses, Your Honor."

"Very well. Mr. Garrett, you may call your first witness."

"Your Honor, Defense calls Manuel Burns."

Burns was sworn in.

"Mr. Burns, what is your occupation?"

"I'm bartender here at the Boots and Saddles."

"And were you a witness to the case we're trying here today?"

"I was."

"Have any of the previous witnesses told of the event as you saw it?"

"No, sir."

"Please tell the court what you saw."

"Well, part of what they're sayin' is true. Proctor did call Cain a son of a bitch, but he done had his gun in his hand when he shouted it out."

"What did Mr. Cain do then?"

"Well, sir, 'n here's the strange thing. He drawed his gun, 'n it was like Miss Lestina said, he didn't shoot at Proctor then, even though Proctor was already aimin' his gun at Cain. First thing he done was he shot Boyle who was standin' up there on the balcony. 'N it turned out that Boyle had his gun out, too, 'n he was pointin' it at Cain, but somehow Cain know'd it, so he shot Boyle first, then he shot Proctor."

"Did either Boyle or Proctor shoot at Mr. Cain?"

"Yes, sir, Proctor, he shot at Cain, 'n hit 'im in the shoulder. But, when all the smoke was done, it was Cain who was still standin', 'n Proctor 'n Boyle what was both of

293

'em a' lyin' dead on the floor."

Garrett called three more witnesses, all of whom testified that Proctor and Boyle drew first, and all stated that there was no doubt that the two men meant to kill Lucas.

"It's only 'cause Cain is fast," Isaac Holloway testified. "He's the fastest I've ever seen, and he didn't even start his draw before Proctor and Boyle already had their guns out."

"Do you think Proctor and Boyle intended to kill Mr. Cain?" Garrett asked.

"Oh, hell yeah, there ain't no doubt that's exactly what they was a' plannin' on doin'."

"Thank you. No further questions."

In cross examination, Northcutt was unable to weaken Holloway's testimony.

Pauline was Garrett's final witness, and she testified as to how Proctor and Boyle had stopped her on the road by killing Duchess, one of her mules, then began to destroy her groceries and set fire to her wagon.

"If Mr. Cain hadn't come along, I don't know what would have happened," she concluded.

It became Northcutt's turn to cross examine Pauline.

"Mrs. Foley, I believe you have testified that one of the two men killed one of your mules?"

"Yes, sir, it was Proctor who killed Duchess. And Duchess was a fine mule, too. Why, she was better 'n any horse."

"So you had but one mule to get you home. Wasn't it difficult on the remaining mule to pull the heavy wagon alone?"

"Oh, Homer didn't have to pull the wagon all by himself. Mr. Cain took Proctor's horse and attached him to the wagon alongside Homer."

"Thank you, Mrs. Foley."

"Redirect, Mr. Garrett?"

"No redirect, Your Honor."

"Defense counsel, you may give your closing argument."

"Gentleman of the jury, all of you know Mrs. Foley. She was made a widow, and since the death of Bill Foley, a man who was loved and respected by every citizen of Higbee, Mrs. Foley has gone on alone. Many thought that she would sell her ranch, and perhaps it would be better for her if she would, but, bravely, she has continued to operate the ranch with naught but her daughter and one hand to help her. What sort of men would attack a woman, struggling to survive? The same kind of men who would try to kill Lucas Cain, and fail at their perfidious attempt, only because of the skill

295

and swiftness of Mr. Cain.

"It has been testified that Proctor justified his attempt to kill Mr. Cain by alleging that Lucas Cain stole his horse. But in fact, Proctor's horse, even at the time of the shooting, was safely stabled in Mitchell's Livery.

"Defense rests, Your Honor."

Northcutt stood to give his close.

"Gentlemen of the jury, there are three facts in evidence here. One," and here, Northcutt raised a finger, "Lem Proctor and Ely Boyle are dead. Two," he raised his second finger, "it is not disputed, even by defense counsel, that the defendant, Lucas Cain was the instrument of their death. And three, the cause of Mr. Proctor's dissent, was the theft of his horse.

"Now defense has sought to mitigate the charge of horse theft by claiming the horse was only borrowed and was returned to the livery. But, and consider this fact very carefully in your deliberation, a horse borrowed without permission is a horse stolen.

"The result of these indisputable facts, is that both Ely Boyle and Lem Proctor are dead, having been killed by Lucas Cain, the very horse thief whose nefarious act had brought about this deadly confrontation in the first place.

"Your Honor, I rest my case."

"Jury will now retire for the verdict," Judge Kramer said.

The twelve men who composed the jury filed out of the room.

Judge Kramer brought his gavel down sharply.

"This court is in recess."

24

When the jury retired for its deliberation, Lucas, Pauline, Sue Ellen, and Garrett went to Waggy's for coffee.

"What do you think the jury will do?" Sue Ellen asked anxiously.

"Well, you never can tell about a jury," Garrett replied. "But Jonathan is a most excellent prosecutor, and I have to say that he made a very strong case."

"Oh, but I thought your case was much better than Mr. Northcutt's case," Pauline said. "After all, you had right on your side."

Lucas chuckled. "Thank you, Mrs. Foley. And thank you for your testimony on my behalf."

"It was easy enough to give," Pauline said. "All I had to do was tell the truth."

Lucas chuckled. "You know, I hadn't even planned to stop here. It was just my intention to get a drink and a supper and then pass on through."

Sue Ellen smiled at him. "Well, I, for one, am glad you did stop here, but I'm sorry that stopping here got you in trouble."

After they had been there for a while, Marshal Forsyth stepped into the restaurant then, and seeing them, came over to their table.

"The jury's announced that they have reached a verdict," he said.

"So soon?" Pauline replied.

"Oh, Mama, what if it's bad?" Sue Ellen asked, the tone of her voice betraying her fear.

"Let's just stay hopeful," Pauline said.

When they returned to the saloon-court room, many were already there. Lucas took his seat beside Garrett at the defense table, while Pauline and Sue Ellen sat behind him.

Neither the jury, nor the judge was present. After a few moments while the gallery took their seats, and the court grew quiet, the jury came in and took their seats. About a minute later, Marshal Forsyth, in his capacity as bailiff came into the room.

"All rise for His Honor, Judge Jeremiah Kramer."

Judge Kramer returned to the bench, then took his seat.

"Be seated," he said. Then, with a rap of his gavel, he said, "This court is in session."

All conversation in the gallery ceased, and it was very quiet as Judge Kramer addressed the jury.

"Gentlemen of the jury, have you reached a verdict?"

The jury foreman stood. "We have, Your Honor."

"Would you publish the verdict, please?"

"We find the defendant, Lucas Cain," and here, the foreman paused for dramatic effect.

Sue Ellen, who was sitting right behind Lucas, reached up to put her hand on his shoulder.

"Not guilty," the foreman said.

The tension broke, and spontaneously Sue Ellen stood and wrapped her arms around Lucas's neck, giving him a kiss on the cheek.

"I knew it was going to come in this way," Pauline said.

"I'm glad you had confidence, because I'm not sure I did," Lucas said. "I mean Northcutt really went after me."

"Yes, he did," Pauline answered, "but look at it this way. The fact that you had a trial and the prosecutor didn't let you off easy, should be enough to prove your innocence, even to the most skeptical."

"I guess so."

"Well, we have to celebrate," Sue Ellen

said. "Mama, let's throw a party for Lucas."

"Well, honey, now just who would show up besides us and Swayne?" Pauline replied.

"No, I mean a real party, a party for the whole town. We could rent the meeting room at the Parker Hotel, and we can get Asa Warnell to play for us, so we could have a dance. Mr. Warnell is always looking for a reason to get his little band to perform."

"I think it is a very good idea. We'll get Mr. Lightfoot to put it in his paper."

"I'd be glad to write an article about it," Lightfoot said, when he was approached. "It's been a while since Higbee has had anything to feel good about. I think a dance could bring the whole town together."

True to his word, Lightfoot wrote an article which came out in the paper the very next day.

Lucas picked up a copy at the front desk of the Parker Hotel, then took it into Waggy's Restaurant to read it over breakfast.

There were two articles that caught his attention.

Cain Found Innocent

Lucas Cain, a recent arrival to our fair community, was put on trial yesterday for the murder of Lem Proctor and Eli Boyle. Proctor and Boyle had recently been riders for the Box Y brand. The incident that preceded the deadly confrontation in the Boots and Saddles Saloon, had its beginning on the Higbee Road, halfway between Higbee and Hillside Ranch.

There, the two men confronted Mrs. Pauline Foley with malicious intent to the end of forcing her to sell her ranch. Lucas Cain came upon the incident and rescued Mrs. Foley, sending Boyle and Proctor cowering, back to town. Shortly thereafter Lucas Cain was set upon in the Boots and Saddles Saloon, and in the engaging shootout, both Proctor and Boyle were killed.

The case was subsequently tried and after a jury deliberation of but forty-seven minutes, Lucas Cain was found innocent.

Gala Dance to be Held

Saturday, June 19th, is the date chosen for a community dance. The dance is to be held in the Parker Hotel meeting room, and though it is ostensibly being given in celebration of the acquittal of the charges facing Lucas Cain, it is indeed a celebration of the spirit of Higbee.

As there has been no community celebration for some several months now, it is anticipated that the dance will be met with enthusiastic response.

"Oh, will you be going to that dance?" Wanda asked as she came to Lucas's table and saw him reading the article.

"I guess I pretty much have to, since it's to celebrate my acquittal."

Wanda laughed. "Yes, I would think you'd be there. It's been a long time since we've had anything like that in Higbee. I know that Waggy and I are going to close the café long enough for both of us to go."

George Rogers had sent word for Jerry Mullins to meet him in the Hog Lot Saloon.

"What do you want?" Mullins asked.

"I've been told you was friends with Proctor and Boyle," Rogers said.

"Yeah, I was."

"How do you feel about the way the verdict turned out?"

"You mean about the son of a bitch that kilt 'em, gettin' off scott free?"

"Yes."

"It pisses me off, that's how I feel. I think they should 'a hung the son of a bitch."

"I share your feelings," Rogers said.

"What? You mean you knew Proctor and Boyle?"

"Yes, they did a job for me once, and as far as I'm concerned, Cain should 'a been found guilty."

"Yeah, I think so, too," Mullins said.

"How about this?" Rogers asked. "How about I give you a hundred dollars to take care of him?"

"What?" Mullins gasped. "Are you serious?"

"I'm very serious. You want revenge for your friends anyway. This way you can get revenge and get paid for it."

"When you say you want me to take care of 'im, are you tellin' me you want me to kill him?"

"That's exactly what I'm telling you."

"Well, look here, I can't just up 'n kill 'im like that. Hell, they'd hang me for murder."

"There's going to be a dance tomorrow night, 'n Cain's going to be there."

"So?"

"You're going to be there, too. We'll work out a way for you to kill 'im without it being murder."

"How is it I can kill 'im without it bein' murder?"

"You just let me take care of that."

Since the dance was being held in the very hotel where Lucas was staying, it was very easy for him to attend, and that evening he walked down the stairs shortly after the dance had started. Because of Lucas's transient nature, it had been a long time since he had attended any sort of social event. Asa Warnell and two other musicians were providing the music, and Marshal Forsyth was calling the square dances. One such dance was on going as Lucas stepped inside. He could see the dancers moving about in response to Marshal Forsyth's calls.

Now it's allemande left with the lady on
    the left
And right to your Nellie and you grand
    right and left
And when you met your Nellie
You promenade her home
Oh you all promenade your Nellie Grey
    home

The room was filled with sun-browned cowboys in their best shirts, cleanest jeans, and slicked down hair. The women, from ranchers' wives, to ranchers' daughters, to saloon girls were wearing brightly colored dresses and wide smiles as they moved through the squares to the music and the calls.

The older attendees stood along the walls, possibly remembering when they were young and had attended such events.

Neither Pauline nor Sue Ellen had arrived yet, so Lucas stood alongside, sipping punch and watching the dancers. Then, he saw a flash of yellow come through the door and he breathed a quiet whistle. It was Sue Ellen, and the change between this walking vision just entering the room, and the young, jeans wearing, rifle bearing person he was used to, was the difference between night and day.

The Foleys were greeted by some who were already there, and the man who had testified against him in court, Jerry Mullins, began talking to Sue Ellen.

Lucas walked over to her. "Miss Foley, may I have the next dance?"

Sue Ellen turned toward him with a big smile. "Why, I would be delighted to dance with you, Mr. Cain."

"Now, just a minute here, Miss Foley, I was about to ask you for the next dance," Mullins said.

"Unfortunately, Mr. Mullins, you didn't

ask quickly enough," Lucas said.

Rather than forming squares, the next dance was a waltz, which gave Lucas the opportunity to be close to Sue Ellen. Although Lucas had little experience as a dancer, he always was light on his feet, and his natural rhythm, combined with Sue Ellen's skill as a dancer, resulted in a few minutes of graceful movement.

The dance was over much too soon as far as Lucas was concerned. Then, as the music ended, Lucas realized that they were the center of attention, as all eyes were on them. Or, rather Lucas saw all eyes were on Sue Ellen. And, why wouldn't they be? She was clearly the most beautiful belle of the ball.

Then he saw a pair of eyes glaring at him. Those eyes belonged to Jerry Mullins.

Within a moment, the movement of people blotted out his view of Mullins.

Lucas asked for another dance with Sue Ellen, who accepted his invitation.

"Lucas, I think you need to be careful around Mullins," she said as they began their dance. "He was a friend of Proctor and Boyle."

"Yes, I gathered that from his testimony against me in the trial, and he's staring daggers at me now."

"He's a dangerous man," Sue Ellen said.

A square dance followed, and when a young cowboy invited Sue Ellen to join him in the square, she accepted.

As the band started the music for the dance, Lucas started toward the door, intending to step outside and get a breath of fresh air. There were a few people coming in from having been outside, so Lucas stopped to give them entry.

As he waited at the door, a young woman came by, then reached up to jerk her dress and camisole down to expose her breasts. At the same time, she screamed, her scream getting the attention of all present. The music stopped and the room grew silent.

"Julie, what happened?" Mullins asked.

"Oh, Jerry," Julie replied. "That man . . ." she pointed to Lucas, "that man grabbed me and jerked my dress down." She pulled the top of her dress back up, as if trying to restore some modesty.

"That's the same man who got away with murderin' Lem and Ely," Mullins said.

Now, Lucas realized that he was the center of attention of everyone present.

"Get that son of a bitch outside," Mullins said. "I'll teach him to attack a young lady like that."

Lucas was a big, strong man, but Mullins was a little bigger, and Lucas didn't doubt if he wasn't stronger, especially since Lucas was still nursing a sore left shoulder, a result of the gunfight with Proctor and Boyle.

"All right," Lucas said, and he stepped out behind the hotel. When he did, several others who were at the dance followed him out.

Mullins mixed in with the crowd and moved through the others so that he was right behind Lucas. As soon as Lucas turned around, Mullins, without warning, threw a hard right to Lucas's jaw.

The blow caught him by surprise, and knocked him back so that he had to take several quick steps to keep from falling.

Mullins got a surprised look as well. He had hit Lucas with everything he had and had fully expected Lucas to go down, but Lucas was still standing.

"All right, friend, let's get this settled, shall we?" Lucas said.

"I ain't your friend," Mullins said. He rushed forward, intending to use his size and strength to his advantage. Lucas stepped adroitly to one side, allowing Mullins's inertia to carry him past. As Mullins stumbled by him, Lucas hit him hard in his ear.

Mullins let out a cry of pain, and slapped his right hand over his ear. He turned and shouted at Lucas. "Fight fair, you son of a bitch!"

"How can I make this even?" Lucas asked. "You want me to fight with only one arm? Oh, wait I'm already fighting with only one arm, aren't I?" Lucas put his left arm, the wounded arm, behind his back. "All right, try it now."

"Arrgh!" Mullins shouted as once more, he rushed toward Lucas like a charging bull.

Again Lucas stepped nimbly to the side to avoid the rush this time, slamming his right fist into Mullins's nose. He felt the nose go under his hand, and when Mullins looked back toward him, blood was streaming across his mouth, and down his chin.

Mullins made one more try, a powerful right cross aimed at Lucas's jaw. Lucas avoided that attack as he had all the others, this time merely by bending back at the waist so that Mullins's swing found nothing but air. Lucas countered with a powerful punch catching Mullins on the jaw, and dropping him like a sack of potatoes.

Lucas stepped forward, his left arm still behind his back. He looked down at Mullins, lying unconscious on the ground.

"Damn, and right when we were having so much fun, he decided to take a nap," Lucas said sarcastically.

Those who had gathered to watch the fight, and that was well over half the people who had come to the dance, now broke out laughing.

"Now, where's that woman that said I ripped the top of her dress down. I want her to tell what really happened."

"I done told ever'body, honey," Julie said, her modesty having been restored. She pointed toward Mullins, who was now, very groggily, regaining his feet. "Mullins paid me ten dollars to say that Mr. Cain done this, but Mr. Cain, he didn't do nothin'," she announced to the others.

"Ha!" one of the cowboys said. "Cain whipped Mullins's ass, 'n he had one hand behind his back while he was a' doin' it. Now that's 'bout the damnedest thing I ever seen."

"Come on," one of the cowboys shouted. "Let's get this dance a' goin, again. They's lots of pretty girls I ain't danced with yet."

25

Sue Ellen had been one of those who had come out to watch the fight. A part of her realized that she should be shocked and mortified by such a display. Instead, she had to admit that she was excited and stimulated by what she saw. She found that Lucas's strength and ability to handle an even larger, and more muscular man than himself was, unexpectedly, arousing.

"All right, break it up out here, break it up!" Marshal Forsyth said. "We've got a dance goin' on inside, but there ain't hardly nobody that's left inside."

Someone gave Mullins a handkerchief, and holding the handkerchief to his bloody and broken nose, he shuffled off down the alley.

Sue Ellen moved back into the building with the others, and after a few minutes of getting everyone settled down, the caller announced the next dance. With a smile, Sue

Ellen walked over to Lucas, and without a word, extended her hand.

They began to move with the callers' calls.

Allemande left with your corners
Go right hand to your partner and its
   grand old right and left
When you meet your own
Then you promenade her home
Yes, you promenade your mountain girl
   home

Lucas danced with no one other than Sue Ellen for the next several dances, then he smiled at her.

"If you don't mind, I'm going to dance the next one with someone else," he said.

"Oh? Who?" she asked, obviously a little upset with him for abandoning her.

"Your mama."

Sue Ellen flashed a relieved smile. "Go ahead, Mama will enjoy that."

Lucas sought Pauline out, and as he held his hand out in invitation to dance, she smiled and accepted.

"How's your shoulder?" Pauline asked.

"Thanks for the concern, but it's doing fine."

"I thought it might be. I mean it certainly hasn't slowed you down any. You've been dancing all night and you've had a fight. But I must say, I was a little concerned for you."

"Well, if you're that concerned, when we're allemanding around in the square, let's just not allemande too hard."

"I'll be gentle with you," Pauline replied with a little laugh.

Mullins had not come back inside with the others, and now he was standing out in front of the hotel. There was a watering trough to one end of the hitching rails and he had been dipping the bloody handkerchief into the water, then using it to wash away the blood that came from his nose. What had once been a rather substantial flow of crimson had now stopped. His nose was still quite painful, however, from the punch Cain had inflicted upon him.

And with one arm behind his back, he thought. He had been humiliated by the son of a bitch. He went back into the hotel to retrieve the gun he had checked in when he first arrived.

When the dance ended, everyone who had checked their guns strapped them back on, and began leaving the hotel. Lucas strapped on his pistol as well, but he didn't actually have to leave the hotel because he was staying there. However, he was engaged in conversation with Sue Ellen and Pauline, so he stepped out on the porch with them, intending to walk them to the buckboard.

As soon as they stepped off the porch, they heard a loud, angry yell.

"Pull your gun, you son of a bitch!" Mullins shouted, firing his pistol concurrent with his shout.

"Uhh," Pauline said.

Lucas drew his own gun and fired, and he saw Mullins drop his gun and grab his chest as he fell.

"Mama!" Sue Ellen called out in a frightened voice.

Quickly, Lucas holstered his pistol, and knelt beside Pauline to check her wound. The bullet had hit her in the hip, and blood was soaking through her dress.

By now several of those who had left the dance had gathered around the wounded woman. One of those was Dr. Conway.

"Get her down to my office," he said.

"Yes, sir," Lucas answered, then he reached down to help her get into the doctor's surrey. He and Sue Ellen rode with Dr. Conway to his office.

Lucas and Sue Ellen remained in the waiting room, while Dr. Conway worked on Pauline.

Marshal Forsyth came into the doctor's office as they were waiting.

"I've interviewed several witnesses, but I'd like to hear your story as to what happened back there."

"As soon as I stepped out of the hotel, Mullins yelled at me to pull my gun. He already had his gun out and was shooting, and his bullet hit Mrs. Foley. I shot him before he could get off another shot."

"Lucas is telling the truth, Marshal. I saw it all," Sue Ellen said.

Marshal Forsyth nodded. "That seems to coincide with what everyone else is telling me. I'll tell you this, you sure seem to have the ability to rid the town of some of its riff-raff. I won't be filing charges, and I'm sure no one else will either. Now, I'd like to know how Pauline is doing. What does the doctor say?"

"He says —" Lucas started, then he stopped in mid-sentence. "Well, I'll just let the doctor tell you."

Dr. Conway had just come out into the waiting room at that moment, and all three looked anxiously toward him. Even before he said a word, the smile on his face eased their fear.

"Mrs. Foley is going to be just fine," Dr. Conway said. "The bullet just creased her. It was painful of course, and she bled a little, but she'll be up and around in no time at all."

"When can she go home?" Sue Ellen asked.

"Oh, I'd say in another half-hour or so. I gave her some ether while I cleaned her wound and sewed it shut. I want to keep her here until that wears off."

"Thank you, Doctor, thank you so much," Sue Ellen said.

One hour later, they returned to Hillside. Lucas drove the buckboard and Sue Ellen stayed in the back with her mother. Charley was tied onto the back. When they got to the ranch, Swayne saw that Pauline needed help to walk into the house, so he came over quickly.

"What happened?"

"Nothing much. We didn't eat before the dance, so I think I should get started on a late supper," Pauline said.

"Mama, you'll do no such thing," Sue Ellen said. "You just go in the parlor and rest. I'll do the cooking."

"All right, dear."

"Sue Ellen, would you let me help you?"

Lucas asked.

"You mean you can cook?"

"When you spend as much time alone on the trail as I have, you either learn to cook, or you starve."

Sue Ellen laughed. "Well then, by all means, come help out."

When they got into the kitchen, Sue Ellen looked around. "We have some smoked ham that I could fry, but I need something that I can fix quick."

"I'll take care of that," Lucas said. "Do you have potatoes?"

"Yes, and I've got some bacon fat to use to fry them."

"What about eggs? I'll need half a dozen or maybe more."

"We've got plenty," Sue Ellen said.

As Sue Ellen cut off slices of ham, Lucas peeled the potatoes and cut them into thin rounds and put them in the bacon grease. Just before the potatoes were cooked, Lucas scrambled up the eggs in a bowl, then poured them into the frying potatoes. He stirred them as he cooked, so that the finished product was fried potatoes with scrambled eggs, doing so in such a way that it was difficult to separate them.

"My, my," Sue Ellen said. "I've never seen potatoes cooked with eggs like that."

"It was something my grandmother liked to do," Lucas said.

At supper, Lucas's potatoes and eggs were a great hit, especially with Swayne.

After supper, Swayne said he had something he wanted to talk about.

"All right, Swayne, we're listening."

"While you folks was all gone, I found a cow and her calf 'n they was both kilt."

"A wild animal?" Pauline asked.

"No, ma'am, it warn't no animal, lessen animals has taken to usin' guns now. Both of 'em was shot."

"How many does that make, now?"

"They's been eight of 'em was kilt so far in the last two or three months."

"Oh, Mama," Sue Ellen said.

"They's somethin' else," Swayne added.

"What is it?"

"This here note was on the mama cow." Swayne handed a sheet of paper to Pauline. There was a smear of blood on the paper.

"Oh, dear," Pauline said as she examined it.

"Read it out loud, Mama," Sue Ellen said.

Pauline began to read. *"We're willing to pay you a good price for your ranch as it is now. But the longer you wait, you will lose more and more cattle. When you are ready to sell, place an ad in the Ledger."*

When she finished reading the message, she held it down by her side. "This is just the same as saying they'll make it so we can't earn any money until we agree to sell. I don't understand," Pauline said. "Why does anyone want this ranch so bad that they would try to starve us off our land?"

"There's something about this that we don't know," Lucas said. "There must be something about the land that is more valuable than the ranch itself."

"Well, what could it possibly be?" Sue Ellen asked.

"I don't know. But if I can figure out what it is, I could get to the bottom of this whole thing."

"How are you going to do that?" Sue Ellen asked.

"I think I'll start by visiting some of your neighbors."

26

After breakfast the next morning, Lucas bade Sue Ellen and Pauline goodbye, then started on his mission of visiting Hillside's neighbors. The first ranch Lucas visited the next morning was the Bar P which was the closest. It was a much larger, and obviously more successful ranch than Hillside. That was immediately noticeable by the size of the cattle herd he saw and by the size of the main house and the number of all the auxiliary buildings that surrounded the house. There were also several of the ranch hands visible as they tended to the various jobs that kept them occupied.

Two of the hands, seeing Lucas as he came across the Las Animus, rode out to meet him.

"What are you doin' on the Bar P land, Mister?" The question was asked in a way that was more of a challenge than an inquiry.

"I've come to speak with Mr. Pogue," Lucas answered.

"Mr. Pogue don't do the hirin'. That would be Frank Adams, he's the foreman." The speaker was an average-sized man with a face that was scarred. Dark eyes looked out at him from beneath heavy brows.

The other rider was a little smaller, a very thin man with a prominent Adam's apple.

"Well, I'm not looking for a job, but right now, I'd like to speak to Mr. Pogue."

"What do you want to talk to 'im about?"

"That would be between Mr. Pogue and me."

"It ain't goin' to be between you 'n Mr. Pogue, 'til after it's 'tween you 'n me."

"What if we just ride with 'im, up to the Big House?" the other man suggested.

"All right, Mister, we'll take you to see Mr. Pogue. But don't you be tryin' no funny stuff, you hear me?"

"All I want to do is talk to him," Lucas said.

The rider nodded, then motioned for Lucas to follow them.

The road continued on about half a mile until they reached the big white house Lucas had seen as soon as he had crossed the river. When they rode up to it, one of the riders dismounted. "Wait here," he said.

Lucas watched him as the man went into the house without even knocking on the door.

A few moments later, he reappeared.

"You can come on in. Mr. Pogue said he's willin' to talk to you."

Lucas dismounted, then followed the cowboy inside.

"He's back there, in the office," he said, pointing toward an open door.

When Lucas stepped into the office, he saw a balding, heavy-set man sitting behind a desk. He didn't rise when Lucas entered.

"Thank you, Arnie," Pogue said to the cowboy, then he turned his attention to Lucas. "Who are you, and what do you want?"

"Mr. Pogue, my name is Lucas Cain, and I —"

"Cain?" Pogue said, interrupting Lucas in mid-sentence. "I heard about you. Are you the one that kilt Boyle 'n Proctor?"

"Uh, yes, sir, I am," Lucas replied, surprised by the question.

Pogue nodded, then smiled. "Good for you. Them two sons of bitches needed to be kilt. Now, what can I do for you?"

"Are you interested in buying Hillside?"

"No, why the hell should I be? I've got more land now than I need to manage the number of cows I'm runnin'. Besides which,

I didn't even know Mrs. Foley was wantin' to sell. Did she send you over here to see if I was wantin' to buy?"

"No, sir, quite the contrary. There are some people trying to force her to sell, and we're trying to find out who's behind it."

"Well, for heaven's sake, man, all the hell she has to do is tell them no."

Lucas shook his head. "It's not as easy as that. Ever since she said no, things have been happening. Cows have been rustled and even killed. Oh, and you mentioned my killing Proctor and Boyle. That all started when I came up on Mrs. Foley out on the road. They had shot one of her mules, and one of them was holding a gun on her while the other one was throwing her supplies into the road, and then setting fire to her buckboard."

"I'll be damned," Pogue said. "You was right to kill them two sons of bitches. But they weren't trying to buy the ranch, were they? Hell, they hardly ever had enough to buy a couple of beers."

"No, I'm sure they weren't acting for themselves. I believe someone paid those two to harass Mrs. Foley. Someone who wanted to buy the ranch, and they hoped this would persuade her to sell."

"Damn, that's a rotten thing for someone

to do," Pogue said, "and as far as I'm concerned, that's all the more reason for you to kill those two no-accounts. By the way, forgive me for not offering it earlier, but would you like a cup of coffee?"

"Yes, thank you, I believe I would like a cup."

"Cream or sugar?"

"No, just black."

Pogue chuckled. "You must travel a lot. You can always carry coffee with you, but not cream and sugar."

Lucas chuckled as well. "You got that right."

Several minutes later, and after more conversation which, while friendly, had not led Lucas any closer to the truth, he sat his empty cup down.

"Mr. Pogue, I appreciate the coffee, but even more than that I appreciate the conversation."

"I'm sorry I wasn't able to give you any more information," Pogue said.

"But you did," Lucas replied with a smile.

"Oh? And how so?"

"You told me that you have no interest in buying the ranch, and I believe you. So, that eliminates one of the people I wanted to find out about. Now, I only have two more to investigate, the Rocking R, and the Box Y."

"The Box Y. Yes, well, the truth is, I wouldn't put it past Bertis Yancey to do something like that. Mind you, I'm not saying he's the one, but he's more 'n doubled the size of his ranch since I've known him, and I believe he's the kind of person who *could* do something like that if he thought it would get him more land."

"Thank you. As it happens, though, Mr. Richards is next on my list."

"We'll ride with you 'till you're offen the Circle P land," Arnie said, rather gruffly, when Lucas stepped down from the front porch.

"Thank you," Lucas said. "That's very nice of you."

"Yeah, well I didn't mean, uh, that's all right. I, uh, well, never mind, reckon you can get yourself off without 'ny trouble," Arnie said.

"I expect I can," Lucas said, smiling at Arnie's reaction.

Lucas rode west for about three miles, until he came upon a sign that read:

ROCKING R RANCH
Duke Richards Owner

He followed the access road for about a mile before he reached the ranch. Everything about the ranch indicated prosperity, from the large main house, which set on an actual lawn, to the well-kept outer buildings. He saw three cowboys at the corral; one appeared to be breaking a horse, and the other two were sitting on the fence watching him.

One of the cowboys saw Lucas, then came over to him.

"Are you looking for someone, Mister?"

"Yes, I'd like to speak with Mr. Richards," Lucas answered. "Would he be at home?"

"Oh, yeah, he's here all right. Just go on up and yank on the bell cord. Someone'll come to the door."

"Thank you," Lucas said.

Lucas stepped up onto the porch and pulled the bell cord. He heard the bell from inside, and a moment later the door was opened by a rather small olive-skinned man. Lucas's thought that he was Mexican was verified when the man spoke.

"Si, señor?"

"I would like to speak with Mr. Richards."

"Su nombre, señor?"

"My name is Lucas Cain."

"Un momento por favor, Señor Cain."

Lucas waited as asked, and a moment

327

later the Mexican returned. He didn't speak this time, but made a motion with his head indicating that Lucas should follow him. They went into the ranch office where Lucas was met by a powerfully built man who looked more like a saloon bouncer, than a successful ranch owner.

Richards held his hand out toward a chair. "Sit," he invited. "Tell me why you're here in my house."

"I befriended Mrs. Foley recently, and —"

"A delightful lady," Richards said interrupting Lucas. "But please, pardon me for the interruption. If you've recently met her, you are already aware of that."

"Yes, sir, I am," Lucas said.

"Please, continue."

"Mr. Richards, are you interested in buying Hillside?"

"Of course I am, and I made her a most generous offer after Bill died. To be honest, I made the offer because I thought she might want out of the operation, but she refused my offer. Are you telling me Pauline's ready to sell now, because if she is, tell her my offer still stands."

"No, sir, she doesn't want to sell."

"Then, I don't understand. Why did you pose the question?"

"Because someone is bringing a lot of

pressure on her, trying to force here to sell."

"Pressure? What sort of pressure?"

Lucas told of the incident of Mrs. Foley being stopped on the road.

"Oh, my, I just recently returned from Denver, and I hadn't heard anything about that. Have you told Marshal Forsyth about this?"

"Yes, I have."

"Good, I hope he acted on it, because those two should be in jail. Are they?"

"No, sir."

"They aren't? And why not if you know who they are?"

"They're not in jail because they're dead."

"Dead?"

"Yes, sir. I killed them both."

"You killed them because of what they did to Pauline out on the road?"

"Not exactly. I killed them because they were trying to kill me." And once more Lucas told Richards the story of the confrontation in the saloon.

"Well, then, you were certainly justified."

"Yes, the court trial found me innocent."

"There was a trial? You'll have to pardon my ignorance," Richards said. "As I said, I just got in from Denver yesterday, and I'm afraid I've not caught up on any local news."

"That's understandable," Lucas said as

he rose from his chair. "I appreciate your taking the time to see me."

"Oh, heavens, receiving you didn't put me out any at all. I'm curious, though. Will you be calling on Pogue and Yancey?"

"I've already met with Mr. Pogue."

"And Bertis Yancey?"

"I plan to call on him tomorrow."

"If you'll take my advice, be careful around Yancey," Richards said. "He's not a very friendly fellow."

"Thanks for the warning," Lucas said.

It wasn't quite dark when Lucas rode into Higbee, but he hadn't eaten since breakfast, and as he rode by Waggy's the cooking aromas enticed him to stop for an early supper. He was greeted by Wanda when he stepped inside.

"Lucas," Wanda said with a welcoming smile. "I've missed you. If you'd have a seat over there, I'll bring you your supper."

"What are you serving tonight, Wanda? Never mind, no matter what it is, I'm sure I'll like it."

"Let me put it this way, Mr. Cain. If you don't like it, you won't have to pay for it."

Lucas laughed. "Well, how can I pass on a guarantee like that?"

A few minutes later Wanda brought a

steaming plate to Lucas's table. "Here it is," she said. "Somebody gave Zeke Mitchell a hind quarter of elk and he shared it with us, so here you have it — roast elk and noodles."

"Well, I don't think you'll have to worry about me not liking it as it looks, and smells, delicious."

"I'll wait until you've tasted it," Wanda said.

Lucas took a bite, then smiled broadly. "It is absolutely delicious," he said.

"Good," Wanda said. "Now, you just enjoy your supper, and if there's anything else you need, you just let me know."

After supper, Lucas stopped in at the Boots and Saddles Saloon because he thought a beer might be good before going to bed.

"Howdy, Mr. Cain, how's your shoulder gettin' along?" the bartender asked as he put the beer before Lucas. "I heard it didn't slow you down the night of the dance."

"That's true," Lucas said as he rubbed the site of the bullet wound. "It's a little sore, but it's not really bothering me all that much."

"That's good to hear."

"Hey, are you goin' to stand down there palaverin' with that feller all night, or can you come down here 'n pour me a whiskey?" a man at the other end of the bar called.

The bartender smiled at Lucas. "Don't want to keep the man from his whiskey."

When Lucas went to bed that night, he had a hard time going to sleep. He had visited Pogue and Richards, and he felt sure they were good, honest people who would not be putting the pressure on Mrs. Foley to try to force her to sell her ranch. Tomorrow he would visit with Bertis Yancey. Even though Duke Richards had warned him about Yancey, at this point he had nothing to indicate that he would get anything more from him.

27

The next morning Lucas was fully dressed and pulling on his boots before he saw a slip of paper lying on the floor by the door. Curious, as soon as his boots were on, he walked over to pick it up.

You have no business getting involved in this. If you value your life, you will leave town.

He had no idea who had left the note, but if he could find out who it was, he believed it might lead him to know who was trying to force Pauline Foley off her ranch.

After breakfast, Lucas showed the note to Marshal Forsyth.

"You wouldn't recognize this writing by any chance, would you?" Lucas asked.

Forsyth shook his head. "I'm afraid I don't, but then I don't get to see that many examples of anybody's writing anyway."

"Yeah, well, I really didn't think that you would, but I just thought I might give it a try."

"Why?"

"Why? Because I hoped if you recognized the writing, we might have a clue as to who is behind this."

"No," Forsyth said. "I mean, why are you getting involved in this? You aren't a local, and the truth is, this doesn't even concern you."

"I beg to differ with you, Marshal Forsyth. I got shot. This does concern me."

"But you killed the two men who attacked you. Three, if you count Mullins."

"And yet, this note proves that it isn't over."

"Ah, but the note also gives you the option of not getting shot again, if you just decide to pull up and leave."

"Marshal, what are you saying? Are you telling me I should leave?"

Forsyth chuckled. "No, I'm not saying that at all. In fact, I've got an idea, that is, if you'd be interested."

"All right. You've aroused my curiosity. What have you got?"

"I could deputize you."

Lucas shook his head. "That wouldn't do any good. You're a city marshal. Once I leave town, I'll have no authority, so I may as well just do it on my own."

"I'm not only a city marshal, I'm also the deputy sheriff for Bent County. I have the authority to appoint more deputies as I need them. This would give you some cover when you begin investigating. The only thing is, I can't put you on the county payroll."

Lucas smiled. "Well, hell, Marshal, I was going to investigate on my own, anyway. And in this case, it would be better if I could do it in some official capacity, so it doesn't matter to me whether I'm paid or not."

"Good, I'm glad to see that you are still with me on this. What did you find out from Mrs. Foley's neighbors?"

"I've only spoken to Pogue and Richards, and I plan to see Yancey today."

"Did you get anything from those two that might help?"

Lucas shook his head. "I'm afraid not."

"But they cooperated with you?"

"Very much so. Seemed like two good old boys who think the world of Pauline Foley."

"I'm afraid that won't be what you get from Bertis Yancey."

"Duke Richards warned me to be careful around him. And now, with you saying that, too, do you think Yancey might be the one behind all this?"

"Not necessarily, but he is one unfriendly bastard. Anyone is lucky to get the time of day from him."

"Thanks for letting me know what I'm getting in to. I'll ride out to try to talk to him, right after breakfast."

"Good luck."

Stopping by Waggy's before he left, Lucas had a good breakfast of eggs, pancakes, and ham.

"You do have a good appetite," Wanda said. She smiled. "I like to see a man who likes to eat."

"I spent a couple of years in Andersonville," Lucas replied. "I've never turned down the opportunity to eat since then."

"Even though Andersonville was on my side, that Henry Wirz didn't treat you boys right," Wanda said. "Bless your heart, as long as you come in here, I'll see to it that you have plenty to eat."

"Wanda, you're a good woman."

"Tell Waggy that."

Lucas chuckled. "That's what I think they would call preaching to the choir. There's absolutely no doubt in my mind but that Waggy already knows that."

"I know you're right about that," she said with a broad smile. She poured coffee into

Lucas's cup. "Let me know when you need more coffee."

Lucas enjoyed his breakfast and his coffee, as he was thinking about his trip out to see Bertis Yancey.

Pogue, Richards, and even Marshal Forsyth had made negative comments about Yancey. Of the three neighboring ranchers, Lucas thought that with those negative comments about him, and given the fact that Proctor, Boyle, and Mullins had all three worked for him, Yancey became the number one suspect. Keeping that in mind, Lucas headed out to the Box Y.

The main dwelling, unlike Hillside and the other two ranches Lucas had visited, was not a large structure. It was instead a single-story house, no larger than the house he had left to his Aunt Tillie, back in Missouri. The rest of the buildings were equal to the others, though. There was a bunkhouse, a kitchen, a good barn, and a corral.

Unlike the previous two ranches he had visited, nobody came to meet him until he began to tie Charley off in front of the cabin. The cabin door opened, and a tall, thin man with dark hair and well-manicured Van Dyke beard stepped outside. He was carrying a shotgun, though he wasn't pointing it at Lucas.

"What do you want?"

"Mr. Yancey?"

"I know my name, I don't know who you are," Yancey said in as gruff a voice as his greeting had been.

"I'd like to talk to you for a few minutes, if you don't mind."

"I ain't hirin'."

"I'm not looking for a job."

"If you ain't lookin' for a job, then why do you want to talk to me?"

"I'd rather have the opportunity to discuss it with you, rather than just blurt it out here."

"You ain't give me your name yet, why should I discuss anything with you. Who are you, anyway?"

"I'm sorry, I thought you already knew."

"Now, just how would I be knowin' your name?"

"I haven't exactly been hiding out since I arrived in Higbee. My name's Lucas Cain and I —"

"Wait a minute," Yancey said, raising his shotgun. "You're the one that killed Proctor 'n Boyle, 'n Mullins, ain't you?"

"Yes, I am."

"I thought you was. I was at the trial for the killin' of Proctor 'n Boyle, 'n there didn' nothin' happen to you. Is there goin' to be another 'n for you killin' Mullins?"

"No, I don't think so," Lucas said without any further comment. "I've been told those three men worked for you."

"They did."

"Mr. Yancey, did you send Lem Proctor and Ely Boyle out to intercept Pauline Foley?"

"Naw, I didn't have nothin' to do with that. I fired them two sons of bitches afore any o' that happened, 'n I should 'a fired 'em long before that. Mullins was still workin' for me, but I would 'a fired him pretty soon, too, iffin you hadn't a' killed him. You said you wanted to talk to me, so all right, let's hear what you got to say," Yancey said as he headed into the cabin.

Lucas followed Yancey in where he was met by an exceptionally beautiful woman.

"Good morning, sir. I'm Nonnie. Would you care for a cup of coffee?"

"Your name ain't Nonnie to no one but me," Yancey said in a gruff voice.

"Thank you, ma'am," Lucas said. "I'd like a cup of coffee."

"Pour us the coffee, then get," Yancey said.

Nonnie poured two cups of coffee, then withdrew to another part of the house.

"All right, now talk," Yancey said.

339

"Mr. Yancey, are you trying to buy Hillside Ranch?"

"Why are you askin'? It ain't yours to sell, is it?"

"No, sir, it isn't mine to sell. But someone is interested in the property, and whoever it is, is putting pressure on Mrs. Foley to sell it. It's now gotten to the point where someone is killing off her stock. And you obviously know what Proctor and Boyle did on the road."

"I don't know why Proctor 'n Boyle took it on themselves to do somethin' like that. You say they was tryin' to force her to sell her ranch — well that don't make no sense a' tall. Them two would have to put their money together just to buy a half a plug of tobaccy."

"Yes, I understand that. They were obviously hired by someone else. Do you have any idea who would want the ranch so much that they would hire the likes of those two?"

"Duke Richards. He wants her ranch. He's been tryin' to buy it ever since Bill died."

"Yes, but he said he was only offering to buy it to relieve Mrs. Foley the need of having to run the ranch alone," Lucas said.

"Maybe so, but what I don't understand,

is why anybody'd want that piece of worthless property in the first place? Who's tryin' to buy it?"

"That's precisely what I'm trying to find out."

"Well, I can't tell you who it is that's a' wantin' it, but I can tell you who it ain't, 'n it ain't me."

Lucas nodded his head. "Thank you, Mr. Yancey. That's good to know."

"Yeah, well, since we got that all talked out, I don't see no sense in you stayin' here any longer, 'n I don't see no sense in you comin' back neither."

"I'll take my leave, then."

"Oh, don't leave yet," Nonnie said, stepping out of the back of the house. "Not until you've finished your coffee. I brought you a sinker to go with it."

"Woman, what are you doin' in here?" Yancey scolded. "You ain't got no need to be a' bringin' him somethin' to eat. You done brung him coffee, 'n that's enough. He don't need nothin' more."

"Thank you for the offer, Miss Yancey, but I needed only to have a few words with your father, so I suppose I'll be on my way."

"She ain't my daughter, she's my wife," Yancey said gruffly.

"I beg your pardon, please forgive my

mistake."

"There ain't no need for forgivin', on account of we ain't friends, 'n we ain't goin' to be. You've had your coffee, 'n you've had your say, so you need to be gettin' on your way, now."

"So I've gathered. Good bye, Mrs. Yancey," Lucas said, purposely addressing her, rather than her husband.

As Lucas was riding away from the Box Y, he felt a need to take a drink of water, but when he tried to lift his canteen, it hung up. Lucas leaned over to free the canteen, and that proved to be a most fortuitous move, because the rifle bullet that would have been a fatal head shot made a popping sound as it snapped over his head.

Staying bent over, Lucas urged his horse off the road and down into a gulley that ran parallel to the road. He heard a second shot, but like the first, it passed over his head.

The gulley provided some cover for him and his horse and he snaked his rifle out of the saddle sheath, then dismounted and worked his way back up to the rim of the ravine where he searched the opposite side of the road for the shooter.

Finding a stick, he put his hat on the stick, then held it up to draw fire. The ruse worked and there was another shot.

His attacker was in the brush on the opposite side of the road. Lucas knew that it would be a dangerous move, but he knew, also, that he was going to have to cross the road to confront the shooter.

He raised up just far enough to bring up his rifle, then he shot at the place where he had seen the smoke. After that he ducked back down and ran several feet back down the gulley, in the same direction from which he had just come. He heard another shot fired as he was running, and he took some satisfaction in knowing that his attacker was still shooting at the place he had just vacated.

After running about fifty yards, he looked over the berm toward where he knew the shooter was, then determined that the shooter was probably still studying what he thought was the target area. He darted across the road, then into the scrub brush on the same side of the road as the shooter.

After dropping into the brush, he remained motionless for a moment to catch his breath, and have a moment of thankfulness that he had crossed unobserved. Then, once he was recovered, he started moving up through the saplings toward the shooter.

He had a couple of advantages. The

shooter hadn't seen him cross the road, and there were no leaves to give away his approach. Before he got there, though, he heard the sound of a horse galloping away.

He had not gotten a look at the shooter, so he had no idea who it was.

28

With Dan Lindell

When Dan arrived in Robinson, Colorado, he unloaded his horse from the stock car, then went to see Clyde James, the person he was supposed to contact here.

Clyde James's office was at one end of the depot and when Dan looked in, he saw a man with a well-trimmed moustache, wearing a suit, and studying some papers that were on his desk.

"Mr. James?" Dan called out.

James looked up. "Yes?"

"Mr. James, I'm Dan Lindell, and I'm here to —"

"I know why you're here," James said with a broad smile. "Tom Allen sent me a telegram about you. He says you can work miracles."

Dan chuckled. "The only miracle I can actually work is convincing him that I can work miracles. But I'll do the best for you

345

that I can."

"Well, we're going to need a miracle, I'm afraid. We want a spur from here to Higbee, but there's privately owned land between here and there, and though we have clearance all the way to the Las Animus River, we've been unable to get any clearance beyond that."

"Do we have an agent there?"

"If by agent you mean a representative of the railroad, no. But we do have someone we have been working with in Higbee, yes," James said

"How far is it from here to Higbee?"

"Eighteen miles. And we have clearance for all but one mile."

"All right, I'll see what I can do," Dan promised. "Who is the person in Higbee that you say has been working with us?"

"That would be David Garrett. He's a lawyer there." James chuckled. "You shouldn't have any trouble finding him — there are only two lawyers in the whole town."

With George Rogers
Eighteen miles south of Robinson, George Rogers was eating a meal of bacon and beans in the Hog Lot Saloon. The Foley woman was the only one who was keeping

346

him from earning his twenty-five hundred dollars. He had tried with Proctor and Boyle, and they failed. Then, when he decided that the man standing in his way was Lucas Cain, he hired Jerry Mullens to get rid of him, but Mullens failed. He was going to have to come up with some way of making the Foley woman sell Hillside Ranch.

After considering all the possibilities, he came to the inescapable conclusion that he was going to have to do it himself. But to do it himself would require a much greater risk than merely hiring someone else for the job. And that greater risk meant that twenty-five hundred dollars just wasn't enough. He was going to have to go see the man behind all this, and ask for more money.

"Five thousand dollars? Why, that's outrageous!"

"I've had three men killed so far, trying to get this ranch for you. The only one who is going to be able to get this done is me," Rogers said. "So you're either going to pay me five thousand dollars, or find somebody else."

"Five thousand dollars is quite unreasonable."

"I was getting tired of hanging around

here anyway," Rogers said. "Find yourself another man." Rogers got up and started toward the door.

"No, no, wait. All right, five thousand dollars. But if I'm to pay such an exorbitant fee, then I expect for you to absolutely do the job yourself. Bring me proof that Mrs. Foley has agreed to sell the ranch. Do anything you have to do."

Rogers smiled. "All right, I'll take care of her."

"When can I expect the job to be done? Time is running out and I don't intend to miss this opportunity."

"I'll get it done for you," Rogers said. "And soon."

"Good. Go now, and don't come back to see me again until you can report that ranch is mine."

With Dan Lindell

Dan Lindell rode into Higbee at a little after nine the next morning. He had been given the name of the man he was supposed to see, and as he rode through town, he studied the buildings and the signs until he found the one he was looking for.

David Garrett
Attorney at Law

348

"Mr. Garrett, my name is Dan Lindell, and I represent the Missouri Pacific Railroad. I was told that you would be my contact here, with regard to getting clearance for the spur line."

"Yes," Garrett said with a big smile. "A spur connection to the main line would mean a great deal to Higbee."

"I'm sure it would, but it is my understanding that we haven't been able to get the right of way we need to build the track."

"Don't you worry about that," Garrett said. "I'm working on it now, and I can guarantee you that I'll have all the paperwork for you within another week."

"I'll tell you what I'll do," Dan said. "I'll wait for one week before I start moving in the rails and ties. I don't want to get everything here and then be stopped for the lack of one mile of right of way."

"One week," Garrett said.

"All right, I'm telling you now. If we don't have signed clearance for this track right of way, I will have to recommend that we bypass Higbee and find another location for our spur line."

"Don't worry, we'll have everything in order within a week."

"Good. I'll go back to Robinson now, but I will be scouting other locations while I wait. When we're building a railroad, time is money, and this eighteen-mile spur has cost the Missouri Pacific more than I would want to say. Mr. Garrett, I cannot impress upon you how important this is. Do you understand?"

"I understand," Garrett said. "It will be done."

After Dan had left Garrett's office he wrote a message to Rogers.

> It is imperative that I own Hillside Ranch within one week. Arrange to see me today. I believe it is time I got more actively involved in the planning of this job, since your methods have not worked.
>
> Garrett

Finishing the letter, Garrett left his office, and walked down to the general store where Jimmy Reynolds worked. He gave the boy half a dollar to take the message to George Rogers.

"You'll most likely find him in the Hog Lot Saloon," Garrett told Jimmy.

"Mr. Rafferty, is it all right if I deliver this note for Mr. Garrett?" Jimmy asked his boss. "I'll be right back."

"It's a matter of the court," Garrett told

Rafferty.

"All right, but hurry back. You've got shelves to stock," Rafferty said.

Rogers was sitting at a table by himself, playing a game of solitaire when Jimmy Reynolds approached his table.

"Mr. Rogers, I have a message for you from Mr. Garrett."

"What is it?"

"I don't know what it is, I didn't read it." Jimmy handed the note to Rogers. He stood there for a second, hoping for a tip from Rogers, but when it didn't materialize, he left the saloon and returned to the store.

Arrange to see me today.

Rogers walked down to Garrett's office, then looking around to see if anyone was watching him, he stepped inside. At first, he thought no one was there.

"Anybody here?" he called.

"I'm back here, Rogers," Garrett called.

When Rogers stepped into Garrett's office, Garrett handed him a glass of whiskey.

"Have a seat, we need to talk," Garrett said.

"All right," Rogers said, accepting the glass.

"Let's put it on the table," Garrett said. "I agreed that for a fee of five thousand dollars, you would bring me the proof that I own Hillside Ranch. Have you made any progress?"

"Hell, no, not yet."

"Well, you're running out of time. If the old lady won't sell, you'll have to get rid of her and her daughter."

"Let me get this clear — now you're a sayin' I'm gonna kill the woman and her daughter," Rogers said.

"Yes, that is what I'm saying. But it has to be done quick. And that's why I'm willing to increase the compensation."

"You're willin' to do what?"

"I'm willing to pay you more."

"How much more?"

"Ten thousand dollars if you get rid of both of them."

"Ten thousand dollars, you say?"

"Yes, and there's an old coot who works for Mrs. Foley. If he's around, get rid of him, too. We don't need to take a chance that he could see anything."

Rogers smiled, broadly. "You can consider them dead."

"No, Mr. Rogers. I won't consider them dead until they actually are dead. You've told me this before, and you didn't get it done."

After leaving Garrett's office earlier, Dan Lindell had gone to the Cattlemen's Restaurant for supper. Now, having finished a good meal, he decided it was too late to ride back to Robinson. He stepped into the Boots and Saddles Saloon to get a beer before taking a room at the hotel.

He started toward the bar, and then he saw something that made him stop in his tracks. Sitting alone at a table in the far corner of the room was someone who looked exactly like Lucas Cain. Then, as Dan examined him more closely, he realized that it was Lucas Cain.

"Lucas?" he called out. "Lucas, is that you?"

Lucas looked up, then a huge smile spread across his face and he stood then walked across to greet him.

"Dan Lindell," Lucas said. "What are you doing in Higbee, Colorado? I thought you were in St. Louis."

"I am still there, but I get out quite often. But the question is, what's the rambling man doing in this little town? Last I heard you were somewhere in Kansas."

"Well, it's a complicated story," Lucas

said. "Here, let me buy you a drink and I'll tell you all about it."

The two men stepped up to the bar, then Lucas called out to Manny Burns.

"Manny, this is Dan Lindell. He's probably my best friend in the world, so I want you to give him a drink from your best bottle of whiskey. Dan, this is Manny Burns, the best bartender the Boots and Saddles has."

Manny laughed. "Bein' as I'm a modest fellow, I'd probably deny that. But, as I'm the only bartender Boots and Saddles has, I guess I'll have to say that Lucas is right."

Manny poured two glasses of whiskey from a bottle he took from below the bar.

"This is the best we have," he said.

"Come on over to my table, and let's catch up," Lucas said, as he and Dan took up the glasses Manny had poured.

"I thought you were working for the railroad," Lucas said, when they were seated.

"I am. That's the reason I'm here. We're planning on running a spur line from Robinson to Higbee."

"Damn, really? That'll be great for Higbee," Lucas replied, enthusiastically.

"You would think so, wouldn't you? But we've got a problem. There's one land owner that's stopping us."

"Who would that be?" Lucas asked, in a much more subdued tone. He was afraid that he already knew the answer.

"I don't know the owner's name, but the property is the Hillside Ranch."

"The owner is Pauline Foley. She's a widow."

"So, it's a woman owner? I wonder why she's giving us so much trouble. You would think that she'd welcome the railroad."

"I think it's the personal attacks and the killing of her cattle that's stopping her from selling," Lucas said in a low, troubled voice.

"Stopping her from selling? Who's trying to buy her ranch?"

"Until this very moment, we didn't know it was the railroad trying to buy, but why the underhanded tactics? Attacking her on the road, killing her cows? That's kind of low," Lucas said.

"Lucas, the railroad's not trying to buy the ranch. We don't even want the ranch."

"What are you talking about?"

"We just want an easement that will allow us to build the railroad through the ranch."

As Dan explained what kind of arrangement the railroad actually wanted, Lucas smiled broadly.

"I'll be damned. I know what this is all

about now," Lucas said. "Tomorrow morning, I want you to go meet Mrs. Foley and tell her what you just told me."

The next morning, Sue Ellen greeted the men with a smile, and an expression of curiosity as to who the man accompanying Lucas might be. Lucas satisfied everyone's curiosity when they gathered around the kitchen table for coffee.

"This is Dan Lindell, a long-time friend of mine. He works for the Missouri Pacific Railroad, and the mystery as to why someone has been wanting to buy your ranch has been solved. The Missouri Pacific Railroad wants to build a spur track, from the main line that passes through Robinson, down to Higbee. And they need right of way to pass through your ranch."

"No," Pauline said, shaking her head. "Lucas, after all we've been through, I thought you knew better. Mr. Lindell might be a good friend of yours, but that doesn't change anything. I still have no intention of selling the ranch."

Lucas chuckled. "That's the beauty of it, Pauline. You don't have to sell; the railroad doesn't want to buy."

"What? I don't understand. Then who has been pressuring us to sell?"

"My guess is Garrett. He hasn't been representing anyone, he wants it for himself. Tell them why, Dan."

"We signed an agreement with David Garrett to make arrangements for us to lease an easement through all the land along our proposed route. You are the only one he hasn't been able to procure. You'll still be able to use the rest of your acreage to ranch or do whatever you want. All we want is a strip of land, a hundred feet wide, from the northern border of your land to the southern border. We figure that's a distance of three thousand five hundred feet, and for that lease, we will pay you five dollars a foot. That would be seventeen thousand, five hundred dollars."

"What?" Pauline gasped. "You mean you'll pay us just to let the track pass through, but we keep the ranch?"

"That's exactly what I'm saying," Dan said with a smile.

"Mama, say yes!" Sue Ellen said.

"Why, yes, of course I'll let the track pass through our land," Pauline said with a wide, happy, smile.

"But, I don't understand," Sue Ellen said, her face registering her confusion. "Why would Mr. Garrett be willing to pay us twenty thousand dollars for the ranch, if the railroad is only going to pay seventeen thousand five hundred?"

"Oh, Miss Foley, you really don't understand, do you?" Dan said. "The railroad will pay that seventeen thousand, five hundred dollars every year, in perpetuity."

"What?" Pauline and Sue Ellen shouted, at the same time.

"Do you see now why Garrett is trying to buy Hillside?" Lucas asked.

"Why that's . . . that's not right! That's cheating!" Sue Ellen said. "So much for David Garrett's integrity and ethics."

29

Swayne Evans was in the barn feeding Henry, and Barney, the new mule, as well as Sue Ellen's horse, Dolly. He put Lucas's horse, Charley, and the horse of the man who had ridden in with Lucas in the corral. He left the saddles on just in case the two men would be visiting the neighboring ranches again.

When he finished his work, Swayne went to the well to carry in a bucket of water. That way, he would have a reason to find out who the man was that had come with Lucas. He was pretty sure that the visitor didn't represent a threat, or Lucas would not have brought him.

Swayne stepped up onto the back porch, set the bucket down, then knocked on the door.

"Come on in, Swayne," Pauline called out.

When Swayne stepped into the kitchen, he was acknowledged by everyone, then Lucas introduced the man with him.

"Swayne, this is Dan Lindell," Lucas said. "We have been close friends since we served together in the war. And we were in Andersonville together. Dan, this is Swayne Evans, and if you can get over his being a cantankerous old varmint, why you'll learn he's a pretty good man to know."

"Don't go gettin' too high-falutin' on your braggin' on me now, 'cause I ain't goin' to be braggin' nothin' on you back," Swayne said.

"Well then, I'll brag on him," Dan said. "We were on the *Sultana* together when it sank in the Mississippi River. I wouldn't be here today if Lucas hadn't saved my life."

"Are we goin' to stay here and palaver all day, or are we goin' to eat a bite?" Swayne asked as he lifted a lid on a pot of stew that was simmering on the cook stove.

Pauline laughed. "Swayne, you always did have the best manners."

"Wait 'till you hear why Mr. Lindell is here," Sue Ellen said.

"From the way you're talkin', it sounds like it might be a good thing."

"It saves Hillside Ranch, and we'll be able to keep it from now on," Pauline said with a wide smile.

During dinner, Dan explained the concept

of leasing an easement, telling also that the ranch would stay in the hands of the Foleys.

"Damn, that's the best news I've heard in a long time," Swayne said. "Excuse my language, ladies."

"That's quite all right, Swayne," Pauline said. "News this good deserves a damn or two."

George Rogers had left the road before he reached Hillside Ranch, then rode through open fields and trees so that he could approach the house from the rear. He knew that the Foleys wouldn't be expecting anyone to come up to the house from the back side.

He was thinking about the money he had been promised. All he had to do to earn it was kill three people, two of them women and one old man, and none of them would be armed. He might even set the place on fire when he was done. Hell, killing was fun, and it was even more fun when he was being paid a lot of money for it.

When Rogers saw the house, he moved over so that he was coming toward it from directly behind. In addition, he took advantage of trees and shrubbery to move into position. When he reached the house, he bent forward at the waist, so he could come up alongside without being seen through the window. Once he reached the front, he stepped up onto the porch, pulled his pistol, pushed the door open, then stepped inside.

"Who are you?" Sue Ellen called to him. "How dare you break into our house!"

"Ben Brodie!" Lucas and Dan said together.

"Wait," Sue Ellen said. "Do you two know this man?"

"Oh yeah, they know me. We're old friends from Andersonville, ain't we, boys?" Brodie said, with an evil chuckle.

"We were never friends, you traitorous bastard," Dan said.

"No, I guess we weren't, were we?" Brodie said. "Miz Foley, you should 'a sold out to Garrett when you had your chance. But as for me, I'm glad you didn't on account of now, I'm gonna make ten thousand dollars to kill you. Goodbye," he said with an evil smile.

Brodie had just raised his pistol, when the first blast from a shotgun took his gun-hand arm off at the elbow. Then, before he could even shout out in pain, the second blast opened up a huge wound in the side of his head, spilling some of his brains.

Swayne Evans stood to one side, holding

the smoking, double-barrel shotgun in his hands.

"Well, I'm glad I went to get that water bucket," Swayne said.

"Yeah," Lucas said. "I'd say that we are, too."

Garrett was sitting at his desk when he saw Lucas Cain, Dan Lindell, and Marshal Forsyth come into his office. Seeing the three of them together didn't bode well, and he greeted them with a strained smile.

"Well, to what do I owe the pleasure of a visit from three such important citizens?" he asked.

"There's no pleasure in it, Garrett," Marshal Forsyth said. "I have no proof yet, but Ben Brodie has implicated you in this business to get Mrs. Foley to sell her ranch."

"Who's Ben Brodie?"

"I just learned his real name. He's been passing himself off as George Rogers," Forsyth said.

"And you say this man, Rogers, or Brodie, or whoever he is has implicated me?"

"Yes."

"And you're going to take the word of someone who hasn't even been using his real name, over mine, a respected lawyer. Wait until I face him in court. We'll let the judge decide which of us is telling the truth."

"That won't be possible. Brodie is dead."

Garrett smiled. "Then you don't have a case, do you?"

"This might be something a good lawyer would use against you," Lucas said as he pulled out a piece of paper. "This note happened to be in Brodie's pocket. Shall I read it to you?"

"That doesn't mean anything," Garrett said. "Anybody could have signed my name to a piece of paper."

"Oh? And tell me, Garrett, since we didn't say anything about a signature, how did you know your name was on the note?" Lucas asked.

"I'll bet the judge can decide if this is your handwriting. If I were you, I wouldn't be leaving town anytime soon," Marshal Forsyth said.

From the Higbee *Ledger:*

Railroad to Come to Higbee

Plans have been announced and all arrangements have been made for a spur railroad line to connect Higbee with Robinson on the main line of the Missouri Pacific Railroad. Passengers will be able to go anywhere in America, riding in comfort. In addition to passenger travel, the produce from our farms and the cattle and sheep of our ranches, will have the entire nation as customers.

Mrs. Pauline Foley, the last holdout, was convinced to make a deal with the railroad after she learned that it was an easement the railroad wanted, and not her entire ranch.

Two days after the announcement of the railroad coming to Higbee, there was another story that attracted the attention of every citizen of the town.

Local Lawyer Takes Own Life

In what must come as a shock to every citizen of our fair community, the body of David Garrett was found face down on the desk in his office. There was a pistol beside him with one bullet having been expended. The entry wound of the bullet was his right temple, the wound being sufficient to bring about the well-known lawyer's demise.

The finding of the coroner and the county sheriff say that the wounds are consistent with that of someone who has committed suicide.

Though the means of death are not a mystery, the reason for it has caused everyone to wonder. Why would a very successful, prominent, and popular lawyer commit suicide? Alas, that is a mystery that Mr. Garrett took to his grave.

30

Lucas and Dan were having breakfast at Waggy's when William Lightfoot and Marshal Forsythe came into the little café. Seeing Lucas and Dan at the table, they came over to them both wearing big smiles.

"You two are the most popular men in town," Forsythe said. "Why either one of you could be elected mayor, if you wanted the job."

"And don't think Mayor Ericson doesn't know this," Lightfoot added.

"You can tell the mayor for both of us, that he has no worries," Lucas said. "Dan will be going back to St. Louis, and I'll be on my way as well."

"Really?" Forsythe said. "You mean I'm going to lose the best deputy I ever had?"

Lucas chuckled. "The thing you liked most about me, was that you didn't have to pay me."

The marshal joined Lucas with a little

laugh. "Well, there is that," he said.

Forsythe and Lightfoot had a cup of coffee to join Lucas and Dan at their breakfast. Then, when the meal was completed, Lucas shook hands with the editor and the marshal. He went over to where Wanda was standing.

"This is goodbye, Wanda," he said, "and I want you to know that I haven't had meals this good since my own mother was the cook."

"You're leaving town?"

"Yes."

Wanda's eyes brimmed with tears, and she opened her arms, inviting him for a hug. Waggy came out of the kitchen to tell him goodbye as well.

"I'll wait out here while you tell the Foleys goodbye," Dan offered when they rode up to the house.

"Yeah, thanks, that might be better."

Lucas dismounted but even before he reached the door, Swayne stepped out onto the porch to welcome him.

"What are you doing loafing around here?" Lucas teased. "Don't you have any work to do?"

"Since you're going to be telling the ladies you're a pullin' out, I thought it might be a good idee if I was to sort'a hang around until you was actual gone," Swayne said.

"You haven't told them?"

Swayne shook his head. "Huh, uh, that's for you to do."

Pauline and Sue Ellen greeted Lucas warmly.

"Are you going to stay for dinner?" Pauline asked.

"No," Lucas said. "I need to be going and staying for dinner would just make it harder."

"Going? Going where?" Sue Ellen asked.

"I don't know," Lucas said. "I just know that it's time to go. I stopped by to say goodbye."

"I . . . I'm glad you didn't just go off and leave us without so much as a word," Sue Ellen said, the tone of her voice showing her distress over his announcement.

"You stay safe, and think of us now and then," Pauline said, embracing Lucas warmly.

Lucas turned to Sue Ellen with open arms. "Sue Ellen?"

"I . . . I . . ." Sue Ellen said, then putting aside her disappointment she spread her arms and embraced him for a long moment. There were tears in her eyes when she stepped back. "Thank you so much for everything you have done for us."

When Lucas went back outside, Swayne was still standing on the porch.

"Goodbye, Lucas, and don't do anything I wouldn't do."

Lucas chuckled. "Thanks for that, Swayne. Since there's very little you haven't done, that pretty much means I can do anything I want to, doesn't it?"

Swayne laughed as well. "Yeah, that's pretty much it."

It was quiet for the first few minutes of their ride back to Robinson, then Dan broke the silence.

"That was hard for you, wasn't it?"

"Yes, harder than I thought it would be."

"Listen, when we get back to Robinson and the train, why don't you come back to St. Louis with me?"

Lucas shook his head. "No, I'll be going the other way."

"Why?"

"I don't know, Dan. I guess you can just call me a rambling man."

ABOUT THE AUTHOR

Robert Vaughan sold his first book when he was 19. That was 57 years and nearly 500 books ago. He wrote the novelization for the miniseries *Andersonville.* Vaughan wrote, produced, and appeared in the History Channel documentary *Vietnam Homecoming.* His books have hit the NYT bestseller list seven times. He has won the Spur Award, the PORGIE Award (Best Paperback Original), the Western Fictioneers Lifetime Achievement Award, received the Readwest President's Award for Excellence in Western Fiction, is a member of the American Writers Hall of Fame and is a Pulitzer Prize nominee. Vaughn is also a retired army officer, helicopter pilot with three tours in Vietnam. And received the Distinguished Flying Cross, the Purple Heart, The Bronze Star with three oak leaf clusters, the Air Medal for valor with 35 oak leaf clusters, the Army Commendation

Medal, the Meritorious Service Medal, and the Vietnamese Cross of Gallantry.

The employees of Thorndike Press hope you have enjoyed this Large Print book. All our Thorndike Large Print titles are designed for easy reading, and all our books are made to last. Other Thorndike Press Large Print books are available at your library, through selected bookstores, or directly from us.

For information about titles, please call:
(800) 223-1244

or visit our website at:
gale.com/thorndike